Alumni Affairs

Marshall Critchfield

ALUMNI AFFAIRS

First edition. February 15, 2021.

Chapter One

The Alachua County Historical Society had for years tried to assume some sort of control over 1308 University Avenue in Gainesville, located right across the street from the University of Florida's iconic Ben Hill Griffin Stadium. Owned by distinguished alum and former football star Bart Johnson, the house was about as far from a museum as a fast food joint. Johnson kept it in the *family* and rented mostly to football players. There always had to be one resident who wasn't on the football team – someone had to manage the tailgating operation on game days. As early as 7:00 a.m. Johnson and his friends would pull up in everything from hundred thousand dollar motorhomes to orange and blue classic cars for home games. The guys would light up smokers and tap kegs while the ladies decorated the yard and put out appetizers.

Most of the properties on University Avenue were no longer zoned 'residential.' 1308 was built of brick in the twenties for visiting professors. There were three stories and the floors were oak. The property was pretty sizable for college living. Set on nearly an acre, it provided an optimal setting for general rowdiness.

Charles MacIntosh III, known widely as Chip, moved to the 1308 house as a freshman. Since most freshmen at UF weren't twenty-one year old Marines, he never underwent any hazing or disrespect. The rent was half of the fancy apartments on the west side of town and while it was often tough to concentrate in a place with eight other people, Chip found a way to hit the books with diligence.

His parents also lived in Gainesville, in the home where he grew up. The oak lined streets on the north end of town were seldom visited by the student body. The Northwood section had a stipulation on the books whereby no more than two unrelated individuals could reside in the same home. That's not to say that a few families didn't rent a room to a student every now and then, but those candidates were usually graduate students or undergrads beholden to rigorous majors like *Dentistry*.

Chip's mom, Mary Wallace, came from a wealthy Virginia family. Her great grandfather was one of the largest private landowners in the state and they made their family fortune farming tobacco. Ironically enough, Mary became the head volunteer at the Shands Cancer Center in Gainesville.

Their home was warm and inviting. They had the resources to make it perfect and, unlike 1308 University, it *did* look like a museum. Over the years, the boys' playroom was converted into a cozy lounge/workroom that Chip used for quiet evenings with dates or to study for finals. The main campus library was of no use to Chip. It was more like a cosmopolitan coffee lounge than a place to absorb knowledge.

The best part about his childhood home was the unlimited, and unmonitored, access Chip had in the summer months, when mom and dad escaped the sweltering heat of north central Florida for the cool, ocean breezes of coastal Maine.

And then there was Jay. John Stuart MacIntosh was Chip's younger brother and he was too smart for his own good. He was a junior at Florida – a Computer Science & Engineering (CSE) Major and was holding down an A+ average. He preferred dorm life to living in an off campus apartment or with his folks. He was the Resident Assistant in his hall and was often summoned by the head of IT to troubleshoot the university's mainframe system, sometimes in the middle of the night.

For a computer super freak, Jay was quite the nature lover. He enjoyed leading friends on nature walks at Paynes Prairie Preserve State Park and canoe trips on the Santa Fe River.

Chip drove along the side of 1308 and saw a familiar Honda Accord parked in the back of the home. It was the 26th of December, Christmas break. Gainesville was a ghost town. He didn't think anyone would be at the house. The plan was to grab his hunting gear and head to his family's ranch.

Chip headed up the back steps to the kitchen door.

His occasional girlfriend Jessica Van Zandt was watching television in the bar area that once housed a formal dining room. She heard Chip when the screen door slammed. "Hey – you scared me," she said. "When are you going hunting?"

"Hey. What are you doing here Jess?" he asked.

"My parents went on a cruise for their anniversary. They left at dawn - I decided to come back early. Hey, why do you have like forty boxes of Wheaties in your pantry?"

"Somebody sends them to us – we don't know where... they," Chip was in a daze, he didn't know what to think of her being there. Part of him wanted to take advantage of not having roommates around and part of him wanted her to leave.

Jessica was a Tampa girl, she was 20 and she was absolutely a four-alarm fire. She was Chip's on again/off again girlfriend and was the social director of her sorority, Delta Delta Delta. She was way too into Greek Life for Chip. As a high-profile athlete, he was welcome in nearly any fraternity house at any time. Most of his friends were SAEs and he had spent quite a bit of time at the house in his earlier years. Jess, however, was over-the-top for the per-petual social regiment offered by the Greek system.

After twice failing *Organic Chemistry*, Jessica switched from being Pre-Med to *Physical Therapy*. She was one of the pony-tailed girls often seen on the sidelines during games in khaki chinos, loose-fitting polo shirts and spot-less cross-trainer sneakers. She liked to be around athletes, but was never con-sidered to have "been around."

"Can we talk?" she asked him.

"Let me take a quick shower," he replied then headed up the squeaky staircase. "Jay got a sweet canoe for Christmas and we took it for a test run earlier!"

Chip was the only resident of 1308 with his own, private bathroom. It was attached to his room, which was always locked. Chip's room was nice-looking; he had help decorating it from Jessica and a few others. There was evidence that he was with the Marines and that he played football, but noth-ing was overdone. His bedspread was a Ralph Lauren plaid and his furniture was all very old and handsome but lacked the condition for top dollar resale. Covering the wide pine plank floor was a massive, tattered oriental rug. Just above the cherry headboard was a poster of ZZ Top that had been there since the nineties. None of the room's many occupants over a thirty year period saw the need to remove it. Chip also had a stuffed pheasant he had shot in Iowa with his dad and his cousins. On his dresser was an awesome cigar humidor he scored cheap while serving overseas. It housed a few decent cigars from trips to the ranch and a few alumni events.

Chip used his shower to reflect and strategize. He wanted to think about the Pittsburgh Panthers' offense in preparation for the Sugar Bowl but he couldn't really focus on the game. He thought about what to say to Jessica. Part of him wanted to go downstairs and tell her that he never wanted to see her again. There had been an incident after the SEC Championship Game - she got wasted drunk and tried to make him jealous.

Chip threw on a pair of Levis and a long sleeve t-shirt. He slid his feet into a pair of Birkenstocks and headed downstairs.

"Hey."

"Hey."

Chip went to the kitchen, still in sight of Jessica, and grabbed from the cabinet a massive plastic souvenir cup from a local deli. He filled it with tap water and walked over to the couch where Jessica was seated.

"Sit," she said, "sit right here. Chip are you going to play – what are you going to do when you graduate? I heard the Canadian Football League was..."

He calmly interrupted her. "I'm not playing for the CFL."

"Well what if you don't get - *drafted*..."

He interrupted her again "what difference does it make anyway. I mean – why are we talking about this right now?"

She looked down at the nicked-up coffee table, her voice changed a little. "I care. I mean, I still have feelings for you – I wonder what this place will be like without you and it makes me – I don't know – sad maybe? Chip when we're apart I meet all these guys – I know the whole team – I feel like all the other guys at this school are so cocky, jealous, and crude. I have never seen any of that in you. You are always so calm and like – cool. I've walked with you, across campus. Literally hundreds of other people walk up and tap fists with you saying 'good luck Saturday MacIntosh!' How do you – aren't you going to miss that?"

"I'm part of something special – I realize that and I'm fired up to be a part of it – believe me. But it's a game. If you asked me if I thought I'd start for the Gators – hell. Don't forget that it took two talented dumbasses to get caught breaking and entering for me to get my shot at actual playing time."

"Yea – then you earned a starting slot then made captain. I guess it's not really football I'm talking about. Like, I just think I'm going to miss you. And it bothers me. Plus I don't know what *we* are."

"It seems we've covered this before," said Chip. "I thought we agreed that we were better off without trying to make something – we both said it would be fine if we weren't - like - a *couple* – right?"

She kept it up. "Do you still have feelings for me?"

Chip had an out, all he had to say, in theory, was "no." But the honest SOB said "Of course I do Jess. How could I not still have feelings for you?"

She began to tear-up a little. Then she laughed – "I don't deserve to be with you - and that's what really kills me." Jessica threw herself into his arms and held him tightly. Then she got up and composed herself. She walked across the room to the front window and looked across University Avenue.

He wasn't in the mood for romantic drama but he caught himself checking her out. She had on little white shorts and a tiny, mint colored t-shirt with small sleeves that barely covered her shoulders. Her legs were long and tan and she wore beach-style flip flops with navy and pink straps. Her blonde hair barely touched her shoulders and she had the body of a track star.

Chip pulled a football from within the couch and started tossing it up in the air and catching it. He wasn't stupid, he knew he could have chased her up the stairs and celebrated the New Year a few days early. It wasn't his style, especially given her apparent fragile state of mind.

"Jess?" he asked.

She removed her flips and sat Indian style on the chair by the window. She was facing him now, but there was still a good twenty feet between them.

"Jess – I told my dad I was – I can't stay here with you right now," he said.

"I think of you as an *era* in my life Chip. I'm happiest when I'm with you; I love our chats, staying at the ranch together, that river house, parties... I feel great – happy when I'm with you. I know I turned into a psycho a few times, but I've changed. The sorority means less and less to me-"

This wasn't what he wanted to hear, he considered getting up and walking out. "I never said anything about the sorority."

"Let me finish. Please. That night at The Swamp – when we had just broken up – I was with that Phi Delt guy – you came in with your buddies and the guy got all mouthy."

"Yeah?" Chip said.

"You just nodded and walked out. The fact that you didn't care that night – the way you calmly left – that isn't normal."

"It's not that I didn't care Jess... it's – where are you going with this anyway? What's the point?" Chip asked.

"The point is that..." she hesitated slightly. "The point is that whatever happens – whatever you end up doing I want you to know that you are a huge part of my life. I've screwed up – I know that. You deserve better than me. And that's tough on me. Maybe I haven't changed. I can't help it. I came over here today – I hoped we could be together, even if just through the break. If we can't be together, if we can't you know – *that* – I want to be friends with you."

He wasn't sure what to do. He didn't want to hurt her by brushing her off, but he knew if they would have gone upstairs he'd be signing on for a semester of Greek-style hayrides, date nights, formals, slight alcohol abuse and a fair number of jealous outrages.

Chip took the mature, brave route.

"Jess," he said confidently, "I have loved being part of your life. And you've shaped me. It's been a great adventure - and I'll miss you. Terribly."

She stood helplessly with tears in her eyes - hoping he would hug her and tell her that he loved her. He offered understanding through his eyes but didn't get up.

Jess half-stormed out the back door through the kitchen. Chip held his breath until he heard her Honda start up and back out the driveway.

A feeling of freedom came over him as he returned to his room to grab his hunting gear.

Chapter Two

Chip was the first one up. He flipped on the light in the kitchen and opened the sky blue cabinet that housed the Folgers coffee. He filled the coffee maker with water from a gallon jug in the refrigerator and began the process of brewing a massive pot for the camp. The coffee cups were Styrofoam and stacked on a shelf just above the counter. Chip pulled a cup from the tall sleeve and wrote his name on it with a black magic marker.

He went into the main room and lit a fire in the old wood-burning stove. The sun wasn't up yet and neither were the other hunters. Chip turned on a few lamps and walked back into the kitchen.

As he waited for the coffee he studied the pictures on the wall. There were shots that dated back thirty-five years; they were the stories of all the great hunters and friends who had gathered at this ranch among the pine forests of northern Florida.

Chip filled up his cup and walked on to the cold, damp porch. It was screened in and covered with peeling white paint. The floor was painted gray and lined with coolers of canned beer, juice for cocktails, and ten-pound bags of ice. Most had the block-printed last names of their owners across the tops. There was nothing to see in the yard, just a bunch of upscale SUVs and a few ranch trucks. He returned to the main room to check on his fire.

The room started to warm up as the pine sticks burned. The floor looked like wood recovered from the bottom of a slow-moving river. It was dark - stained with coffee, liquor, and cigar smoke. The paneled walls were barely noticeable amid all of the photographs and ammunition advertising signs of varying vintage. There were two tables with ashtrays and playing cards and a dusty old couch someone donated in the eighties.

There wasn't much in the way of taxidermy. Just an old stuffed rattlesnake Chip's grandfather killed in South Carolina years ago, a feisty looking bob-cat, and one six-point whitetail taken on the ranch by a guest whose wife wouldn't permit it in their home.

The pictures were all there, some hanging on by a mere thread, some neatly fastened to corkboards. Chip studied the walls as he sipped his coffee. This was his favorite place; he grew up on this ranch.

Chip heard the screen door to the back door bang shut. An excited young Black Labrador came rambling through the old house and up on the couch next to him. It was Bruce's dog: "Rex." Chip embraced the pup then Rex proceeded to sniff out the entire room for a piece of dropped food.

Bruce Hudson walked in with a look on his face like he had never been so cold in his life. He had on outdated prescription glasses and a discount cigarette between his frigid-looking lips. His face was weathered and he wore the sideburns of his daddy. He had on an old flannel jacket and a pair of flea market jeans. Bruce shuffled his feet when he walked as if to get the full effect of the tattered wood floor. His boots were sturdy leather Wellingtons and Chip used to wonder if Bruce had ever actually removed them.

Bruce hacked a bit while he poured his coffee. He quickly scribbled his name on his cup and shoveled into the great room. He looked over at Chip on the couch and said, in a groggy but deep southern twang, "Mornin' Chip. Where's everyone else – the sun's half way up you know. What time you get in last night?"

"About eleven I think - everyone was already asleep. Great to see you... How've you been?" asked Chip.

"Oh pretty good I'd say," Bruce replied. "Switched over to light cigarettes."

Chip was a big fan of Bruce. He was the caretaker and lived in a trailer about a thousand yards south of the ranch house. He was a field biologist with the Division of Fish and Game but looked after the ranch and its guests throughout the year. He couldn't have been the town dentist's best customer, but he had a warm and genuine smile.

Bruce never seemed to sit down. He smoked tons of cigarettes so he usually hovered around the doorways to the porch. He would let out a loud fart during the middle of a conversation as if there was nothing abnormal about it. Then he'd catch the youngest guy in the room laughing and he'd give him a little wink.

The hunters started to clamor down the old steps and into the kitchen where they'd dutifully brand their cups and top them off with coffee. Bruce was the only resident so he knew of every deer in the woods. Everyone shook hands with Chip and asked Bruce where they should sit as they pulled out photocopies of the property map.

Within twenty minutes the base map was marked with each hunter's location and only Bruce and Rex remained in the main room. Chip's dad and one other guy had slept in – no doubt due to the cold weather.

Chip drove to his spot alone; his Toyota Land Cruiser was one of the older, boxy ones with four doors. The beige paint had flattened a bit and the tires were the chunkiest he could fit on there. He had one of those "Reward" stickers on the chrome bumper. It was part of the state's effort to crack down on poachers – they offered a *reward* to those who turned in people who took illegal game.

He stashed the Cruiser into a huge patch of palmettos and shut off the motor. He dipped his hand into the lever of his Winchester 94, shoved it up over his shoulder and walked toward his deer stand. In his preteen years, he referred to this morning jaunt into the woods as the "scary walk." One small flashlight in a sea of palmettos and slash pines isn't terribly illuminating. But it was different now. Chip knew every tree, every stump, and every trail.

There was still plenty of darkness on the horizon as he settled into his spot. The aluminum tower stand had four legs and stood about ten feet off the ground. The flat metal seat was wet and uncomfortable, but Chip had remembered to bring a seat cushion.

Rays of sunshine slowly started to show through the pines. There was so much moisture in the air that the air above the ground appeared like smoke from a wildfire. As the woods began to light up, a decent sized whitetail buck appeared. Chip had the shot, the deer was respectable, but he didn't want to shoot because it might scare the rest of the game away and ruin it for the other hunters, his dad's friends.

As the buck moved on, Chip sat motionless and absorbed the sounds of the pine forest. The turkeys and deer always moved around palmettos undetected but swallows and squirrels would sometimes crash into the palmate leaves like kamikaze pilots.

Even with the sounds of nature present, it felt quiet for Chip. His mind was on other things. He had just finished his best regular-season as Middle Linebacker for the Florida Gators. With the SEC Championship in his back pocket, he was focused on the Sugar Bowl. The Gators had two losses under their belt, so they weren't playing for the National Title, but Chip was under the impression that this game would decide whether he be invited to the NFL or be looking for a regular job in May.

In the distance, a shot was fired. He thought he recognized it as a .243 caliber - the gun being used by his dad's accountant Jimmy Reese. Chip gave his spot another ten minutes then carefully unloaded his firearm.

The drive back to the ranch house felt like a safari. Chip saw game at every turn but he wanted to get back and see if his help was needed with whatever Jimmy had shot. The kid was pleased to see his dad's truck wasn't still at the ranch house. 'The old man made it out there after all,' he thought to himself.

One of the best things about the whole experience, for most guests of the ranch, was the smell of bacon upon returning from a morning in the woods. Pete Hilton stood in the kitchen in full hunting apparel with not a snowball's chance in The Keys that he was heading into the woods.

Pete was the ranch cook. He had hunted years ago but basically gave it up to cook, sleep-in, drink, and tell bullshit stories around the campfire at night. He was a very good guy and everyone liked him. And at a towering six foot five, no one would dare speak ill of his food – even though the young kids usually puked their first time out. Nearly every recipe contained butter, flour, grease, and possibly even lard.

Like clock-work, the first words that a hunter would hear when he made it back to camp were "Did ya' see anything?" This day was slightly different – Pete had heard the shot. The .243 rifle. Chip said he thought it had been Jimmy who fired.

Pete played both offense and defense for the Miami Hurricanes years ago so he and Chip had somewhat of a special bond. Chip roamed the house for his coffee cup so he and Pete could chat and watch over the dirt road for whoever took that shot.

They found vacant rockers on the porch and took in the fresh air while breakfast was on cruise control.

"Big times for you son," Pete said as he crossed his legs and took a sip of his coffee.

"I know," said Chip, "it's been quite a year. I know, I just don't know where it's all going."

"Are there any options you can't handle?"

"I don't know. I have this feeling… I don't know what I want. I *knew* I didn't want to be a career Marine. I never thought I'd have gotten this far in football. Even if I were offered an invitation to play in the league, I don't know if I'd want to."

Pete nodded. "Take your pick – what would you do?"

"Anything?" Chip asked.

"Yea. If you had a choice – you could do anything in the world, money no object – a real – a *dream* job. Hunting guide?"

Chip smiled. "Sort of. No, I can't see myself being a hunting guide forever. If I had my choice I'd be in the FBI for thirty years. But that means law school and a fighting chance or cop for ten years and little probability."

Pete rose slowly, as if his knee was bothering him. "I have to check on that bacon. Let me think about it."

Just then a Lexus SUV pulled up from the woods and out jumped Jimmy. Chip yelled out the big question. Jimmy approached with a bit of a grin. Either Chip was headed back to Gainesville to watch films or he was headed into the woods with Rex and Bruce.

Jimmy, as predicted, had shot a deer but never found him. Chip couldn't help being a little fired up. He drained his coffee and went to find Bruce.

Pete met Jimmy at the porch door and began the hazing. Whenever a hunter missed a deer a Camp Tribunal was held and the other hunters voted on whether or not to cut a piece of clothing off the unfortunate shooter in front of everyone in attendance. Once the sacred cloth was removed, usually by skinning knife whilst still attached to the victim, details of the miss were recorded with a black, permanent marker.

Jimmy assured Pete Hilton that he hit the big deer – no question – just that he had lost the blood trail.

There was some laughter and some cuss words between the two then Bruce and Chip reappeared with knee-high snake boots and Rex.

Bruce managed a few quick questions for Jimmy in a polite but hardly understandable fashion.

"We'll take my truck, we'd better go," urged Bruce. Pete stuck his giant head out of the kitchen and yelled "breakfast'll be here when ya get back!"

Bruce's truck was the most uncomfortable and messy piece of crap in the South. It was an antique Chevy LUV diesel 2 wheel drive. Chip never understood how a guy could live on a ranch like this and drive a 2WD vehicle. Bruce wasn't the only old red who was sure they could get by without all four wheels spinning. Chip hopped in the bed of the small truck amid the gas cans, logging chains, random chunks of wood, and a few "empties." Even Rex wouldn't ride in the back of that truck. Chip found an Army green cooler and used it for a chair.

Jimmy rode shotgun and Rex sat perched between the two men as they headed out.

Halfway to Jimmy's spot the group found Chip's dad Charles headed back to the house in his navy blue Suburban. Charles MacIntosh Jr. was a History professor at Florida. His specialty was the Civil War and he actually resembled a Civil War General. He was a tall, full guy with slightly longer hair than his contemporaries. His beard was graying – it wasn't quite a goatee and it wasn't quite a full beard either. His students called it a "Civil War beard."

Charles heard the story of Jimmy's down deer and said "Go get 'em." He gave a nod through a silver cloud of cigar smoke and slowly drove off.

Jimmy pointed to his trail and the men got out of the truck. Rex was wagging his tail furiously, making it clear he knew exactly what was going on. Jimmy could do taxes with his eyes closed. He could testify in court about complex financial matters and he could do long division in his head. But he sure sounded like a wind bag when it came to tracking a wounded animal in the bush.

He had given Bruce an earful then finally Bruce politely turned to him and said "Don't worry yerself Jimmy, Rex here will have that buck for us quicker'n shit."

Bruce let his trusty canine off his lead and the two of them went straight into the palmettos. Chip found himself alone with Jimmy Reese, who was back in his regular mode now that Bruce had reassured him.

"That was some game against Tennessee, kiddo," Jimmy said as he stood beside Chip.

"Thanks. We had luck on our side that night," replied Chip.

"So – uh, what's next for you? Are you going to play pro ball?"

"I still don't know to be honest. If I had to guess I'd say 'no.' The truth is I'm finally starting to worry. I've still got a few months until graduation, but I'm pretty sure my football career will be over after the Sugar Bowl."

"What's your degree in again Chip?"

"I'm a Forestry major. Minoring in criminal justice. So... *Park Ranger.* Right?"

"Nothing wrong with being a park ranger. You'd get to live in a National Park, be out in the woods all day, organize rescues or whatever. Chip if you saw some of the low-lifes I have to deal with everyday – believe me – thirty years with Smokey Bear – retire with premium bennies. Sign me up man."

Just then Bruce whistled like a train horn and yelled for those two to drive the truck up to him. Chip took the helm of the little diesel and they did as they were told. The driver's seat was almost as rough as the cooler in the bed. They spotted Bruce's ironic blaze orange *and* camo hat out in the scrub and exited the vehicle.

"We got em!" yelled Bruce.

Jimmy started to shake a little, he was pumped. "Oh thank God," Jimmy said as they traipsed out into the woods.

Bruce went over the whole scenario about what happened, he lived for this stuff and both Chip and Jimmy listened intently. Bruce reviewed the blood trail, the entry and exit wounds... It reminded Jimmy of the Warren Commission, but he enjoyed the explanation just the same. Chip, albeit a Bruce supporter, couldn't stop thinking about breakfast.

Just as Bruce was wrapping up his lesson on aging a whitetail buck Chip suggested loading him up and heading back. Meanwhile Rex was off looking for another deer. Bruce called for him and he came flying over.

When they got back to the ranch house, they spotted the Ford Excursion of Walt Davenport, the owner of the largest Ford Dealership in the South. This truck had a flat black, custom paint job, a ten inch lift, and 38" Ground Hawg mudders wrapped around wide, black wheels. The inside was trimmed in private-jet-style leather, had plush leather captains chairs, walnut trimmed dash, wheel, and shifter, and a pair of flat screen televisions – wifi, satellite TV, phone – everything.

The fellas all came clamoring out of the house at the sight of Bruce's truck. There was some rowdiness – some hollering – as there always was when someone showed up with an animal.

"Nice deer Jimbo," said Charles as he shook Jimmy's hand and herded the guys back inside.

Breakfast always started with a quick prayer in the old kitchen. Then everyone would grab a heavy-duty paper plate and line up.

Pete liked to load up the scrambled eggs with olives and a bunch of other arbitrary items that Chip didn't care for. He never understood the idea behind white, breakfast gravy so he stuck to grits, bacon and heavily pre-buttered English muffin. The picky eaters always got a bunch of shit from Pete about not going for the gravy or corned beef hash, but it was all in good fun.

Chip was basically a talker, but when he was the only young guy at camp, he usually just listened – a lesson he learned at the ranch at an early age. Chip's younger brother Jay didn't hunt much. He had spent plenty of time at the ranch when he was a kid. Once when Jay was in high school, Bruce caught him and his buddies looking for psychoactive mushrooms in the cow pasture. Charles never got wind of it, but Jay had pretty much stayed away from the big hunt weekends since then.

Chip tuned out during Jimmy's deer story. He looked around at the guys in the room and wondered how he was going to make his mark. For a twenty-four year old guy, he had accomplished quite a bit.

At seventeen he graduated high school and joined the Marines. After three years in the Corps he enrolled at UF and became a long-shot walk-on. In his sophomore year, as a back-up linebacker, the two starters were caught robbing an Indian Casino in Brighton and Chip made it to the starting line up overnight.

Two-year starters at Florida were expected to excel on the field beyond their undergraduate years. But with little hope of playing in the League and a degree in Forestry, Chip was starting to lose sleep over it all.

The room was full of well-tested guys. They were all friends as kids in Miami and all of them ended up being very successful. Chip had known these guys since he was a child and he knew he wanted to have a similar life. He had this feeling that the key to his future was in the room – enjoying olive-laced scrambled eggs and sawmill gravy.

Walt Davenport was sitting next to Chip and he had a newspaper opened up to his side. Chip asked if it was today's paper and Walt said he got it on a butter run to the store when he got out of the woods. Chip knew there was going to be an AP article about the Sugar Bowl. "Can I see the sports section real quick Walt?" he asked. "Surely," said Walt handing it over.

Charles didn't much like when people read the paper or watched TV during hunt weekends. He'd rather everyone tell bullshit stories about hunting or whatever. Chip read the article on the Sugar Bowl to himself. The Gators were favored and Chip was noted only briefly. He put the pages back in the general vicinity of Walt and went back to his English muffin.

"Interesting, very interesting," Walt said as he studied the A Section through his half glasses. "What is it," asked another fellow from across the room. Walt continued, "Reynolds is hanging it up after fourteen terms." A round of "Hmmms" filled the room.

Most of these guys knew Congressman Robert Reynolds personally. He was a Democrat with nearly thirty years in the House and he was the type who was loved by all.

Hank Hoover got up to get seconds. As the bank VP got to the doorway of the kitchen, he turned around with an empty plate in his hand and a fork in the other. He looked over at Chip and said "How old are you now?"

Chip swallowed a sip of orange juice and answered "Twenty four."

"Well when do you turn twenty-five?" asked Hank.

"I just turned 24, in November. Why? You think I should run for Congress? You think my first job out of college should be a Member of Congress?"

Everyone in the room turned to Chip. There were some nods and some grunts. It got silent.

Walt Davenport spoke first. "I fish the tarpon run in Pine Island with a big time political consultant – has offices in Boca and D.C. – he could tell you if you have a shot. It's not a bad idea."

"Are you guys insane?" Chip asked. "On what grounds would I – look, look, the second this paper hit the stands – no – probably before that – there was a state rep licking his chops right now – someone with experience. Think about it for chrissakes!"

Chip's dad jumped in. "You *did* join the Marines in spite of a full ride to play linebacker for Georgia Southern, you're a hell of a student, and you're one of the captains on one of the most marketable college football teams in the country."

"Think of the gals in D.C.... Oh man." added Jimmy.

"It's not that insane Chip," his dad said.

Chip couldn't help suppress a slight grin. He stood and walked his plate into the kitchen. Hank was still in there. "Chip... I honestly think you could pull it off. Didn't you intern for someone in local government – you know the drill don't you?"

"Hank I not only do not 'know the drill,' I don't think I even know how a bill becomes a law. I don't – where do Congressmen even live? DC or in their district? How much does it cost to run a campaign? There's gotta be – I can't believe we're even having this discussion."

"People don't vote for politicians – they used to. Now they want leaders. It's all about *branding* kid. Believe me. And if every guy in this – hell, look at Walt – if every guy in this ranch house made ten phone calls, you'd have a very solid financial launchpad. Money is the last thing you should be worried about."

Chip could hear the other men grumbling in the great room as he looked out the window at Jimmy's buck, hanging in the attached pole barn. Hank whistled as he reloaded his paper plate with eggs and white gravy.

Pete stood in the doorway with a big smile. "Congressman Charles Robert MacIntosh the Third. Did you get some of that gravy?" He put his giant arm around Chip and rumbled out a deep chuckle. He was excited for the kid.

The kid couldn't believe any of this. He picked up his coffee and headed out the propped-open door to the porch. There was about a four foot wooden wall with a ledge beneath the screen. Chip set his coffee down and rubbed his face. The sun was way up at this point and the porch felt warm. He looked out over the barnyard and reconsidered his fate – his destiny. The men inside were chatting it up pretty good. They all seemed to be strategizing on behalf of the young man on the porch.

Chapter Three

The Florida Gators arrived via chartered buses on New Year's Eve. As a captain, Chip was responsible, at least in part, for keeping the guys on a tight leash. Sixty young men filled with testosterone being unleashed on one of America's wildest cities could have had consequences. Add the players from Pittsburgh into that mix and *trouble* becomes a near certainty.

Skip Haynes was the head coach of the Gators. He passed out a printed schedule back in Gainesville and told his players not to screw up. Then he left to board a private jet with an elite group of alums and benefactors.

The boys had a day and a half to prepare for the game. There were team breakfasts and team lunches, but the dinners were "on your own" plus there were voluntary receptions hosted every night.

Chip's parents were in town as well. They were at a historic bed and breakfast with a few other couples.

The eight hour ride down I-10 had taken its toll on most of the team. Chip and the other captains reminded the players that breakfast was at seven in the morning as they filed into their hotel rooms. It was 3PM; there were no meetings, films, or receptions that night. The players could exercise at the YMCA if they so desired.

Chip's suite-mate was the quarterback and fellow captain Christian Ross. He was an easy going, effective leader. Off the field, his vice was girls. He was just as much of a heartbreaker as Chip but he was a somewhat lousy student and chased women every chance he could. Coach Haynes specifically asked Chip to "keep an eye on that goddamn *hound dog* while we're in New Orleans."

Christian was a junior from North Carolina. His dad was an Air Force Colonel and kept his son on a pretty tight leash. When he got to Gainesville, he let loose, just like many who came before him. Chip helped keep him in line.

They were situating their stuff when Christian's phone started playing the cell phone version of some ridiculous song. He studied the tiny screen then hesitated for a minute. "Hey man – I just got a text from my folks, I'm meeting them for dinner, do you want to join us MacIntosh?"

Yea, Chip thought – a text from *mom and dad*... "I appreciate it, but I already have plans with my folks. I'll call you afterwards though, so make sure your phone is on."

Christian gave Chip a smile and a nod. Chip knew damn well that the text message came from some little group of honeys who caravanned in from G-ville but he figured he only had to worry about his teammate during what college kids call "late-night." So he let it slide.

"I'm going to see if anyone's hanging out – wanna come?" Christian asked.

"Nah dude, I'm gonna take a shower. I feel kinda gross."

"Cool. Later" he said as he dashed out into the hallway in warm-up clothes.

Chip finished unpacking and locked himself in the bathroom while Christian was out exploring the Embassy Suites hotel. The different types of rooms had all been established within an hour of their arrival. There was a video game room, a beer room, a Texas Hold-em room, a Bible Study room, and a film room showing Pittsburgh's last game – against Penn State.

Some of the guys napped, mostly big lineman.

The hotel was atrium style and the entire courtyard was nicely landscaped and the restaurant and bar were right in the middle of it. Fans from both teams littered the ground level with their blue, orange, black and yellow clothing. Some of the players were on the ground floor signing autographs and taking pictures.

Just as Chip got out of the shower, his cell phone started vibrating on the bureau. It was his dad. "Hey dad. Sure. Why? Okay. But-. Right. Not really. Seven AM. I think so. Mom was going to. No. I don't know. Yea – I'm in. Roger that. Thanks. Bye."

Chip had just learned he would be dining with the Lieutenant Governor of the great state of Florida on New Year's Eve. Apparently Charles' friends had made some calls.

Chip stared out the window of his hotel room and studied the character of the architecture unique to New Orleans. The thought of running for Congress was back on his mind. He wanted to go for a run, but there were too many people and he didn't care for treadmills. Plus he had just showered and was due at dinner in two hours.

With his face in his hands Chip sat on the edge of his bed. He was still wearing a towel and a pair of flips. He didn't feel right sitting in his hotel room and he couldn't really leave, so he threw on some clothes and decided to check on his teammates.

Before he could leave his room his phone started humming again. Without looking at the number, he answered it. It was Jessica. He told her he couldn't talk and she let him go. She and the rest of the training staff had made it to town and were staying at the Holiday Inn around the corner. He promised he'd call her after dinner.

The younger players were all fired up. Most of them were acting like kids at camp. Chip empathized with their elation and opted not to give any of them a hard time – as long as they were playing by the rules. He went from room to room saying 'hey' to everyone. Nearly all of the rooms had the security latch thrown the opposite way to allow unlimited access. Even the nappers left their doors ajar so they wouldn't have to contend with sleep-ruining knocks.

While hanging around the wide open door of the video game room, Chip looked down the hall and saw a manager-type guy heading his way. Chip asked the fellows to keep it down a bit as the man approached.

"Sir, are you with the University of Florida Gator football team?" asked the man.

"Indeed I am sir, everything okay?" Chip responded.

"Yes sir, fine. I was told to let everyone on the team know that there is food for you in the Bayou Room."

"Oh – thanks – thank you, I'll tell the crew – that's great."

The man smiled and said "my pleasure sir. Good luck in the big game."

"Wait – mister... I mean *sir* – where is the *Bayou Room*?" asked Chip.

"It's just off the main lobby, there's a pedestal sign that points the way."

Chip swept the hallway telling everyone about the free food in the Bayou Room. A sea of athletes swarmed the hallways, stairways and elevators. Free food was free food. No one even wanted to know what it was. Chip joined the circus and made his way to the Bayou Room.

The room was lined with banquet tables. Some tables had thick deli sandwiches made with real croissants. There was a huge bag of Kaiser Rolls next to a few bins of pulled, barbecue pork and beef. There was a tin of

French fries, one of sweet potatoes, and there was a huge chilled bowl of coleslaw. Another table was stacked with bottled water and Gatorade. The last table looked more like a salad bar but instead of greens it was loaded down with boxes of candy bars, moon pies, and a host of other snack cake items – like Twinkies. There were plenty of round tables with sturdy banquet chairs. It got loud pretty quickly.

Once the boys all got settled in to chow down, a heavy-set fellow in a charcoal suit came storming through the double doors to the room. He started out by greeting the tables individually then made his way up to the previously unnoticed podium toward the side of the room.

Just then a bunch of other people showed up – coaches, boosters, a few reporters. One guy had an SEC lapel pin on. There were a few nice-looking older ladies.

The man at the podium began to speak. "Good afternoon everybody! I hope you boys are enjoying these fine eats – courtesy of *your* Florida Gators Booster Club!" There were some whistles, cheers and grunts. The food, likely brought in by a local barbecue joint, was exceptional. The man in the suit continued, "I'm proud to be a part of this extraordinary event this week. 'Cause I know only the finest teams in the country get to play in *the* Sugar Bowl! And I can tell you from the *heart* – that this is a great time *indeed* – to *be* a Flor-i-da Gator!" The howling continued as the boys filled up.

By the time half the team had gone back to the line for second servings, Coach Haynes fast-walked into the Bayou Room with a clipboard. The man with the microphone introduced the coach but quickly reminded the squad that there were huge boxes near the door filled with Sugar Bowl t-shirts.

Coach Haynes took the mic and thanked the Booster Club – it didn't appear that he even knew the speaker's name.

"Williams! Save some for your coaching staff son!" yelled the coach as he saw the giant right tackle heading back to his table with three pork sandwiches and about a pound of slaw. Williams just laughed. Someone threw something harmlessly at the 300-pounder from Clewiston.

The head coach continued with a big smile and in his southern drawl, "Gents, I know this meeting wasn't on the schedule. So don't think of it as a meeting. I just wanted to make sure you realized a few things before you head out for the night. First and foremost – you guys are *men*. I won't treat you like children but I will say this... I'm proud of this ball club. We've fought hard and come a long way. Don't give up on yourselves by screwing off tonight. I know a lot of parents are already in town for the game – go spend a nice evening with your folks and call it a night. I don't want to get a phone call in the middle of the – hell I won't be – my phone is going to be *off* this evening. You have earned the right to be here and I want you to enjoy yourselves – but I also expect a hundred and ten percent on that practice field tomorrow. So stay outta the sauce tonight, tell your girls you'll see 'em after practice and don't do anything that could jeopardize our mission here this week. Now y'all eat up and rest up – and I'll see you at breakfast. GO GATORS!"

The man in the suit returned to the podium – shook hands with the coach and took the mic again. "Fellas – we're almost done talking here – an' we'll let you get back to..." he didn't know how to finish that line. "I'd like to introduce to you the Director of Alumni Affairs of our fine university – Ms. Cheryl West!"

There was some clapping and a few slight cheers – they knew better than to actually whistle.

Cheryl had graduated about ten years earlier; she was pretty tall, though not for a room of football players. She was slender and almost tough looking yet she had a softness about her. When she got to the podium, the light was better – she was very attractive indeed. She wore the glasses of a younger woman but her outfit was mature. Chip studied her as she thanked the team for "continuing to improve the university's strong, national presence."

She talked about the university's heritage and went over some enrollment facts, numbers of programs, and the geographic range of the alumni base. She mentioned "Gator Nation." It didn't seem like many players were giving her their undivided attention. Chip was certainly the exception.

Finally, she mentioned the "seniors" in attendance today and she looked directly at Chip – almost as if she knew him well. He smiled. His heart began to beat a little faster.

Chip was a calm guy but he was a *talker* when he wanted to be. He had rallied his defense during pregame and halftime meetings; he had actually addressed tens of thousands at Gator Growl – the night before the homecoming last October (a severe beating against a non-conference opponent).

The alumni lady continued "Where are my seniors? Can the graduates stand up and be recognized?" Now the whistling fired back up a little – empty water bottles were chucked as about a dozen slightly embarrassed upperclassmen slowly made it to their feet. "I want to remind you guys that whatever your plans for the future involve – wherever you end up – you will *always* be a part of our awesome network of Florida grads."

On that note, Chip made the decision to give an impromptu speech – he had to leave soon to make his dinner date but something had come over him. His initial rationalization was that he was finally leaving the university that had given him so much over the years. Then he wondered if he might just be trying to impress the Director of Alumni Affairs.

He approached the podium while the applause was still sort of going. Cheryl holstered the microphone and greeted Chip a few steps away. "Cheryl West, pleasure to meet you." She extended her hand to him and flashed a warm smile. She seemed to blush a bit. Chip smiled back, shook her hand and reminded himself not to call her 'ma'am.' "Nice to see you Cheryl, Chip MacIntosh" Chip replied – where did that come from? He had never said 'nice to see you.'

Chip took a deep breath as he stood at the podium. Cheryl stood about four feet from him.

"While I'm not quite authorized to speak on behalf of Gators Football, I thought I'd say a few words that have been racing around in my head these last few days. I spent my Christmas vacation thinking about the Sugar Bowl and reflecting on the SEC Championship. And, somewhat selfishly, I've thought a lot about my future. I'm the oldest member of this family and, yet – I feel like I've grown up with you guys. I've seen some of you guys really blossom and I don't mean that to sound..." Chip was struggling a bit. What was he doing up there? He looked over at Cheryl who smiled at him as if to say – 'keep it up Killer. You can do this.'

He exhaled slowly. "I'm not one for giving speeches, but as the old man in the club and as a captain; I want you guys to know that I'm proud to have been a part of this team – this family. In three or perhaps four days, I'll turn into a *has-been* – that's just the nature of the game."

The crowd got quiet. Chip looked down for a second or two. He took another deep breath, raised his chin and continued. "We've all been blessed by God with talent – strength and speed. But God only planted the seed. The rest of our success is attributable to those who have guided us on this journey – our coaches, our families, and our school. I wasn't going to say anything – I didn't even know we were going to be in here today – but the word *alumni* has a new meaning to me lately. When I was in the service, I never fully understood what it would mean for me down the road – I don't mean the skills I learned or the work I did – I mean the *legacy* that carries with being a Marine. It's become a part of me yet it's as if I had nothing to do with it. My point is that today we are the team that made it to the Sugar Bowl – regardless of the outcome – we are winners. And because I have experienced a legacy – I wanted to share with you guys that this experience has been a dream come true for me. I love you guys and I will never forget the memories we've made together – both on and off the field."

There were lumpy throats at every table – no one moved. Chip was emotional – the guys made it to their feet and started clapping. The Marine linebacker smiled and yelled – "Now let's win this ballgame – for *The Legacy*!"

The crowd was all fired up. Chip knew this would be the last time he spoke to so many teammates at once. It made him sad – he was going to miss this crew and he knew he'd never again lay eyes on the majority of them.

As he turned to his side, Cheryl West was in tears – she was slightly embarrassed – her eyeliner was streaming down her tan cheeks. She was touched. Chip extended his hand to hers but she pulled him in for a hug. He held her more than the unwritten rules would have called for – she smelled like a high-end hair salon and she got better looking by the second.

Cheryl composed herself. She was blown away by the sensitivity of this offensive-line battering Marine who had just made her heart pound and her knees shake.

The applause and general rowdiness calmed down as Chip bumped a few fists on his way to the door. He shook hands with some of the guests and hosts then raced up to his room to get ready for the big dinner.

Jackson Square was slightly damp from an earlier sun shower. The slate covered ground was shining in the remaining sunlight. It was five forty-five, Chip was surprised it wasn't more crowded in spite of the rain. He had a few minutes to visit with President Jackson – who, with the St. Louis Cathedral as his background – looked like the king of the city. His monument was flanked by stately live oaks, blooming oleanders and small hybrid date palms. There were even banana trees at the entrance gates; it was a beautiful site. Chip knew Jackson pretty well. His dad had a painting of the seventh president in his study and though he didn't openly admit it, Charles Junior was a big fan of the hell-raiser president from Tennessee.

Jackson's militia had played a big role in the shaping of Florida's history. Charles was once summoned to an archeological dig near Kissimmee to examine artifacts thought to have been a part of one of the Seminole Indian Wars.

It was five until six and Chip had to turn on the charm.

Maxes on the Square was one of the best restaurants in the Quarter. The interior walls were clad in a patterned red wallpaper and had a walnut trim. There were candles burning in every corner and everyone there seemed to look great to Chip as he waited for a hostess.

He wore starched chinos, a white shirt, striped Nautica tie and a pair of Brooks loafers. His navy blazer was an Orvis traveller with dulling silver buttons.

The French-seeming maître d welcomed Chip with a fake smile beneath a real albeit ridiculous-looking mustache. "Right this way Monsieur MacIntosh," the man said as he snatched a one page menu from behind his post.

The linebacker was impressed "How did you know my name?"

"It is my 'pwofession' to know Monsieur."

The Frenchman briskly escorted Chip to a private room on the second floor. It was fancier than he was used to. He noted the richly colored curtains pulled back against mahogany columns, the white linen table cloths, oil paintings, and crystal chandeliers dangling sturdily from a pecky cypress ceiling.

"There he is," someone at the table slightly yelled.

"No hurricane damage here!" Chip proclaimed with a smile as he began the process of shaking hands and dolling out masculine hugs. His opening line was met with laughter.

Kirk Osborne was the last to greet Chip. "Pleasure to meet you Chip – great season son – you make the Orange and Blue proud!"

"Thank you sir, very nice to meet you, Lieutenant Governor," replied Chip as he took his seat next to the distinguished gentleman.

Charles was motioning for Chip to adjust his necktie. "Where's mom?" Chip mouthed to his dad. Charles cocked his head slightly over his left shoulder, closed his eyes and shook his head for a second or two.

He looked around the table at the group of men with whom he was dining. It was dad, along with his childhood pals-hunting buddies and fellow UF Grads: Jimmy Reese, Walt Davenport and Hank Hoover. Also at the table were LG Osborne and the very popular President of the University of Florida: G. Thomas Walker.

The Miami guys were singing the praises of Chip while Walker and Osborne listened and chewed on baguettes. Chip just studied the menu and politely smiled every time they said – "Eh Chip – Eh!"

"Chip my boy – what are your plans for after graduation?" asked Osborne as he drew heavily from his slightly diluted glass of bourbon. "Actually, hang on." He took another big swill and lowered his voice slightly. "Chip have you ever used the N word publicly, been arrested, mistook 'no' for 'yes,' or insulted a minority in any fashion?"

Walker jumped up like his ass was on fire "I, uh, need to use the men's room - excuse me."

Chip felt like his face was turning bright white. His menu fell from his hands like a bag of oranges. He wasn't sure what to think. He looked at each of the men at the table for a sign – something – anything. They all seemed serious. Osborne turned in his seat, now he was face to face with the Marine. He looked him in the eye with a cold stare and said "...cause if you answered *no* to all of those questions, I want you to run for Reynolds' House seat. And I want to leak it to the press *tomorrow*."

"Could you guys – I need a... Would you excuse me for a sec?" Chip asked respectfully. He rose to his feet, looked at his father and tilted his head towards the main section of the restaurant.

Charles met his son at the bar on the second level. "Well... What do you think?" asked Charles. Chip just looked at the floor and shook his head. He took a deep breath. "Okay – here's the deal. The truth is I *have* thought about it a lot lately. I think it would be cool to serve my country in another – another *way*. But I have so many questions and I don't think they can be... why tomorrow anyway? It has to be tomorrow?"

"Osborne thinks it will change the dynamics of the Sugar Bowl and it's like getting free airspace that would otherwise cost about a million dollars to achieve. How many hours are you taking this spring?"

"Nine I guess."

"What are they?" Charles asked – he sounded like a chief strategist.

"Ho-*ly* Shit," Chip said as he peered at the top of the stairway.

The Vice President of Alumni Affairs was making his way to the upstairs bar and trailing closely behind him was the *Director* of Alumni Affairs. She had gone back to her room and traded her suit for a pretty dress.

Charles turned to see what his son was staring at. "Jack – how are you?"

Jack Griffin was the nephew of the University's most generous donor of all time. He was a shoe-in for his position. The guy *bled* orange and blue but was pushing sixty and his way of bringing the bacon back to the university was becoming noticeably antiquated.

"Good to see you here Professor – this must be Chip. Delighted to meet you son."

"Yes sir" said Chip.

"Permit me to introduce Cheryl West. Cheryl these are two of the biggest Gators in the country – Dr. Charles MacIntosh and his son, our star tailback (he didn't watch the games) Chip MacIntosh."

She shook the professor's hand but never took her eyes off Chip's eyes. He felt his heart racing a bit. "Hello again Ms. West," Chip said with a smile.

She also smiled, "Hello again to you. I really liked what you said to your teammates earlier."

Charles nudged his kid in the elbow, "Folks, I don't mean to be rude, but we've got to get back to our table."

"Of course, of course – please," urged Jack Griffin. Just then Tom Walker appeared on his way back from the restroom. "Hey there Jack!" yelped Tom as he approached the group.

The conversation shifted to the three older men. Chip and Cheryl found themselves face to face – shielded from the rest of the world by a sea of blue blazers. There was chemistry – though she fought it with everything she had.

Chip was thinking about how nice it would be to stroll around the French Quarter with her. He found untapped romantic confidence and leaned in toward her studded diamond earrings. "Come up with a reason you have to leave and meet me at the Jackson Monument as soon as you can." He broke up the group of men next to him, brought Cheryl back to their loop and left the bar area. Even if she wasn't up for it – he had nothing to lose and he lost interest in dining with the older gentlemen.

He rushed to the private room where the men were drinking and talking. "Chip!" one of them said, he didn't care who.

"Mr. Lieutenant Governor," Chip began. The table got totally quiet – Chip remained standing. "Count me in sir!" The guys all jumped up to express their joy. "But I'm afraid I have to leave right away. I've been charged with looking after a teammate this evening and I have to go. Mr. Hoover, would you do me the courtesy of inviting Jack Griffin to sit here in my absence?"

Hank lit up – "sure kid. Is he here though?"

"Yes, he's at the bar with dad and President Walker," Chip replied.

Osborne grabbed Chip by the bicep and stared into his eyes, "You a hundred percent on this Chip?" he asked him.

"I have your blessing sir?" asked the young man dutifully.

"Along with my resources son," he said, seemingly from the heart.

"Then I'm a hundred percent," Chip said with a giant grin. He shook all of their hands and darted off.

Before the men sat down, Chip dashed back in – nearly knocking down a waitress. "Wait a sec! Mr. Osborne – what party?"

"Democrat Chip."

"Aren't you guys Republicans?" Chip asked.

"Yea, but Reynolds is a dem - whoever he endorses is going to win this thing. And though he's no liberal - he isn't going to endorse a Republican for that seat."

"Democrat... I see." The linebacker struggled with the label, "I'm a registered Independent... or maybe Democrat, I'm embarrassed - I can't even recall what my card reads."

The men all looked around at each other.

"You're a winner MacIntosh, don't worry too much. The press will find out that you're a registered Independent if you are. Just go with *Democrat*," said Osborne. "And Chip – winning the Sugar Bowl wouldn't hurt. We'll see you at the Alumni Reception tomorrow night."

"Okay – thanks. Thank you all, we'll talk..." Chip said as he cruised out of the room.

He neared the bar and couldn't see Cheryl. Dad and the others were still there, "Gentleman, I'm sorry – I won't be able to join you for dinner." Tom Walker asked if everything was okay. Chip replied "yes sir, my team needs me though. I'm sorry again. Mr. Griffin it was very nice to have met you sir." Chip shook their hands quickly and gave his old man a hug. He whispered to him: "I'm in Man – don't tell mom." And he took off.

Chapter Four

As far as bed and breakfasts go, the *Maison Metairie* was about the best the South had to offer. The restored mansion with its impeccably manicured grounds was the epitome of the modern southern plantation. All guest and service vehicles were stashed behind a hedge trimmed so tightly it looked like it had been hand-sanded.

The lawn was composed of gorgeous zoysia grass; it looked like rich green carpet made with futuristic fibers. Century-old live oaks, laced with Spanish moss, lined the crushed river stone drive and the back side of the place had a stout row of shiny, mature magnolia trees. There was an authentic, formal French garden area off to the side of the building where guests could receive breakfast service or cocktails.

The attendants wore white gloves and only seemed to show up when needed.

Mary Wallace McIntosh awoke New Year's Day to the sound of mockingbirds singing in the oaks outside. She sat up in the bed, put her feet on the rug and admired the front lawn through the window. The History professor was sound asleep next to her. He had a piece of goose down stuck in his whiskers so she gently removed it to keep him from consuming it.

Just outside the door to the room was a large stainless coffee vessel with a pair of cups, saucers, napkins, and silverware. To the side was a sealed glass bottle of milk and a small box of sugar sticks peeled fresh off the cane.

A crisp, monogrammed linen tote bag contained a national and a local newspaper. Rather than the *USA Today*, the *Maison* had chosen the *Wall Street Journal* for its guests. The local paper was the *Times Picayune*.

Mary picked up the tray and tote bag and brought them to the iron table near the balcony. The balcony was more of a second story wrap around porch with potted, purple bougainvilleas separating the individual rooms.

She fixed her coffee and tried to keep the noise to a minimum. The professor grunted a bit and started to shift around in the sheets. This was her cue to check the national news to see if anything had gotten out of hand on New Year's Eve. She opened the cabinet that housed the 42" flat screen television and clicked on CNN.

The professor moaned a little so she poured him a cup of black coffee and put it on the nightstand next to him. She pulled out a chair at the table, sat down and sipped her coffee. Next she opened the linen tote bag and produced the papers.

Mary noticed a "financial woes" headline across the top of the Journal and glanced over it. The professor emerged from the bed and rubbed his face. "Hey," he said to his wife. "Morning Charles. There's some coffee there," she replied. "Thanks," he said, sitting up.

Charles tugged at his beard then sipped his coffee. "That's not the *Wall Street Journal* is it?" he asked – still half asleep. "Uh-huh," she said. "Anything happen last night? In the world?" he asked. "Not that I can tell," she said as she continued reading.

It had been years since either of them stayed up to watch the ball drop, much less attend an event long enough to see the clock strike twelve. And yet every New Year's Day they awoke wondering if they had 'missed anything.'

Charles got up and walked toward the bathroom, he kissed his wife on the head as he went past. She reached up and touched the hand he placed on her shoulder. "Happy New Year," he said as he entered the bathroom. "Happy New Year – I love you," she said back.

Her husband was half-way through a significant hosing when she slightly yelled "think you could close the door?" He tried to reach the door from his stance but couldn't. He finished, flushed and came back into the room. His voice went up a full octave, "there's a three inch gap under that door." She didn't respond. "Sorry," he offered and he saw her smile at the paper.

Charles had just slipped into a pair of khakis and a sweater when he heard his wife slam her cup down – breaking the thin saucer. She turned to him and stared shockingly into his eyes over her frameless reading glasses.

"What is it?" he asked.

"Chip is – Did you? Look at this!" She was frantic.

In the bottom right hand corner of the front page of the Times Picayune – in bold, black type read: *Gators Standout MacIntosh Seeking Seat in US House.*

Mary reaffixed her glasses, dialed Chip's number, and put the phone to her ear. "Shit! – *voicemail* – mailbox full." She slid the phone into the breast pocket of her cotton pajamas. In a thick but demanding Virginia accent she grilled him "Charles, you had better start talking. Chip can't - What is going on Charles? Talk to me. Talk to me Charles!"

He walked her over to the two alligator-patterned leather lounge chairs. "We were at the ranch – right? Walt read out this article about Reynolds' retiring... Hank picked up on it and said Chip should run for his seat. Hank called his consultant friend in Boca and Walt called the lieutenant governor."

She was trying to absorb it all. "And that's why you two had dinner with those guys last night? What did Chip say? He said 'yes, he wants to run for Congress?' That's what he said? Chip said that? Really Charles?"

"I wasn't quite there when he told Kirk Osborne. But he told me before he left, I was stuck talking with Tom Walker and Jack Griffin – at the bar. They told me he was rock solid," he assured her.

"Where is he? Where is Chip right now?" she asked.

"Practice. Aren't you excited for him? Here's a kid who had no idea what to do for the rest of his life. Sure he'd have landed on his feet – right? Just think about where he's been and compare that to where he *could* go. He's a star Mary – he can't go sell Fords on 13th Street – not from where he's been. You're not happy about this. Why?"

"Of course I'm happy – but how's he going to – is he even old enough to be a Congressman?"

"He'd be 25 just in time. So, yes, he will be old enough."

"But he's just a kid! I mean is he *old* enough?"

"John C. Breckinridge was around 28 when he got to Congress and was elected Buchannan's Vice President at the age of 35. He later ran against Lincoln, left Kentucky to join the Confederacy, became Davis' Secretary of War..."

"Okaaaay! I get it," she pleaded.

"Look, let's just let the boy play tomorrow. He needs to stay focused on football for the next thirty-six hours."

"Fine, but – when can I see him?"

"He'll be at the alumni reception this evening for sure, but I think practice is open to the public," replied Charles in a most agreeable tone.

"Good, get a shower. I need to see him."

Coach Haynes was in the locker room in a closed meeting when his cell rattled the desk in front of him. The caller ID read "unavailable." The coach looked around a bit and decided to answer it. "Hellough!" he yelled in a thick South Carolina accent. "Yes sir! Is that right? Well sir, no. Yes sir. Thank you sir. Tomorrow. Noon your time. Yes sir." He covered the phone for a second – "Smith – find MacIntosh!" He went back to the phone. "Yes sir. Very good." He hit 'end' and set the phone down.

Chip came hustling into the locker room, he saw the coaches meeting through a separate room with giant Plexiglass windows. He knocked. Coach Haynes motioned for one of the coaches to open the door. Chip spoke first "you wanted to see me coach?"

"Dude, you'll never believe who I just got off the phone with," said Coach Haynes.

Oh God Chip thought, the NFL – a coach – a scout – shit! What had he done!

"I don't uh – who – I don't know..." offered Chip.

"I've got the biggest game of my career tomorrow and I just got a call from a goddam Congressman. Oh yea – a dimmacrat to boot! And do you know WHY the sumbitch is calling me?" asked the most unpredictable coach in college football.

"I think I could speculate sir," Chip tried not to grin.

The head coach stood with his star linebacker while the three other men remained seated. "This little fucker... (a half-foot taller and forty pounds heavier than Haynes) is running FOR CONGRESS!"

No one could tell if the coach was fuming with rage or excited for Chip. It could be seen as a distraction for the program. It could take away from the true essence of the Sugar Bowl or make the opponents more resentful.

"Put 'er there MacIntosh – that's big time!" the coach yelled as he extended an open hand to Chip. The other coaches smiled and relaxed a bit. "Thank you Coach Haynes – thanks," said Chip as he too breathed a sigh of relief. The other coaches joined in with praise.

"Allright – that'll do men. Chip – get back out there with your teammates and focus on tomorrow's contest – can you do that for me?" The coach was amused but ready to get back to the drawing board.

"Of course coach – thanks again." Chip remarked as he trotted out of the locker room.

"Sonofa'bitch" coach Haynes mumbled as he threw a pinch of Skoal into his face.

It was freezing cold in Washington, D.C. on New Year's Day. Jeff Schick had spent the evening at a private party composed mostly of senior congressional staffers. The event was held at a roomy Capitol Hill row house just three blocks from the US Supreme Court building.

Jeff awoke at 10:45 AM clutching a wool comforter and listening to the television ramble out national news. He was the only one in his house who had stuck around for New Year's. Both of his roommates had left town – one to Georgia and one to Snowshoe Mountain in West Virginia.

Unable to really see and unwilling to get out of the warm bed, Jeff slid his arm around his bed looking for the remote. He located it and, without looking at the buttons, turned on *College Gameday*. The broadcast was live from New Orleans but Jeff's hangover made it nearly impossible to fully listen to it. The volume proved too much for his stinging ears so he muted it and tried to go back to sleep.

It was cold, he was tired and felt like hell, but he had to pee. Rather than stand and run the risk of missing the bowl, Jeff sat down on the small commode. Just as he sat down, he could faintly see the red indicator light on his cell phone flashing on his bureau. And then there was the unmistakable vibration that accompanied a new email.

Jeff wondered if his boss, the Honorable Robert Reynolds, was trying to reach him – perhaps to wish him Happy New Year. But the old man never emailed, he hadn't learned how. He was a "caller." Jeff brushed his teeth to rid his mouth of the Canadian Whiskey that had put him in such a state.

He was awake now and knew sleep wouldn't come again until later in the day. Jeff was hopeful for a rare afternoon nap.

His boxer shorts weren't doing the trick against the cold so he threw on a pair of cords, a t-shirt from his softball team and a zippered fleece. Jeff turned off the TV in his room, stepped into a pair of running shoes, grabbed his mini computer from its charger and headed downstairs to make a cup of tea. He preferred a mix of green and Earl Grey tea for hangovers.

Jeff filled a copper-lined tea kettle with a pitcher of filtered water from the fridge and threw it on the stove. The kitchen was reminiscent of the 1950's. It looked like one of those retro-diners that had popped up all over during the eighties – when the fifties made a slight comeback. Everything was pink or aqua or stainless steel. The tile floor was finished in black and white tile, though it was not quite checkerboard.

While the water made its way up the thermometer, Jeff decided to thumb through his iPhone. It was an email from Karen Jared, a Committee staffer close to the Reynolds office that read: WHERE IS REYNOLDS?!

Jeff quickly phoned Karen. "Hey!" he said. "He's at the river house. Palatka – why what's wrong?"

"Jeff!" Karen seemed to scream. He held the phone a foot and a half away from his head and squeezed his eyes shut.

"Yea?" he replied. "What the hell? What?"

"Chip MacIntosh is running for Reynolds' seat!" she yelled.

"The linebacker!?"

"I thought he was a quarterback – yes – the 'linebacker.' For the Gators. Do you think Reynolds is watching the College Gameday? *No* – right?"

"He's definitely not watching ESPN, the man declines Super Bowl tickets. But he also reads the Gainesville Sun – cover to cover. Did they?... College Gameday said that Karen? They said *Chip MacIntosh is running for Reynolds' house seat*?"

"I swear to God! Like, five minutes ago. Where's David?"

"Home I guess – he's here. I've got to go. I need a fountain Coke and a couple slices of pizza. I'll call you later."

Karen had been with the Reynolds Team for four years before she left to help manage the very powerful Ways and Means Committee, of which Reynolds was the Chairman. This was commonplace on Capitol Hill - loyal staffers could, with certainty, count on being taken care of as long as their boss remained in a position of power.

David W. Jasper was Reynolds' most loyal confidant. He had been with the Congressman for fifteen years and was like a son to the old man. Without seeming like a total sucko, Dave was everywhere his boss was. He was always ready with a pen, pad, marker, checkbook, phone, tissue, statistic, car, what-ever – whenever the bossman needed him.

Dave pulled down the highest pay allowable. And he earned it. He had also made some lucrative, completely legitimate, land deals with Reynolds. His place was in Georgetown, a three-story federal style pad just off Wiscon-sin Avenue he had scored cheap during the housing crunch. Dave didn't have time for a pet iguana much less a family. He lived alone but seemed happy. His brother's daughter in California was the light of his life and he often sent the kid expensive gifts.

The news of Chip's plans circled around the Florida Delegation – mem-bers, staffers, former-staffers, and lobbyists with ties to the Sunshine State. Phones and iPads lit up for hours in DC on New Year's Day. Those outside the Florida 'loop' wouldn't have cared – it wasn't big enough news. But to those with a link to the state, this was *serious* gossip.

It was just before noon when the Suburban pulled into the packed park-ing lot at the SuperDome. "What is this?" Mary asked as she observed from the passenger's seat. "These folks are all here for the game – tomorrow's game? Or the practice or what?"

"I can't believe – try his cell again," replied Charles as he tried to avoid a frisbee-slinger in the middle of the lane.

Mary dialed her son and got him, "Chip! Honey where are you? Are you at this stadium? Where? Yes, I do. When? Okay Hun. Chip?"

She pointed to an obscure gated area near the corner of the parking lot "He's going to meet us at that – Gate Seven – in two minutes."

Her phone rang two seconds later, it was an old friend from Virginia, this really brought that accent out. "Hiiiiii – I KNOW – I don't know – No – I KNOW! – You just wouldn't belieeeeve it – I KNOW!"

Charles could hear his wife's friend stretching her words too. He picked up on the whole "I NOAUGH!" thing for the first time at their wedding, nearly thirty years ago. He thought it was an inside joke or something. But it wasn't, it was four or five generations of *Veh-GIN-yah*.

Just then Chip was seen jogging out of the SuperDome wearing dark sun-glasses. Mary jumped up in her seat "Chip is – love to Frederick – Bye!"

Mary opened the door just as Chip yelled to shut it. He bolted into the back seat and slid to the middle. "Drive!" he said. "Hey Momma."

Chapter Five

The Honorable Robert Reynolds had much in common with Northern Florida's most successful guys: *Diversified Agriculture*. He had his hands in citrus down in Vero Beach, pine timber near Deland, cattle in Okeechobee, hay in Ocala, sod in Belle Glade, and – just to really fit in – he owned half of a crab shack on his beloved St. Johns River in Palatka. Almost every good ol boy in Florida owned at least a part of a restaurant at one point in their life. It was a rite of passage for anyone in Wrangler jeans, a gold watch, and a pair of pull-on Wellington boots.

The icing on the cake for these sorts was a Chevrolet Silverado 3500 4x4 with a leathery crew cab and dual rear wheels. Reynolds bought a new one every three and a half years, just shy of the four-year mark for massive depreciation.

His river home was straight off a movie set; weathered wooden siding, unfinished tin roof, wrap around porch, huge, latticed crawl space to accommodate flooding and stash canoes, and just under eight acres of land. Most of the original oaks had been creamed in back-to-back hurricanes so Reynolds had fast-growing mahogany trees planted by the dozens. The original sabal palms had weathered the storms and framed the view of the river beautifully.

Near the bank of the St. Johns was Reynolds' favorite place on the planet – his 'den.' Originally built as a smokehouse in the fifties, Bob's den was damaged during the storms. He had it rebuilt nearly ten years ago with salvaged timber and antique fixtures to the specs of an old Florida Cracker House he'd seen in Chiefland. The *Den* was about twenty by thirty and had a premium view of the river, the pier and boat dock. The inside was cased in tongue and groove cedar planks with tarnished old lanterns to make it glow. There was a hidden door to a spacious bathroom with a two-headed shower and a sauna. He had become quite fond of the private john located in his congressional office so he decided to replicate that privacy at home.

The main room in the den overlooked the river on one side and the main house on the opposite. The other walls were loaded down with shelved books and photographs. In the corner was a cast iron, wood-burning stove. Adjacent to the old cooker was a stack of yellowing newspapers and a bundle of fancy, lightweight firewood his wife had ordered from a catalog retailer in New England.

In the other corner was a personal fly-tying factory complete with vise, magnifying lamp, stainless instruments, and trays of natural and synthetic feathers, fibers, and lines.

Reynolds enjoyed novels and sportsman magazines from a bull hide chair and ottoman. He kept a humidor for pipe tobacco he scored during fishing trips in the Keys. And though he fogged up the Den with the sweet grey smoke, he wouldn't be caught dead smoking a pipe in the District of Columbia.

The main house belonged to Mrs. Robert Reynolds. She collected French china and sixty percent of the house was reflective of their vast collection. The key to the river house was hidden atop the closest shutter to the door. Everyone from staffer to second cousin had stayed there on their own. Being a Member of Congress certainly had its perks, but privacy was not typically one of them. There were always people around Reynolds, especially during the campaign.

Reynolds loved Christmas on the St. Johns. It was warm enough to fish and explore the river and it cooled way down at night creating the perfect setting for an outdoor fire pit surrounded by grandchildren.

At the end of the long pier-like dock was a thirty-three foot sportfishing boat. Reynolds had enjoyed nearly twenty different boats over the course of his lifetime, but he had always wanted a bigwater diesel cruiser that would get him way out in the ocean if he'd ever committed the time necessary to pilot it up to Jacksonville. The thing cost him over fifty grand but it could easily handle twelve adult passengers and it provided comfortable sleeping quarters for four people. It had a head, air conditioning, a galley, even a carbon monoxide detector. It was a little out of place on the tea-colored river lined with live oaks and palmettos, but Reynolds loved the boat almost as much as his family. He bought it in Stuart, Florida. It originally had a big tower with a hardtop and a bunch of outriggers. Since the Congressman only really wanted it for river cruising, he had the extras removed and relied simply on a Bimini top for sun protection. His family loved the boat as well.

It was after the New Year and the kids had all gone back to their homes. The Congressman used the quiet time to reflect and think about his last year in the House. He wouldn't be back at the river house until the Blues Festival in February.

The thought of a young kid running for his seat appealed to him. He was a Gator, but he never found time for football games. Reynolds knew Chip's name, Charles and Mary were donors and supporters. It meant a lot that Chip was in the Corps and a Gator, but the old man just didn't understand football.

Reynolds was born in St. Augustine to Irish immigrants. His parents worked for one of the upscale resorts on the beach. He fished the ocean as a kid, but the rivers, lakes and streams to the west of town are what really peaked his interest.

During Christmas break from middle school, Robert would help out at a private quail hunting club. By the time he was in high school, he was taking wealthy wing shooters from up north on guided quail hunts. The tips alone were more than he could make in an entire summer of bussing tables at the resort.

Reynolds had always credited *the woods* for teaching him about people; he said 'when you spend time with someone in the woods, only then could you really get to know them.'

He once guided a Senator from New York for three straight days. On the final day of hunting, the man handed him a 150% tip and said "you've got a good way about you kid, you should run for Congress some day."

Those words stuck with Reynolds and he read up on civic affairs and followed the elections closely. His time at the university went quickly; he worked more than most undergrads and became very active in politics.

Chapter Six

Chip spent the afternoon with his parents but they hardly had any time to actually talk to each other. All three of them were on their cell phones fielding questions from family and close friends. Finally Charles found a wayside park on the Mississippi and pulled in. "All right goddam it, everyone just turn their phone off for two seconds."

Chip got out of the Suburban and stretched as he watched a barge coming down the river. His parents got out and joined him. "Chip," his mom started. Chip wasn't listening "Dad! Look at those canvasbacks!" he yelled.

His mom was losing it. "Dammit Chip, you're looking at ducks! Will you please talk to me?"

"Sorry Momma, go ahead" Chip said nicely.

"Hun, what's the matter?" Mary asked.

He wanted to yell at her – this was her stock question at any given moment, like she was a psychotherapist. Charles saw a bench nearby, produced a cigar from his shirt pocket and strolled away from his wife and son.

"Mom, there's nothing wrong. I can do this."

"Chip this isn't about what you *can* do, we know you can *do* anything. It's about wanting to – it's about needing…" She was lost for words; she looked to Charles who was enjoying his smoke and the fine view of the big river. Mary continued, "Why don't you – it's okay if you don't know what you want, you're still so young, it will – why don't you get a graduate degree or go to Europe or something?"

"Europe? Mom I want to do this. People don't elect 'representatives,' they elect 'leaders.' I wouldn't do it if I didn't think I could win. Hell no one else has even announced yet."

"I think – Chip there's a good chance you can win. I don't know – someone will run against you – someone with more experience in politics – but it's not that – I'm not worried about – Honey do you have any idea what they'll write about you? They will attack your character – your family…"

"My family?" Chip asked.

"These people – Chip I – your great great grandfather had a plantation…"

"I know – I know. Look. Mom, I have no more football practice or games or anything after tomorrow. I have three cupcake classes in the spring and I've got plenty of time to get the ball rolling – do research – find help – I – I've got this. I think it will be fun. We've got months still – this thing is practically a year out. Don't worry – for once – don't worry so much. I need your help. Will you help me?"

"Of course I'll help you. Have you really thought?"

"No, I haven't thought it all out. The truth is I have no idea what I'm doing. But it makes sense to me somehow. Doesn't it sound kind of cool? MacIntosh for U.S. Congress!"

"That's what worries me – it's more than a 'cool sounding' sticker on your truck. Its peoples'..."

"Lives?" Chip asked. "I know that – don't worry."

Chip joined his dad on the bench while Mary stood by the truck looking spent. She worried about everyone, it was her nature. The idea of a negative write up about her son in the local paper made her fists clench. She took a few deep breaths and looked over at her boys. She shook her head slightly and walked over to them. She stood upwind of the cigar smoke and watched the tugboats do their thing.

Charles looked at both of them "We all on the same page now?" he asked.

Mary stood there with her hands upside down on her hips. "I wish someone would have – Chip you're going to need to let that hair grow out a little – and we've got to get Reynolds on board ASAP, that's a solid gold endorsement and you need him on your side if you want to win. Charles, I want you to have a T.A. present in every student meeting from now 'til November. I have a few friends I want you to meet with Chip - in D.C.. And someone needs to talk to Jay – is he here Charles? Is Jay in New Orleans?"

"Did he end up coming out here?" Charles asked his son.

"I thought so. He hasn't called you guys? I haven't..."

Mary went to get her phone from the truck.

Chip could not focus on the game or the campaign; he could not stop thinking about the Director of Alumni Affairs. He could still smell her perfume. "What time is it?" he asked his dad.

"Quarter to four," replied Charles.

"We've gotta split. Are you and mom going to that reception *thing* tonight?" Chip asked, trying to make it sound like a total drag of an event.

"Of course," he said.

"Lets go – I've got to get to the hotel."

Mary walked toward the men, "He's here. He's been at some Murphy bar or something all day – he has no idea – Chip can you call him?"

Chip put his arm around his mom as he walked her back to the Suburban. "I'll call him. But I've got to get back to the hotel. I'll call him when I get to my room" Chip assured her.

Chip secretly thought that if anyone could mess things up for his chances at Congress, it was Jay. He was clever and operated under the radar, but he hung around a lot of younger kids. And younger kids *talk*.

The hotel looked different to Chip when his parents dropped him off. The number of girls wandering the halls had at least doubled. There were players and fans hanging out in every corner. Signed jerseys dangled from shoulders, coolers were being wheeled around, and Gator chants could be heard from every level in the atrium. "Bluuuuuuue!.............Orrraaaaannge!"

Chip stepped out of the elevator and looked down the hall. He could see a group of people hanging around his room or the room next door. "Please don't be my room," he said to himself as he walked closer.

The room next door to his was the place to be. There were people spilling into the hallway with beer, music and dancing.

A few people said hello to the linebacker as he danced through the crowd to his door. Someone mentioned 'Congress' but he got through in time, and without any forearm shivers.

Apparently the music was too loud for Christian Ross to hear his suitemate enter. Ross was wedged between white sheets and a nineteen year old girl wearing nothing but makeup.

"Ross!" Chip yelled. The girl didn't even care. She turned and smiled at Chip as she continued to straddle the quarterback.

"Hey - man – sorry – do – you mind..."

"No, I'm – taking - a - shower. But," Chip said.

"Ten – minutes – tops – bro – thanks!" Ross managed.

Chip couldn't help but notice the attractive blonde atop his teammate. She had remarkable tan lines to accentuate her immaculate rear end.

He caught himself staring then quickly grabbed a few items and disappeared into the bathroom.

Chip got out of the shower and was sure he heard a bullhorn. It was one of the coaches breaking up the party. He heard the word "mission" a few times. Just after the music was cut off, Chip deduced that Ross and his friend had reached the 'end' of their activity. 'Lovely' Chip said to himself.

He exited the small bathroom just as the girl was getting her clothes back on. This time he got a look at her front. She wasn't a bit shy but she didn't quite flirt with Chip either. She slid into her flips flops, turned to Ross and said "Bye Christian," she turned to Chip and said "see ya – thanks."

Chip nodded – "you bet. Nice to meet you." And the girl was gone. Just before the door closed all the way, a meaty hand with a wedding band slid into the crack. It was one of the coaches. Chip stood there in a towel "hey coach!"

"What'n'the hell Chip!" the coach asked and yelled at the same time.

Chip motioned his head toward the ruffled sheets of bed number one.

"Why am I not – Dammit Ross! This isn't fucking Mardi gras! You can't store that pecker 'a yours for three days!? Your moment to shine is tomorrow – the biggest game of your life and you want to treat this trip to the Sugar Bowl like it's a goddamn three-day smash-fest!"

Ross sat up in the bed a little – "Coach she was giving me a message. She's an *occupational sports medicine trainer* major..."

Chip tried to hide his grin by rubbing his face with his long fingers.

"I'm not amused – you're just as guilty as *Dumbass* here. Congressman my ass!"

The coach disappeared and yelled at some people in the hall.

"Dude – did you see her ASS – Chip – tell me" asked Ross as if it was worth the chapping he had just received from the coach.

"I can't remember," said the politician with a wink. "I'm sure it was most-satisfactory though. Get dressed man, we've got to be at that reception. She *did* have a nice butt."

Ross got up, placed a ball cap in front of his midsection, walked to the bathroom and shut the door. Chip checked himself in the mirror. He had shaved that morning and was pleased to see a slight shadow occurring on his face. He wanted to look a tad older than his teammates that night.

The Alumni Reception was for "seniors and standouts," and that's exactly how Haynes had described it to the team. "At two-fifty a head," the coach said, "that's just how they want it. It's shitty, but it's the way it is. My hands are tied."

One of New Orleans' nicest hotels was the W on Poydras Street, right around the corner from the Embassy Suites. Chip, Ross, and a few others walked together. They were all wearing oxfords, ties, navy blazers and duffle-bagged cotton chinos (Chip found the iron in the room – Marines don't wear wrinkled trousers). He pressed Ross' too for providing a peek of the hot girl in his room.

The attendants at the ground level wore very sharp uniforms and alert expressions on their faces. The donor class folks all poured in wearing suits and dresses. Shiny lapel pins revealed the red bars of the Florida flag. Some guys had on their orange and blue Brooks Brothers ties. One, obvious former player, had a vintage scarf depicting a championship year dangling from his still-broad shoulders. The older man had a chunky gold ring clinging to his hand and his bride still looked good to Chip in spite of her years.

The top floor was saved for the W's signature four-star restaurant and lounge. Dubbed *Zoe's*, it had a commanding view of the city, the quarter, even Lake Pontchartrain. Chip was delighted not to hear Jazz music when he walked in. He had heard it everywhere he'd been so far in New Orleans and just wasn't into it. He respected it's heritage, but could only handle so much. On a slightly elevated platform between the bar and the fixed dining area was a band of aging hipsters playing Captain Jack by Billy Joel. Hardly a fitting ballad for a floor full of scholars, it sounded great to Chip.

Jessica Van Zandt had done a fine job introducing him to the likes of Billy Joel and Peter Gabriel. Chip was a Tom Petty – Lynyrd Skynyrd – Dwight Yoakam – guy but he was working on broadening his horizons. College did that to him; he found that enlisted Marines either like country or rap.

The bar at the W. was hip and high-end. Lots of glossy cherry wood and brushed aluminum. The immobile bar stools were finished in caramel-colored leather and the backdrop wall displayed bottles of liquor with rays of colored lights beaming through them.

Rather than the against-the-wall, rectangular banquet tables the players were used to, Zoe's had large round tables stacked nearly to the roof with everything from freshly shucked oysters to smoked marlin. Chip overheard a lineman ask a waiter for a bigger plate.

"Oh fuck" thought Chip "not *Mustang Sally*." It reminded him of a few of the way-too-young-to-get-married Marine weddings he had attended.

Chip wandered solo about the great room. He was in a zone as people said "hello" and "Chip! I want you to meet..." He made it through it all without seeming like a total jerk.

He found himself obsessing about having not yet located Cheryl. He needed a beer but couldn't remember if the team was allowed to drink or not. He looked around to see if any other players were drinking. He spotted Ross talking to the daughter of an alumnus. The girl looked fifteen – tops. Ross noticed Chip and gave him a little nod.

Someone tapped at Chip's shoulder. He turned around slowly and there she was - with a guy. "Christ – pleeeeeease don't be her boyfriend!" he thought to himself.

Cheryl spoke first, "Chip? There's someone I want you to meet."

The Marine rallied, "Hi there. Chip MacIntosh – pleasure." Cool as cool gets.

"Very nice to meet you. Shane Thompson," the thirty-something banker type said as the two firmly shook hands. "I was at that Championship Game Chip – Gator football at it's finest! Congratulations on a great season."

Chip found his eyes bouncing back between Cheryl and her friend. The guy couldn't have been nicer and he was a handsome enough dude. It had to be her boyfriend. Chip hated that he cared so much about this situation in spite of his ability to keep his feelings hidden.

"So Chip... Is it true you're running for Reynolds' house seat?" Cheryl asked as she drew a sip of red wine.

"Are you even twenty-five?" asked Shane Thompson albeit playfully. It didn't sound terribly patronizing but Chip wanted to tackle the guy.

"If I'm lucky enough to be elected by the good people of Northern Florida's Eighth Congressional District, I will, in fact, meet the required age upon taking the oath," Chip replied with premium poise.

The older girl lit up a little. It didn't sound a bit fake to her; slightly political, but it seemed genuine and off the cuff. "What brought all this on – I mean – have you always been interested in politics – I don't recall ever seeing you-"

Chip stopped her, respectfully. "Cheryl – Shane – would you excuse me? I just noticed that my folks are here and I'd like to say hello. Can we continue this chat in a bit?"

"Of course" said Shane.

"Yea, please – by all means," Cheryl said with a smile. She briefly touched his elbow as if it was soaked in Holy Water.

Chip knew he could no longer say 'mom and dad' or 'my parents.' *Folks* sounded better, a mature guy would refer to his parents as *his folks*. The linebacker felt good as he left her. He knew it was game-time and he wasn't thinking about the Sugar Bowl. Her eyes briefly trailed him as he confidently walked away.

Coach Haynes got to Chip before Chip could get to anyone else.

"What's this shit about you and Ross and some goddamn tart – *neckid* in your room?" The coach asked. Chip knew the assistant coach never saw her naked.

"She was naked?" Chip asked, busting the head coach.

"MacIntosh – you've got more to lose here 'n any of us. Don't screw up now. I wanna win tomorrow – if I have to board your goddamn door shut tonight, I will."

Chip looked down at the floor and nodded slightly – like a puppy that had just shit on a Persian rug. 'Oh Jesus – no!' thought Chip in his head. Coach Haynes was wearing football cleats and it made Chip chuckle a bit. He couldn't hold it – his large frame started to bounce up and down. Chip scrunched his eyes and prayed to God not to let him crack up.

"What's got you all cracked up – my shoes? Well, asshole, if you must know, I forgot to bring my good shoes with me and didn't have a chance..." The coach started to explain himself. By some miracle, one of the big-dog alums came up to the two men and Chip found an acceptable escape. His eyes were tearing and his face was red. Coach Haynes loved Chip like a son. He was the team's most reliable player. Chip wasn't the best player, but his loyalty and commitment to the team was second to none – that made him reliable – a coach's dream. Haynes talked downward, not quite 'down,' to every player. It was his way. He never called anyone an "asshole" if he didn't love them.

Chip composed himself and saw Cheryl walking towards him. She looked great. She had on a J. Crew strapless dress in satin black with an alligator green cashmere shawl to hide her flawless tan shoulders. Her blonde hair was pulled back and she wore small diamond studs. She carried a small black purse by its tiny strap and in the same hand as her wine glass.

He liked the way she seemed to have gotten through life without a little tattoo on her ankle and by limiting the jewelry to a pair of simple earrings. She had a way about her that set her apart from any girl he had ever met.

"Got a minute Chip?" she asked.

"Sure." He replied.

"Can we talk on the deck outside?"

"There's a deck? Yes – of course," he said, looking around.

She didn't put her arm in his, though they walked off in such a fashion.

It was cool on the deck and the view was impeccable. Chip looked out over the City of New Orleans and attempted to seem as though he was thinking about anything other than the foxy woman who had shuttled him out there.

"Chip – about last night," she started. There it was. Chip lost count of how many times those words had been poured over his head like warm, foamy beer.

"Forget about it. I don't really know where that came from. I have no excuse, I just had this feeling. I'm embarrassed about the whole thing, sincerely." Chip turned away from the city and looked her in the eyes. "Cheryl, I've never been one to sugar-coat things. I call em as I see em and I speak from the heart. Part of me was glad you weren't at the Jackson Memorial. And the truth is – I was supposed to be watching... I was supposed to be looking out for a teammate who tends to make poor decisions – *off* the field anyway." Chip looked around a bit. "Actually... my stomach turned, my heart pounded and my knees rattled. That's not easy for me to-" damn he was good, but he was being honest. "Plus," he continued, "that was the first time I had ever done anything like that, I kid you not."

Cheryl was looking back at the city. She was physically experiencing everything Chip had just described. Her eyes got watery and she was blushing slightly.

He wanted to ask if Shane was her boyfriend but realized it didn't matter at that moment and he might be able to find out without asking. He wanted to hear her side of the story and he was careful not to push her. Chip wanted to know what she was thinking.

He gambled. "Do you need a minute alone?" he asked politely.

She cleared her throat in a very feminine manner. "Chip I've known you for a day. Sure I *knew* you, everyone knows *of* you, but we hadn't met. What am I saying?" There was a slight pause. "Look. Chip. I think of you as a student, in spite of your – I *don't* actually think of you as a student – that's not true. I think of you as a guy I'd like to know in some form or fashion. I hadn't honestly figured out which way I thought of you. I watched you at the Jackson – I saw you out there. I left the restaurant and I was going to meet you but then I got scared, I thought we'd get into trouble. I watched you in the darkness – it was one of the hardest things I have ever done. I should have... I could get fired if I..."

The thought of her watching him while he stood there like an idiot was like falling on a sword for Chip. He remembered playing it so cool.

Chip took the high road. He had to. "Cheryl, why don't we do this... Why don't we take a deep breath and get back to the reception? You and I are here tonight to perform. Right? Let's just do it, get through the game tomorrow, get back to G-ville and we'll figure it out next week or something. The truth is I have a lot going on too. I realized from the moment I met you that I had a special fondness for you. I know it doesn't seem conventional right now – for either of us. Let's just let this wine breathe a little and we'll see if there's something there in a few days or whatever."

"Okay – that's a good plan. I like that. Why don't you go in first? That way it won't look..."

"No, no – please," he held his hand out showing her the way to the door. She gave the deck a quick glance and kissed him on the pressure point under his left ear. Chip swore to himself her mouth opened slightly. She was alluring. Cheryl walked to the door then stopped half way. She turned to the schoolboy Marine. "You don't live in that big brick house across from the stadium do you?"

"Shittt," Chip said – not loud enough for her to hear. He curled in his lips and nodded affirmatively.

Cheryl lowered her long eyelashes, smirked and slowly shook her head. She then winked playfully at Chip and went back inside.

Chapter Seven

The third of January came after most of the Florida Gators had enjoyed a decent amount of sleep; even Ross slept alone. The team made it to breakfast on time and to the stadium with very little yelling from the coaching staff. It was a gorgeous day in New Orleans. The parking lot at the SuperDome was lit up by nine a.m. Fans in the Southeastern Conference prided themselves on their innovative tailgating set-ups.

It looked like a yuppie Woodstock around the big dome. The diehards all set up shop with tents and grills and smokers. It was a sea of Blue and Orange. Most Pittsburgh fans seemed to be nursing hangovers or taking in the sites – the Panthers hadn't seen a Sugar Bowl in twenty years.

The scene was different from games in Gainesville. Only the hardcore fans with the means to blow a grand in the Big Easy made it to this one. Home games had a 'redder' feel about them. Students were the exception to the rule. Students are like damaging water, they find a way. Some had slept in cars, tents, Bates Motels, etc. And with all of the online networking, it's likely some kids found strange houses to crash in.

Jay MacIntosh had spent the past two nights in a tent at a nearby campground. The place was well maintained and well lit and everyone was there to have a good time. Some Pittsburgh fans had even road-tripped down to stay at the campground. There was no rivalry among the campers; these were the "friendly" fans who shared resources – everything from pot to pancakes. Half of them didn't have tickets to the game and half of those who actually had tickets sold them for gas or beer money.

The standard provision list for student campers was a twelve pack per person, per day, a loaf of bread, peanut butter, jelly, a few gallons of spring water, pop-tarts, bagels, tons of granola bars and, if it's the South, numerous bags of Golden Flake potato chips.

Nearly all of them had brought sleeping bags and some had procured roomy family tents. Some kids even owned, or at least possessed, actual vans. The weather had been perfect for sleeping under the stars.

Every now and then some crafty camper would engineer a way to make coffee on site, but it was rarely good and didn't seem necessary in the alarm-clock-less world of college camping. These kids were fans of their schools, but most could care less about the game.

Jay awoke in a daze at around nine. He had slept with a friend in the back of his inherited Ford Explorer. He walked around rubbing his eyes and scratching his midsection. He wore an orange sweatshirt and cutoff, olive green cargos. The ground was dry enough to go barefoot. A Louisiana park ranger rode past on a John Deere Gator utility vehicle and eyed Jay as if to say 'goddamn hippie!' Jay just nodded politely.

He had two missed calls and a voicemail - from Chip: "Hey man! Mom said you were here in New Orleans – call me – I've got some pretty big news. Oh- and uh – if you and a buddy need tickets, I can probably hook you up. Call me, I should be around. See ya."

'Nice enough,' thought Jay as he studied the other campsites. Chip and Jay were different but they liked each other. Jay hit the red button on his phone and went to see if his friend was awake. She wasn't, so Jay slid into his flips, grabbed his bath towel and shaving kit and headed over toward the showers before it became a madhouse.

The shower was warm but the floor reminded Jay of a seventh grade science project he presented on 'Algae in Lake Alice' thus his flips remained on throughout the cleansing. The guy in the next shower was singing *Uncle John's Band* and Jay didn't think it was half bad. Jay stood under the water and thought about the message his brother had left him. Regardless of the big news, he wanted to see his older brother's last football game at the University of Florida.

Sara Walden was half awake when Jay returned to the Explorer. She was swimming in a weathered Dave Matthews shirt and had on a pair of flannel PJ bottoms. She had long brown hair, messy at that point, and wore low-profile bifocals accentuated by a tiny nose ring. She was from Connecticut and had spent summers in Florida at her grandparents' condominium on Flagler Beach. Sara hated the cold weather up north and had decided early on that she would attend school in the Sunshine State.

"Should we go to the game?" Jay asked his friend.

She looked around at the campsite. "I kind of wanted to see the city. Y'know – the 'sites.' But if you want to go... I thought you didn't have tickets," she said, playing with her hair.

"I can get tickets, let's do it. Cool?" he urged.

"Sure, I'll go," she said. This is why Jay liked younger girls; they always went along with whatever he wanted to do.

Sara grabbed a small tote bag and headed to the showers. She was an adapter, and deep down, Jay was too. Both could turn from hippie campers into spirited, average undergrads in about five minutes. Although football wasn't Jay's thing, he enjoyed the games he had attended over the years.

Sara was an eighteen year old freshman and Jay was a twenty-one year old junior. He had never taken advantage of her youth though; they weren't having sex or really even hooking up. Jay learned from his older brother not to let sex corrupt a good situation. He sort of thought of Sara as a buddy anyway. If he wanted to go to the game, and she didn't, he would have gone to the game without her. That was the beauty of 'just hanging out.'

The Eddie Bauer Explorer had the off road package with four wheel drive, beefed up suspension and *best in its class* towing capacity. It was hunter green with tan molding. The seats were leather and at one point very comfortable. The carpet and mats were soiled with everything from smokeless tobacco to cow shit. The inside smelled like a package of artificial bass fishing worms crossed with Rem-Oil gun cleaner.

Jay had traded a questionably legal version of operating software for a top of the line Yakima rack for the roof. He used it for his mountain bike, canoe, and the occasional borrowed kayak. Out of respect for the old man, Jay left a faded Ducks Unlimited sticker on the rear window. Plus it looked good with the oval *WP* sticker that flanked the other side of the glass. He hadn't hunted in years, it wasn't really him, but he respected the sport and was aware of the benefits to conservation. He often found himself at odds with campus environmentalists over hunting and even fishing. If he met someone who protested fishing, he immediately turned and walked away, that was a meaningless debate. At least the anti-hunters had realistic expectations, albeit statistically inaccurate data. Jay found that most people were anti "assholes with firearms" and not "anti hunting." He had spent hours explaining the difference to freshmen.

Sara returned from the shower in a pair of wide-bottom khakis and a white halter top with "UF" in orange and a washed denim over-shirt. She had on a small, curled cowboy hat and black Reef flips. She had traded her bifocals for contact lenses and shielded the sunlight with small-framed avia-tors from Ray Ban.

"Who are you?" asked Jay as she approached *Camp Explorer*.

"Shut up Dork!" she said as she smiled.

Jay had settled on a long-sleeve, gray "College of Computer Science and Engineering" t-shirt and a fresh pair of khaki shorts. He had on New Balance 990s with quarter socks and wore Smith polarized wrap-around shades.

"You look – really good Sara," he remarked as she heaved her canvas tote into the back of the Explorer.

"Are you flirting with me?" she asked with a bright smile.

"Hell no." her friend said.

"What do we do with these towels?" she asked.

"Here. Let me see em. Watch this." Jay stood on the running boards and secured the towels to his Yakima roof rack with Eagle Scout precision. "By the time we get to the stadium, they'll be dry as a bone."

"You're such a dork!" she said as she dipped into the SUV.

He didn't care, he knew she wouldn't have been in Louisiana with him if she really thought he was a dork – it was a term of affection. They both smiled as they pulled out of the field.

"My dad gave me extra money to come here for this," she admitted. "This was a good idea; I won't have to lie to him about having actually gone to the game."

"I hear ya," Jay said. "It's kind of important to my family too. Shoot – I've gotta get tickets!"

Jay reached for his cell phone, found Chip's name and hit the call button.

Chip answered "I've got like thirty seconds. What's up?"

"Can you still get me tickets?" Jay asked in a slight panic.

"I think – how many?"

"Just two."

"Okay, but you're going to have to find will call, I have no idea where that is," Chip said hurriedly. "I've gotta go Jay."

"Wait! What was the big news?"

"I can't talk, I'll tell you later!"

"Wait – Chip?"

"Yea?"

"Good Luck Man," Jay said to his brother.

"Thanks. I appreciate it – come find me after the game." Chip said sincerely before he flipped his phone down. He was slightly choked up.

The fans had been pouring in for hours. The bands had rehearsed; the players were all fired up. Some of the younger guys kept bashing into each other at half speed with ferocious-sounding war calls. The locker room was loud and the Gators were in their blue jerseys and ready for action.

Coach Haynes and the others had said their pieces earlier. This time was for the boys. It was time to *turn them butterflies into bull balls* as the head coach had explained a half hour earlier.

Jay and Sara pulled into one of the last semi-vacant private parking lots. "Shit – twenty bucks! Screw that," Jay said as he hit the brakes and went for the shifter. "Just do it Jay, I'll pay for it," Sara said. He kept going in. "Are you sure?" he asked her. "Yea man, you got the tickets," she said as she produced a crisp pair of ten dollar bills. "Thanks" he said, totally impressed.

They rushed through the lots on foot, looking for the right gate. "What in the HELL?" Jay was totally stopped in his tracks. Sara followed his site path. "What?" she asked in a confused tone.

He took her hand and led her over to a street vendor with a stack of signs that read: "CHIP MACINTOSH for CONGRESS" in orange and blue. Jay slid his shades to the top of his scalp and studied one of the signs up close.

"Hey – what is this? Is this a joke or something?" he asked the entrepreneur of mixed ethnicity.

"No joke – fi' bucks!" he retorted. "I got some gator jerky too man – best you ever had. Asso fi' bucks!"

Sara tried not to laugh. She looked to Jay to see what his next move was. "Come on dude, we're going to miss the game, we still don't have the tickets yet." She took him by the hand this time. "I'm sure there's an explanation for all of this."

Jay reaffixed his Smiths and produced his cell phone. With one hand he called his mom. "Voicemail" he muttered. He couldn't go through his mom's entire voicemail greeting; it was too long and sounded like a guided tour of Colonial Williamsburg.

Jay tried his dad, whose phone wasn't likely to be on his person. Charles was the type who thought it had to be charging in the car for it to work.

"Hello?" Charles answered.

"Dad!" he said

"Hey Pal! We're at the game! Are you here?" asked the professor.

"Wait – is Chip?" the call went dead. "Fuck!"

Sara jumped in. "Jay, there's no need to…"

"I know – I know – sorry" he interrupted.

"Look! Will call! Run!" she urged.

There was only so much ground she could cover in her attire. "Hi," Jay said to the clerk, buried in a newspaper, "I've got tickets waiting for me. Jay MacIntosh. They were left by a *Chip* MacIntosh."

"Yea yea – the boy-Congressman from Florida. ID please?"

"What did you just say?" Jay asked as he stared at her gold teeth.

"ID please?" she said through a pair of thick glasses.

"No – before that – what did you say? Did you say 'boy Congressman from Florida? What are you talking about?" Jay asked as he produced his driver's license.

The neck-less woman turned in her swivel seat, grabbed the tickets and the sports page from the Times Picayune and handed it to Jay. "This is what I'm talking about. Enjoy the game Baby."

"Uh… Thanks," Jay managed as he walked away studying the paper. "Here," he said as he handed his friend their tickets without looking up.

Sara was far from stupid, she knew what was going on and tried to stay away but she couldn't help it. Jay read the article twice. Half way through the third reading he felt Sara's small hand on the back of his shoulder. She rubbed it gently then softly rested the side of her cowboy hat on his arm.

Jay was confused, worried, nervous, shocked and slightly envious all at once. He turned to his friend cautiously and said "my brother… is running for Congress."

"Aren't you excited for him?" she asked as the crowd jumped to their feet and cheered. The Gators had taken the field. Jay looked up at the concrete deck as if to look at the sounds of the fans.

"You bet," he said. "You bet I am."

Sara smiled, leaned into Jay and wrapped around his left arm like a boa constrictor. They walked up the ramp towards their seats.

Chapter Eight

With a minute left in the first half of the Sugar Bowl, Florida was up 35 to 3. Chip had already broken two SEC records and, he was fairly confident, his left ring finger. And for the first time in NCAA history, a candidate for the US Congress was actively participating in a collegiate athletic contest.

Lieutenant Governor Kirk Osborne was right in encouraging the linebacker to leak his intentions to the press prior to the game. The sportscasters and national media ran with Chip's announcement like a herd of antelope. The street vendor outside the SuperDome had sold at least a couple thousand of those 'CHIP MACINTOSH for CONGRESS' signs and fans waved them with gusto.

Jessica Van Zandt had been eyeing Chip from the trainer's area since the moment he and his team stormed out of the locker room tunnel. She had not yet had a chance to talk to him about his big news and he had tried like hell to avoid her, despite the broken finger that needed attention.

The announcer came on as the clock hit zero "And that will bring us to halftime ladies and gentlemen with the Florida Gators on top thirty-five to three!"

The UF fans jumped to their feet and cheered as the boys in blue headed for the locker room. The head coach got stopped for a quick interview with an attractive redhead from the network.

The locker room was almost as noisy as the stands. The kids were most excited to have such a commanding lead in such a key game. They used their tightly clutched helmets as extensions of their hands. Butt pads were patted, shoulder pads were smacked and the yelling was nearly ear-damaging.

Coach Haynes was never an early celebrant though. He reminded his squad that there was plenty of time left and that Pittsburgh's coach was a very capable fellow and how he'd seen teams come back against greater odds than the Panthers. Chip was all smiles but his finger was in bad shape. He located a male trainer in a polo shirt and went to get his finger taped, perhaps even splinted.

He sat up on the examination table and motioned to his finger. "Jeez," the bald, mustached trainer said as he looked over Chip's ring finger. "You shouldn't really be playing with this finger like this. You could do permanent damage to it. Seriously. Doc!? Come here a sec' can you?"

The head coach overheard and beat the team physician to the examination area. "What's 'a matter?" Haynes asked. "It ain't broke – I know it ain't broken!" He waited for the doctor.

The doctor took Chip's filthy left hand in his. "I'm sorry Coach Haynes, but this finger is definitely broken."

The coach threw his palms up into his eyebrows "DAMN!"

Chip jumped in "I played against FSU with a broken toe, I can still..."

Haynes cut him off "Yea – but no one knew at the time!" He lowered his voice significantly. "And we weren't up more than four touchdowns that time. You done good kid, take a little break." The coach looked at the doctor respectfully and said "Don't give him anything stronger than aspirin; I still may need him yet."

The doc fixed up Chip's finger with a padded aluminum splint and some tape, and then incorporated the finger repair into the rest of Chip's hand with even more tape. He then fitted the linebacker with a sling to keep the broken finger iced and elevated.

Chip was immediately excited that his friend and backup, Kevin Williams, would get to play the entire second half of the Sugar Bowl.

Jay and Sara watched as the halftime show got underway. Jay was reluctant to point out all of the members of the Florida band who lived in his residence hall.

"We – I – should probably try to find my folks," he said to her as he looked around the stadium.

"I'll come with you – can you call them again?" Sara replied.

Jay nodded and reached for his cell phone. He got his dad and asked him where they were.

"They're in a skybox – should we?"

"Yea. Are we dressed okay?" she asked.

"We're fine, you look – c'mon," he said.

The two of them slowly high-stepped up the stands toward an exit tunnel. Sara took his hand to get better leverage but didn't let go of it when they made it to the hallway. He felt a little nervous.

Jay was too handsome and too outgoing to be the perennial friend-only to attractive girls. He simply feared commitment and often hid under the flags of immaturity and mystery to keep relationship-style girls at arm's length. He stereotypically liked video games and computers, but he was active and outdoorsy and many girls liked the simplicity and respectfulness that *was* Jay.

The two walked through the loud breezeway hand in hand. He tried not to look at her as he considered the possibility that they were becoming a 'couple.' The floor in the breezeway was stamped concrete and sticky with spilled beer. Most of the fans had passed the buzzed state by the second half and there was a fair amount of general rowdiness. Jay saw a fat girl eating nachos against the wall and tried not to smirk.

The elevator to the sky boxes was guarded by a giant man with a beard and a camo trucker's cap with the CAT logo in the front. His EVENT STAFF vest was bisected by his massive belly and the straps of his overalls were holding on for dear life. He had a few decent-sized bits of fried chicken stuck to his lower whiskers and gripped with ease the largest sized soft drink available in the retail market.

Sara clung to Jay as they approached the giant. Jay looked up with a smile and a nod. "Hello, my name is Jay MacIntosh and I'm trying to get to a certain skybox."

"I'll need to know your name sir," replied the big man.

Jay tried not to laugh. Sara squeezed him but didn't look at him.

"Sure, yes, it's Jay MacIntosh," he said extra-politely.

The man turned and grabbed a clipboard from the stool that certainly wouldn't hold him. He checked out Sara from head to toe then studied the clipboard. Just then the elevator beeped and out stepped Charles.

"Look who's here!" Charles yelled as he walked toward his son. "He's with me – thanks – they're both with me," the professor said to the big man.

Charles and the kids hopped on the elevator.

"Dad, this is Sara," Jay said.

"Glad to know you Sara," the professor said as the two shook hands.

"Thank you Doctor MacIntosh, nice to meet you too," she said, still smiling about the grizzly fellow guarding the elevator.

"Man did you see that guy?" Jay asked his father.

"Just be glad he's not a guard for Pittsburgh," Charles said with a grin and a nod. "Your mother is glad you're here. Sara, where are you from?"

The door opened and Mary was standing there with her arms open. "Honey!" Jay stepped out and hugged his mom. "And who's your friend?" Mary asked as she sniffed for pot smoke and stared at Sara's tiny nose ring.

Introductions were made and pleasantries were exchanged as the four of them stood in the lobby area.

"Chip has a broken finger, he isn't going back in the football game," Mary said with a frown.

Sara tried to recall the accents in *Gone with the Wind* to see if they matched Jay's moms. She had never actually heard anyone talk like that in real life. Jay wasn't quite without an accent, albeit he sounded nothing like his mom.

"Hey when did Chip decide he was running for freaking Congress?" Jay asked as his eyes bounced from parent to parent.

"Your dad was there – Charles? Tell him the story. I need to use the ladies room. Sara did you need to freshen up a bit hun?" Mary asked with a smile.

"Oh, no thank you, I'm all set," replied Sara.

"Dad?" Jay continued, "what's the deal with Chip running for Congress – and how come no one told me?"

"We were out at the ranch house last week – hunting – having breakfast – and there was a write-up in the paper about Bob Reynolds' not seeking re-election. The guys all started talking about it." Charles started to sound like a college professor. He rubbed his hands together and raised his chin a bit. "He didn't know what he wanted to do for the rest of his life – the NFL – professional football was seemingly beyond his potential. He had been searching for an alternate career path and he – nothing appealed to him."

Jay interrupted the lecture. "Nothing appealed to him? So he's running for Congress?"

"I think it's... At first it seemed like an uncultivated idea but I think he'd be excellent at it – if he's elected of course," Charles said as he looked around. "I could use a – lets go inside, they've got all sorts of provisions in there. C'mon."

Sara detached from the MacIntosh clan for a closer look at the halftime show. She inched through the skybox, slipping between the big shots and gripping her elbows.

Charles and Jay were at the private bar. "Do you still like Crown Jay?" He didn't hear the old man. He watched Sara looking out the opening to the field. "Jay?"

"Yea?" Jay asked blankly. Charles nodded in the direction of the bartender and lifted an eyebrow. "Oh – uh – Crown 'n Coke please. Sorry," Jay said.

"And I'd like a J&B on the rocks with a splash of soda," requested the professor. He turned back to Jay. "So who's the girl? Seems nice. Easy on the eyes. Did you two meet here in New Orleans or is she in that dorm of yours?"

Both of Jay's parents referred to his residence in a negative fashion as far as he was concerned. They had encouraged him to get an apartment like most upperclassmen. Jay knew they were worried he'd get nailed with liquor on school property, a far greater concern than with off-campus housing. With Chip knocking on the door of the US Capitol, Jay figured their concern had already tripled.

"Sara and I came out here together – in the Explorer. She's a *friend*," Jay said.

"Where are you staying?" asked Charles.

"We're at a campground, actually. Camping. There's a pretty clean shower though and it's basically all students – a lot of kids from Pittsburgh."

"Good. That's real good."

"What?" Jay asked. His dad was struggling with his words, a rarity indeed.

"We all need to sit down and – your mom and brother – we have to talk about this – well – campaign I guess."

Jay knew what this meant.

Mary returned from the restrooms and joined her son and husband near the bar. Sara was still watching through the opening.

"Charles, I wonder if we should go. Well with Chip not going back in and all – what is the plan for after the football game?" Mary asked.

"We're supposed to see Chip briefly downstairs then I guess they're all getting on the bus and going back to Gainesville - the players," Charles replied. "Jay we're here tonight, are you and your friend staying? You must be, right?"

"I haven't – I don't know actually. We haven't gotten that far I guess," Jay answered as he looked around the skybox. "Let me see what Sara wants to do."

"You two are welcome to have dinner with your dad and me if you like," Mary offered.

Jay knew Sara wouldn't want to go to dinner with his parents, even if they weren't quite a couple yet. "Thanks," he said. "Let me talk to her."

The skybox began to get a bit more crowded as the halftime clock ticked toward the third quarter. Jay noticed an attractive blonde woman making her way inside with a friendly smile. Charles' phone rang. "I've never had so many calls in one day," he remarked as he squinted to find his 'answer' button. "Hello? Hey. Of course. Yes. He's right here. Okay. Do you need a place to sleep? I see. Very well. Bye now."

"Who was that?" Jay asked thinking it had to be Chip.

"It was your brother. He's riding home with us." Charles said, almost proudly. "We're meeting him right after the game. Downstairs. Mary, we can't leave. Jay, why don't we all get dinner tonight – together. And bring your friend."

Mary rejoined a few of the other ladies in the room. Jay and Charles overheard her saying that they were staying for the whole game and that Chip was driving back with them.

Jay patted his dad on the back of the shoulder and excused himself. Just then the attractive blonde approached Charles with a bright smile. "Hello Dr. MacIntosh, Cheryl West, I'm with the Alumni Affairs office, we met the other night. At Maxes"

"Of course Ms. West, nice to see you again. I suppose the scoreboard is good for your business." Charles said playfully.

"I'll say! And not to mention the possibility of another Gator on Capitol Hill," she said with confidence. "I'm fascinated by Chip's announcement. I'd actually like to talk to him right away. We've got to get this in the newsletter. I half-wish he wasn't heading back with the team tonight."

"You might be in luck Ms. West," Charles said as he sipped his scotch. "Chip isn't going back with the team tonight. He's staying in New Orleans for another night. I think he's riding back with us tomorrow."

Cheryl hid her enthusiasm. "Oh?" she said. "I wish I had a way to contact him," she said, hoping Charles was buzzed enough to offer Chip's cell number to her.

"Oh I doubt if he'd mind my giving you his phone number," Charles said as he produced his half glasses. "Have you got something to take it down with?"

Cheryl produced her tiny computer phone like it was a Colt Peacemaker. "Sure. I can just enter it in."

Charles took his phone from his shirt pocket and began squinting at it. He set his drink down on a high top and started searching for Chip's number. "He just called – how do I?"

"Would you like for me to?" she asked.

"That'd be fine. Thank you," he said, handing the phone over. She quickly programmed Chip into her phone and handed Charles' back.

"Thank you professor," she was starting to get a bit flustered. "I really think this – well – I met Chip recently and he – I think if the university can be... What I mean is – with the Gator legacy behind him – surely the school can't officially endorse a candidate for – I'm actually not sure what the protocol is. Would you excuse me?"

"Absolutely," said Charles in a comforting tone. He could tell she had something else on her mind.

Cheryl left the skybox hurriedly. Her boss and another wave of VIPs were huddled in the skybox to the left so she veered right.

The crowd began to roar and she deduced that the Gators had taken the field. Cheryl wondered if she should leave Chip a message. She felt like an undergraduate as she silently rehearsed the message she would leave for the linebacker. She rolled her eyes at the fact that she was blushing.

The second half of the Sugar Bowl was hardly watchable; both teams seemed to be allergic to the end zone. The Gators only added three points to their halftime lead and the Pittsburgh Panthers were able to tack on six more points with a pair of decent field goals.

For the group in the press box, the highlight of the second half was a sideline interview with Chip MacIntosh. The linebacker wore a slightly wet, gray t-shirt. His padded pants and cleats were coated with dirt and grass stains. His arm was in a sling and his hand was all taped up.

Chip flashed a huge smile and said all the right things. "It's encouraging to have so much support so early on but I want to stay focused on the task at hand – which is to bring a Sugar Bowl victory home to Florida."

The redhead with the microphone tried hard to get him to talk. "There are four minutes left in this game, you guys are up by 29 points, I think the task at hand is a - uh - *success*. Now Chip, on what platform will you base your run for Congress and what are some of the key issues important to you?"

"I don't think it would be fair to my teammates and my coaches for me to comment on platforms and issues during this moment of great joy – this football team deserves this moment. Everyone on this team has given a hundred 'n ten percent since the moment we all became Florida Gators. This is an emotional time for all of us – especially for my fellow seniors. I'm confident we'll have plenty of opportunities to discuss politics in subsequent weeks and months. Thank you so much."

The reporter looked like she felt better. She frowned and nodded as Chip walked back to his teammates. The 'emotional time for the seniors' got to her but she recovered, spun around to the cameraman and wrapped up the story from 'down on the field.' After she 'sent it back to the guys upstairs' she looked around for Chip but he had disappeared into the sea of blue jerseys.

Just as the two minute whistle was blown, dozens of Sugar Bowl caps were distributed along the Florida sideline. The smiles were wide and the yells were loud. Two linemen heaved a massive cooler of frigid Gatorade over the top of Coach Haynes. He made that "shit that's cold" face and hunched over dramatically. "Motherfucker!" he yelled then looked around to make sure he didn't just say that to the entire world.

The game drew to an end and the players all hustled onto the field to congratulate everyone. Haynes and his State Troopers jogged over to the Pittsburgh coach for handshakes and standard congratulatory remarks.

Sara hugged Jay tightly and the skybox filled with cheers and jeers. Most were just glad it was over. The blowout had caused plenty of fans to exit before the fourth quarter. Bowl Games typically take place in towns where there are always other things to do – and usually with decent weather.

Two men entered the skybox with orange polo shirts and headsets. "We've got field passes for anyone who wants them – for the trophy presentation." Charles darted over "We need four please," he said as one of the men handed them over. A few others snatched them up but most were content to watch the ceremony from up high. "The *field*?" Mary asked Charles. "Well sure the field," he replied. "Jay, here ya go. Come on – when are we going to be able to – this is the last..."

The dome had cleared out even more by the time the skybox crew made it down to the field. A bunch of event staffers wheeled a giant stage draped in blue curtains to the middle of the field. Sara felt like a fish out of water but she was excited and flashed a seemingly proud grin the whole time. "Hook" by Blues Traveler blasted from the sound system and confetti came from every direction. Some people were dancing on the field but no one dared attack the uprights that were fortified by prison guard-looking Louisiana street cops in camo pants.

The executive vice president of the company sponsoring the Sugar Bowl gave a quick speech then Coach Haynes and a bunch of players took over the stage. Haynes thanked his team and the fans and called it a day.

Chip made it to his family as the festivities came to a close. He gave one-arm hugs to his parents and Jay and was introduced to Sara. It was his last football game and he was more emotional than he thought. The run for Congress was a reality. He had something exciting to look forward to – unlike many other seniors on the field, but he was more nervous about it than he thought. He walked with his family and Sara toward the sidelines when the redhead from the network approached him again. "Hi Chip – Erin Sanders – ESPN – can I just get another quick minute with you?" She didn't wait for a response. "Chip there has been some talk in the media that you were hand-selected by Congressman Reynolds to fill his slot in the House?"

Chip looked around a little bit.

"Well, if that's the case, I had no idea. I haven't seen or spoken with Representative Reynolds in over two years," Chip said firmly but with a smile.

"Chip, candidates for Congress with no political experience tend to run for specific reasons – issues dear to their hearts. What will your platform be and what are your key issues?" she asked.

Mary was ready to slide tackle the reporter but Charles was interested in his response. Jay and Sara gently escaped from the field of view.

"Look. Erin, right?

"Uh huh," she confirmed.

"Erin, perhaps too many people head to Washington with 'issues.' I think I can help out, it's that simple. I don't have any *issues* but I've got ten months to travel around northern Florida and find out what's on the minds of those I seek to represent. Thank you."

"Thank you Chip. How's the hand?" she asked.

"Oh, I'll be just fine. Thanks," he said as he nodded and rejoined his parents watching from a few yards away.

"How'd it go?" Charles asked.

"Good I guess. I should probably get some help with that. I feel okay talking to the sports people, but I don't know if that will be the case with the political types. Did you hear those questions though? She had talked to someone. Someone fed her those questions, someone at the network," Chip said.

"Hun what's the plan? You're riding back with us tomorrow? Shall we get you a room with us at the bed and breakfast?" Mary asked.

"Nah – I think I'm gonna - I need to check on a couple of things before I..." Chip stopped himself and looked around. "Where's Jay?"

Jay and Sara were talking near the thirty yard marker. Chip motioned for them to come over and they did.

"Guys, I think Sara and I are going to head back tonight – like soon." Jay said.

"Oh – stay another night," urged Mary. "We'll get you a room so you won't have to go back to that filthy campground."

"You'd better let her take the first shift there *Mr. Crown and Coke*," remarked Charles.

Sara felt way out of step and had told Jay she didn't want to spend the evening with his parents. Jay understood.

"Dad – I'm fine," Jay pleaded. "But if it makes you feel better, I'll let her drive to Mobile. We should actually split, it's going to get dark soon."

Chip approached his brother. "Thanks for being here man," he said.

"Thanks for the tickets dude," Jay said sincerely.

"Sara – nice to meet you. Jay, we'll get together when I get back - I'll try to explain this whole Congress thing to you. Maybe we could catch some bass or something. I'll call you," he said.

"Nice to meet you too Chip. Congratulations on all of this," Sara said looking up at the lights and remaining fans. "And good luck with the campaign."

Jay gave them all a little nod – everyone said their goodbyes and Jay and Sara were gone.

"Are they like – a *couple* couple?" Chip asked his parents.

"I don't think so. Who knows with him..." Charles said, though not disparagingly.

"I saw them hugging and she held his hand when they didn't think I was watching. Did you notice she had an earring in her nose?" Mary asked.

"She's pretty cute. Mom – lots of girls have those things. It's not as weird as you think it is. I'll find out the deal. Though I admit I'm a little surprised he was here today – at the game and then down on the field."

"So what's the plan?" Charles asked hoping the 'plan' was going to involve a nap before dinner or whatever.

"I've got to hit the showers and I'd like to get this hand taped before I leave this place. Tell you what... Why don't you guys go back to your room and freshen up and I'll call you when I finish up here. Is there an event tonight?" Chip asked.

"Well – not really. Some folks we know have a table at the House of Blues – downtown. We can skip it though – or you're welcome to join us if you like," Charles answered.

"Come with us Chip – or *we'll* all go somewhere – the three of us. We never get to see you anymore," Mary said.

"I have to check on a few things," Chip said pointing to the locker room. "Plan on the House of Blues. I'll call you. Where are you – oh – the bed and breakfast right? What is it like four o'clock here?"

"Four fifteen," Charles said, eyeing his two-tone Rolex.

"Why don't you guys go back and rest a little. I'll call you in a couple of hours – plan on the House of Blues."

They parted and Chip walked to the locker room with a few other celebrants in uniform.

Chapter Nine

Chip signed at least twenty programs near the tunnel to the locker room. Fans thanked him and promised to vote for him. Christian Ross was also signing memorabilia. The two walked into the locker room together.

The place was pretty rowdy but the showers were going and a lot of guys were on the phone. Chip went to his locker and removed his duffel bag. He produced his cell phone and checked his messages. Two calls were invitations to the same party at the SAE House the next night and one call was from Cheryl.

"Hi Chip, this is Cheryl West, Director of Alumni Affairs for the University. I wanted to see if you were staying in New Orleans this evening. If I could just get a few minutes of your time – it has to do with the newsletter slash website. We could talk over the phone but I'd prefer if we could do it in person. I'll be at the W hotel – where we held the reception last night. Let me know. Thanks Chip. And congratulations on a spectacular win today."

The linebacker smiled as he saved the message and tossed the phone back in the duffel bag. He wanted to call her right then but figured it was too soon. Many of the Florida Gators were getting on the bus to go back to Gainesville but at least a dozen were staying in town for the night to celebrate – mostly with their families. Chip wondered who was slated to be at his parents table at the House of Blues. He figured if they didn't work for the University that he could convince Cheryl to go. Whoever was at the table was a potential donor and Chip couldn't believe he was thinking about campaign contributions with a Sugar Bowl trophy in the next room.

The Marine needed a shower. He had to think for a minute. Ross approached.

"Hey man – are you staying in town tonight?" he asked Chip, almost in a sneaky fashion.

"Let me guess," Chip started as he began to de-robe. "Your parents aren't in town but you don't want to ride back with the team. You've met some girl and you need a sponsor or someone to convince Haynes that you have a reason to stay in New Orleans. Am I right? Did you find some group of wild chicks who want to celebrate the big win with you – maybe show you the town? Did the girl from yesterday *text* you and say she wants you to meet her two best friends? Am I on the right track Ross? Huh?"

Ross was shaking his head the whole time. "WRONG!" he said. "Well, sort of wrong." He flung his phone to Chip and said "read that message though."

Chip had a confused look on his face. He turned the device upright and read the message silently. "This is some kind of a joke – right?" Chip said half-seriously.

"It's no joke Pal. I just called to confirm," Christian said with a nod. "MacIntosh, she's the highest paid fashion model in New York City. She's been in like three movies."

"Then what 'n the hell is she doing in Gainesville tonight?" Chip asked.

"She's visiting her goddam friend!" Ross said.

Chip read the text message again. "I can't believe women talk – write – like *this*. Which one is this? Is this the girl you were?"

Ross interrupted him "she's the one with the silver BMW convertible. They modeled together in high school," Christian lowered his head, looked around and got a little quieter. "I'm just saying bro..."

Chip was interested. "Damn. I can't Ross." Chip took a loud deep breath. "Shit. I can't go back tonight. I've got to shower. My folks are – let me know how it goes." He paused for a few seconds. "This is real, right? This isn't a fake message? And your friend – the girl – she's for real?"

Ross briefly shut his eyes and nodded. "Swear on it."

"Well I can't go back tonight. I can't," he said, looking up at the ceiling. "I'll be back tomorrow night – maybe tomorrow afternoon."

"It's cool man. And hey, I'm sorry about the hand. It would be hard to – well with the broken finger and all," Ross said pretending to justify Chip's staying in New Orleans.

"Good game today Ross," he said. "I've got to shower. I've got to go."

Chip stood in the stall with his head slung below the hot water. He used his forearms to lean against the wall but he wasn't a bit tired. The hot water felt good on his neck and back. He was able to shut out the sounds of the remaining players and coaches. The steam helped him breathe. He was able to think clearly about the message from Cheryl and how he'd respond but the thoughts of the X-rated text message on Ross' phone kept drifting into his head.

The locker room was almost totally cleared out by the time Chip got back to his locker. Some players had left with their folks, some had secured decent seats on the buses and some were gathering their stuff for the ride back. Chip had a towel around his waist and another in his hand. He was drying off his face and taking his seat when he heard Coach Haynes yell his name from across the room.

"Hows'at hand or finger or whatever?" he barked.

"Oh, I'll be fine coach, it doesn't really hurt," Chip replied.

"You played a hell of a first half kid. I mean a HELL of a first half," he confessed proudly.

"Thank you coach," Chip said. "I wish I could have made it through."

"You did what you could. You gave it all you had and I know that," the coach remarked. "Look Chip." The coach sat down on the bench next to Chip but faced the other direction. There weren't any other players close by. Haynes had his elbows on his knees and his eyes in his hands.

"MacIntosh, look, if this whole bullshit Congressman thing doesn't work out – I want you to know... I'm not one for conversations like this kid. You're not a kid – hell I know that." The coach lifted his head and put his hands on his knees. "You're a *born* leader and I want you to think about coming back and coaching for me – for the Gators. Leonard has offers to be a defensive co-ordinator at a few schools. I'm gonna need an LB coach next season; I know it – two years – tops. But if this is what you want – this politics business, then I know you'll give it your *all* and that you'll probably win. And even though my daddy would roll in his goddamn grave for votin' for a dimmacrat – you've got my vote."

Chip couldn't believe what he was hearing. On an average day, Haynes would make most Marine drill instructors seem softer than pillows. "I appreciate that Coach. That means a lot to me, sincerely. And thank you for considering me for a coaching job. The truth is I have no idea where this all came from – I mean – I do but... It all happened so fast. At one point I thought I might even get invited to work out with a professional organization – then I thought I'd be selling Fords for my dad's friend's dealership. It's like they hit me with this – convinced me I could do it – then – ya know, here I am. Jeez. What am I doing?"

The coach stood up and paced back and forth behind his star linebacker. "The banquet will be in a few weeks. Afterwards, I always invite the seniors to my house for sort of a reception. You're still under my command until then – at least as far as the Athletic Director is concerned. We'll talk again after that MacIntosh. But I wanted to – uh – thank you for a great season and a great four years. I – we – don't get many like you." The coach slapped his hand on Chip's shoulder. Chip knew not to turn around. Two of the toughest guys had tears in their eyes. "I'm goin'," the coach said and he walked away.

Chip turned to watch the coach walk out. He rubbed his face with the towel and stood up. The coach got about a hundred feet away and turned back toward his team captain. "Oh I forgot! Reynolds – the Congressmen – wants to see you – Sunday in Palatka. I told him you'd call him! So do it!" Chip nodded affirmatively. The coach disappeared.

Chip was in shock. He hadn't seen that side of Coach Haynes. He decided not to decode the whole thing and instead dressed himself. He put on a pair of jeans and a long sleeve t-shirt, running shoes and dark glasses. He stashed the ridiculous-looking Sugar Bowl Champions hat in his duffel bag and looked for an exit.

The one thing that hadn't occurred to Chip was where exactly he was going as he scouted for reporters and exited the dome. His hotel was a short walk but he had checked out already. He didn't want to cab it to the bed and breakfast, the idea of staying with mom and dad didn't exactly appeal to him. There were fans still lingering, some were even cooking in the parking lot. Chip felt well-disguised but his frame alone put him in the collegiate-athlete category – not to mention the aluminum splint still fastened to his left ring finger. Dealing with drunken fans wasn't on his list of things to do at that moment.

He had a strange and rare feeling come over him, he didn't want to be around people but he didn't want to be alone. He looked around outside and felt like it was the end of an era for him. He already missed the game of football and being sidelined for half the contest hadn't helped him. He ducked behind a massive structural column, took a knee, and searched for his phone.

He scrolled to the number he thought was Cheryl's and looked at it. But he didn't know what to say if he got her. He checked the message she had left him one more time. Chip's heart pounded a little.

Cheryl was watching the news in bed at the hotel when her phone vibrated next to her. She glanced at the screen and saw that it was Chip. She rushed to clear her voice a few times and even fixed her hair a bit. Not wanting Chip to know she had already programmed him into her phone she rehearsed her greeting twice.

"Hello – Cheryl West," she said like a busy realtor.

Chip held his breath. "I thought we were going to wait 'til we got back to Gainesville," he said mysteriously.

"Who is this?" she lied.

"Sorry – Cheryl, it's Chip MacIntosh," he answered, not knowing whether she was messing with him or not. He felt like a sophomore.

"Right – Chip – of course. I see you got my message, that's great. Hey – good game, I'm sorry about your hand. Chip I think we should get together tonight to – I have an idea for the newsletter. It's a win-win situation, I don't need but a few minutes. What's your schedule like?" she asked.

Her voice had a commanding sex appeal that Chip had never really noticed in a woman. When he had read the dirty text message from Ross' phone, he had used Cheryl's voice in his head. He looked around a little and begged himself not to screw up.

"I checked out this morning then decided to stay an extra night," he said, sounding nearly confused.

"Okay," she said slowly. "Where are you staying tonight then?"

"That's a good question," he replied. "I don't – well – I haven't made any arrangements for that yet."

Cheryl got out of bed and walked around the room straightening up. She was wearing the white oxford shirt she had worn to the game and a pair of bikini-style underwear. "You should stay at the W. – we got a great rate through the University. Jack Griffin went home this afternoon," she said professionally.

"The W.?" he asked. "How *great*? The rate I mean."

She popped in a small mint candy from the dresser. "*Very* great," she replied – not professionally at all. Whatever the rate was, Chip was ready to plunk down his credit card like it was free money. "Where are you right now?" asked Cheryl. "Do you need me to pick you up?"

"No – I'm at the stadium – the SuperDome. I can walk it," the Marine said with a mixture of fear and confidence.

"Good then. Why don't you check in, get a shower or whatever, and call me when you get settled," she said cheerfully. "I'm in 707 if you want to use the hotel phone or whatever."

"Perfect. I'll call you," he said as he slung the strap from his bag over his broad shoulder.

"Sounds good – thanks, I mean – okay," and she hit END.

Use the hotel phone or whatever – what the hell did that mean? He asked himself as he walked along, smiling. It was the first time he had left an *away* game on foot, it felt strange. Any loneliness Chip had felt was gone, he felt great. The mystery and uncertainty associated with Cheryl involved an excitement Chip hadn't felt in a while. He pictured her in his mind as he walked down the street toward the W. Hotel.

Cheryl probed her luggage and closet for the perfect outfit to seduce a younger guy who had just dominated a bowl game. She wondered what *he'd* be wearing. Nothing she had brought to New Orleans was terribly sexy or youthful. She fired up the shower and hung a skirt and blouse on the back of the door. She laid out a bra and a white satin thong then walked to the mirror and began undoing her oxford. Her phone vibrated again. She looked over in the direction of it and decided it might be the football player.

The number was unrecognizable. "Hello - Cheryl West."

"Hi Cheryl, it's Ray Smith how are you?" the man on the other end said.

"Hello Ray, I'm well – thank you. Everything okay?" she asked, wondering why the university's head of Charitable Giving was calling her.

"Sure, yes, everything's fine. Listen, I just spoke with Jack and he said he had gone back but that you were still here. In New Orleans?" he said.

"That's right," Cheryl sounded almost short with him.

"Well – look – I've got some donors in town, we're all getting together tonight, there are some alums and even a professor, at this – uh - House of *Blues* I think it's called. I called Jack to see if he could join us and he asked me to call you – said he'd already gone back to town."

"I see. Well, thank you," she said.

"You're under no obligation obviously but it might be a good opportunity for the University. You don't even have to let me know. Just swing by if you can. Good?"

"Okay, I suppose I..." she hesitated.

"Cheryl, I gotta run. See ya," he said and hung up.

Any time a higher-up said "a good opportunity for the university" it meant 'mandatory attendance.' It was the game. The university had been around for over a century yet many in the back offices treated it like the youngest school in the state university system.

Cheryl studied her nude figure in the mirror. She turned off all but one light then did it again. Her body was feminine and nice. She didn't have the abdominals of a fitness instructor but she was miles from being overweight. Twenty years earlier, she would have been considered a "hardbody" but the times had changed. Fake breasts and sit-up regiments had changed the standard for the female body. Cheryl felt good though. Her most intimate parts were highlighted by a recent tan she secured during Christmas vacation in West Palm Beach.

She slipped into the bathroom and quickly shut the door to contain the steam from the hot water.

"Hey there!" Chip said with a warm smile as he approached the guest desk at the W. Hotel.

The girl behind the desk was around Chip's age. She looked like a newbie flight attendant. "Welcome to the W. Hotel sir. Can I help you?" she asked with a massive smile.

"Yes please, I need a room. I was told to say I was with *the University*," Chip said.

"Very good sir, I'll be happy to check on that for you. Okay – that's the University of..."

"Florida," Chip replied proudly.

"Perfect," she said. "We do have a special rate, it's $175 per night for a single occupancy. Will anyone be staying with you tonight?"

He could have been a real smartass. "No. It'll just be me in there," he said. She smiled and touched her hair briefly.

"Do you have a credit card and a photo ID please?" she asked, looking him straight in the eyes.

Chip handed the two pieces of plastic to the girl and looked away.

"You're all set Mr. MacIntosh. Take the elevator to the seventh floor."

He interrupted her, almost rudely. "The seventh floor?" he asked.

"Is there a problem? I can arrange for a lower level if the height makes you uncomfortable but unfortunately I can't offer you the same rate," she said in an accommodating way.

"No – I – it's fine. I just didn't expect..."

"The whole block for the university is on the seventh floor. Most have already checked out but we are still using seven for the Florida – for you," she said.

"I'm – forgive me. The seventh is fine. Thank you. Thank you very much," he said. He looked tired.

"Do you need help with your luggage?" she asked as she studied his frame. She knew he didn't need help but had to ask.

"No ma'am," he said looking down at his canvas bag.

"Here are your room keys. You're in 706 Mr. MacIntosh; let us know if there's anything we can do to make your stay more comfortable. Thank you for choosing The W," she said with a parade-style wave of her hand.

Chip said "Jesus Christ" under his breath and walked through the lobby past all of the white-gloved attendants and seemingly well-to-do guests.

She was right across the hall and he couldn't figure out what would be wrong with that. He liked barriers but this whole concept was foreign to Chip. She had flirted with him – or so he thought. Then she made him look like an idiot at Jackson Square, even watching him as he stood there waiting for him. Then there was the reception and their chat on the deck. And now she wanted to get his story for the alumni newsletter. He still wasn't sure why he'd signed on for another night in New Orleans. He was, however, pretty sure he couldn't spend eight straight hours on a bus with the team.

Charles and Mary made it back to the bed and breakfast in decent time, considering the traffic. They drove around the back of the beautiful mansion and hid the Suburban behind the great hedge.

The living room on the first floor was like a Mecca for those who could appreciate antique furnishings and the southern way of life. The gas fireplace was always going and the chairs made you want to skip your next outing.

The MacIntosh couple strolled in the back door and saw some friends gathered in the large room. The two groups were segregated male/female as usual. Charles waved and nodded at the ladies and joined the men by the fire.

"Some game, huh professor," said one of the men.

Charles looked over at the women, ordering tea. "That game was a piece of shit," he said. "I'm sorry; I know I shouldn't say that. The kids played well, great outcome, but it was so mismatched. Hell, I'm just tired. And no one likes to see their kid get hurt – injured – what have you."

The other guys asked about Chip then Charles politely excused himself. He needed a nap. "What time are we due at the restaurant?" he asked them all as he pulled on his beard and noticed the artwork on the wall.

"Eight. It's the earliest we could get," one of them replied.

"No, that's good. Eight's fine," he said.

"Go get some rest old man," another commanded in a friendly tone.

Charles yawned, stretched, and nodded at the same time. "Mar' – I'm going up," he half-yelled across the quaint inn. Mary smiled and waved him off. Charles paused for a peek at a painting of a southern-style quail hunt then disappeared up the grand staircase.

Cheryl stood and adjusted the towel around her torso. Her hair was secured turban-style with a matching towel. She pulled a massive hair dryer from her suitcase and headed back to the bathroom.

Directly across the hall, Chip was lying face-down on a stripped, queen bed. His duffel bag was lying on the ground in the little hallway. He hadn't touched it. His cell phone rang so he stood up and retrieved it from his jeans. It was Ross. "Hey buddy," he said as he walked toward the window. Ross had shown the famous text message to at least three other guys on the bus. "Last chance Bro!" Ross said with laughter. Chip smiled as he watched the peaceful looking tourists march through town. "I'm good man. I've got something... I'm good," Chip said, wondering about the night ahead of him.

"Fine – *fag*. I'll let you know what happens," said Christian.

Ross was gone and Chip stared at his iPhone then back out the window. He turned and looked at the hotel phone. He sat back on the bed and picked up the large receiver. A small card beside the lamp read: "For Room to Room Calls, Dial # then the Room Number." He stood up and decided not to rehearse. He hit #707 and drew a deep breath.

"Cheryl West."

"Hi, it's Chip. I thought I would call and let you know I had made it here," he said.

"Oh, hey! Where's 'here' – the W?"

"Yea," he said, thinking that might have been obvious.

"Great! What room are you in? Isn't it nice here?" she asked.

He smirked a bit, "I'm in seven o' *six*."

"Really – what are the odds?" she said as if she bribed the clerk at the front desk. "When should we – I'm just out of the shower. What are you doing in ten minutes?" she asked.

"I'm just unpacking, why don't you come over when you get dressed?" he asked, hoping she would skip the dressing part and show up in a towel.

"Perfect – give me ten minutes – see ya," she said and put the phone down.

Cheryl dropped her towels on the floor and went back in the bathroom. She did a quick and subtle makeup job, rolled on a little antiperspirant and brushed her hair, still quite wet. From her bag she produced a pair of comfortable jeans and a folded white sweater. She strapped on the bra and stepped into the panties she had set out earlier then slipped into the jeans.

The mirror in the bathroom had cleared up completely. She stood there in her bra and jeans and attempted to dry and brush her hair. It got dry enough, but she didn't have time to style it. She tied it back – it was half ponytail, half bun. It looked youthful and fun and she settled on it. Cheryl gave her chest a quick look in the mirror, adjusted her bra a little, and then went for her sweater.

Chip had started to unpack but wasn't making great progress. He had a 24-hour news channel on and couldn't get motivated about pouring a pile of clothes into the bureau that didn't belong to him.

There was a knock at his door. It was her. He opened the door and smiled. He hadn't seen her in such casual clothing and he was instantly feeling good about having stayed in New Orleans. She gave him a hug then snapped back and looked at his splinted finger. Her eyes squinted and she frowned. "Does it hurt?"

"Not really – it's more annoying than anything else. I need to find a drug store, I want to redo the dressing before I – uh"

"Before what?" she asked with devilish eyes.

"Well, I might be going out or meeting up with some people tonight. Maybe you could – uh. Do you have plans tonight?"

Cheryl walked across the room towards the window. She took one of the armchairs by the coffee table and crossed her legs. She was barefoot, Chip was impressed.

"Why don't you come sit down? Charles *the Third*," she said playfully.

The kid was out of his element. She had a presence that set her apart from any girl he had ever been alone with. This might just be how thirty year old women act, he wondered. He stopped thinking and walked in her direction.

Chip sat in the arm chair. She was to his right, on an angle. "So should we talk about the newsletter thing or the other night or last night, or what?" he asked confidently.

"What do you think of me Chip?" she asked, straight as an arrow.

"I'm not sure I know what you mean," he replied. "Think of you..."

"Do you like me?" she asked.

"Possibly," he said, trying not to look away from her. Chip couldn't ever remember telling a girl to ditch her boss, or anyone else, to meet him somewhere. He could easily have played that off though. It didn't have to be about sex. For all he knew, she hadn't taken it that way. He decided on that approach.

"Look. I'll be honest with you Cheryl. I think you're a very attractive woman and you've got a 'way' about you that I find terribly appealing. You're someone I'd like to be with - in some form or fashion – I don't know what that is, really. Be-*with*. It sounds kind of vague – I know. That night in the French Quarter, I think I just wanted to get out of there. I rolled the dice on the chance that you'd want to be *with* me too – and again – I didn't know what that meant at the time – hell I still honestly don't know. It wasn't about sex - or whatever - so if that's what you were thinking - I'm sorry if I made it seem like that. I just wanted to 'know' you, I think. You implied at the reception that you wanted to 'know' me too. Right?"

Her elbow was rested on the arm of her chair and part of her face was in her left hand. She was looking right into his eyes. He had her attention. The sun had dipped rather significantly by the time Chip had finished his monologue. He felt pretty good about it and he sat back in his chair, relieved. He was essentially *covered*, regardless of what she said in response. There was a lamp on the table between them, Chip reached toward it and she put her hand on his. "Leave it off," she said. "Okay," said Chip as he sat back. "Did I say something wrong?" he asked. His eyes waited for a response.

"I have to make an appearance tonight at the *House of Blues*. But I want to be *with* you until I check out tomorrow," she said without reservation. "And I don't really know what... Chip I'm not clear on my own definition of whatever *this* is either. We've got some forces working against us. We would look like a couple if people saw us out. The age issue is a tough one to tackle; I'd be lying if I told you I hadn't thought about what it would be like to date you. That may have never crossed your mind, but the thought popped in my head a few times in the past two days - if we're being honest."

"I'm supposed to go to the House of Blues too," he said.

She propped herself up her chair and in one move crossed her legs and sat on her feet. She leaned toward him and smiled. "I should have known!" she said. "I heard there was a professor coming. I'm glad it's your father. So what should we do?"

"I was just going to ask you that," he said. "Is it one table or a room or what?"

"I think it's like a loft. I've been there before – we saw BB King while we were still in college," she said excitedly. "I think we probably have the whole loft tonight. Are your parents staying here?"

"No, there at a bed and breakfast just outside of town," he said. "What should I wear? I forgot to ask someone."

"Let's take a look. Shall we?" Cheryl got up, turned on some lights and walked to the closet. "It's empty, where's your hanging bag?"

Chip grabbed the clump of hair above his forehead. "I just have *that*." And he motioned to the duffel bag.

She knelt down over the bag. He got up and walked over to her. "You really thought about what it would be like to date me?" he asked her.

Cheryl looked up at him and smiled. "What? Did you think I thought you were too young for me?"

"There's something here, but I'm back to square one. I don't know what I thought about us," he confessed.

The two found themselves sitting on the bed, side by side. "Chip, this apparent indecisiveness is going to hurt you in the primary."

"I've had not-so-great luck with girls, why should *women* be any different." He said, aware of the implication.

"Am I the first *woman* you've ever had alone in a hotel room?" she asked.

"I don't even know how old you are. And please don't make me guess. Someone said you had been out of school around ten years," he said.

"That's pretty accurate. I'll be 32 this year," she confessed.

"So we're talking seven years, that's not that big of a gap actually," he offered.

"I don't think so either, but there's more to it than that I'm afraid. You're still an undergrad – and at the school where I work. Granted, you're not the average senior in college. You've been in the Marines – that probably matured you by three years right there. I've actually put you at 27 and I've shaved three years off of me for working at a college and for never having been married. That puts me at 29, a two year difference. Not to mention, if you won the House seat, that right there tacks another – at least five onto you - making you seem *older* than me," she had finished.

Chip was impressed that she'd given it so much thought – even if she was making it up as she went along, it was good stuff.

"So what do we do?" he asked. It still seemed friendly to him.

"We need to find you something to wear. We can arrive at the *House of Blues* together and if anyone asks any questions we just say that we chatted at the hotel pool or gym and got to know each other etcetera. Let's just see what happens. Can you tape that thing on the way to the restaurant or should we run get the stuff right now?" she asked.

"It's unsightly isn't it?"

"A little, but you just won the Sugar Bowl for chrissakes," she said.

Cheryl went through his bag and found chinos and a nice shirt. "Your blazer is in here? C'mon Chip! You go get the stuff for your finger, I'll iron your outfit. Get spray starch too. Go!" She was in charge.

Chip grabbed his cell phone and his room key and took off.

Chapter Ten

Chip was only gone for about fifteen minutes; there was a drug store just around the corner. When he returned to his room he found Cheryl ironing one of his dress shirts.

"Did you get the starch?" she asked, barely looking up.

Chip walked up to her and handed her the starch. "Why are you doing this – for me?" he asked.

"Cause I like you. And I don't really have anything else to do," she said cheerfully.

"Thank you. Hey, I'm going to take a quick shower – I just need to..." he was daydreaming a little.

"Go ahead, I'm almost done," she replied.

Chip grabbed his shaving kit from his bed. The entire contents of his bag were laid out neatly on the bed, in stacks. His laundry, previously stuffed into an undershirt, had made its way to one of the hotel-provided plastic bags. He sat on the bed and exchanged his sneakers for flip flops but left the rest of his clothes on. Cheryl continued to spray starch and iron his shirt. She had switched the television to local news while he was out.

She looked over at him as he walked toward the shower. He had a puzzled look on his face. "I'll – uh – shave – you think?" he asked her, feeling his face.

"Yea – I would," she affirmed.

Chip spent his ten minutes in the shower thinking about his new friend. He had hard-wired himself never to make the first move and wouldn't dare lean in on an older woman. She would definitely have to strike first. But he couldn't stop thinking of her in that way, she had officially made it into his head and though he was agitated by his broken finger, he remained rather happy and excited.

Cheryl was sitting on the edge of the bed when he emerged from the shower. His towel was wrapped around his waist and he held it there with his right hand. He was clean shaven and still slightly wet from the shower. She stared at him as he stood there outside the door to the bathroom. He was six foot three inches and had muscular arms. Cheryl stood up and walked toward him.

"Do you always bruise so badly when you – play?" she asked, pretending to be focusing on the four or five black and blue marks that dotted his forearms and biceps.

"Yea. It's a contact sport. Right?" he said.

"Right," she said as she inched closer to him. "I think I'll get – uh – ready too Chip. We should probably leave soon." She got right up to him and looked him in the eye. Chip looked nervous, like he wasn't ready for her. Cheryl gently placed her hand on his chest, just below his left collar bone. Her other hand slightly slid into the top of his towel and she pulled him closer. She turned her head and rested it briefly on his bare skin. The contact exited him. He closed his eyes. She smoothly broke free from him and slipped out the door.

The linebacker fell back onto the bed. He took a deep breath and smiled as he stared at the ceiling. Just then his cell phone started to ring. "Fuck," he said quietly. It was his mom. He felt like he had just been dipped in cold water but he hit the answer button. "Hello Mother," he said.

"Hun are ya meeting us at this Blues House?" she asked, seemingly in the car already. Chip could hear his dad "*it's the House of Blues*" he corrected from the other seat in the car. There must have been at least two other couples in the Suburban, it started getting loud.

"Yea we'll be there in an hour – tops," Chip said gritting his teeth, hoping she hadn't caught the "we'll" part of his response.

"Are you bringing a friend with you Chip? I thought everyone'd gone back," she said. He could hear Charles again: "He can't bring someone, he's a guest of the..."

Chip's head rolled back over his shoulders. "Can I talk to dad for a sec?"

"Chip? Hey – you can't bring a buddy to this thing – these are costly affairs man. Didn't you know that?" Charles asked.

"No – I know. Look, I ran into someone who was *already* going. Uh - at the *pool*. We're going to split a cab," he said, rattled.

"A *swimmin'* pool? Where are you staying?" he asked.

"At the – look I'll be at the *House of Blues* in an hour. I've gotta go. Thanks!" and Chip hung up. "Damn."

Chip dressed himself and dug a tiny sample of Burberry cologne from the bottom of his toiletry kit. He didn't wear the juice very often but something made him think it would be a nice touch for an evening with Miss West. He returned to the full-length mirror and looked himself over. The thought of her touching him the way she did made him happy. There *was* someone he could call to discuss her motives but he didn't have time.

Rob Dougherty was Chip's best friend in middle and high school. He was a pure ladies man and was in LA waiting on tables, parking cars, and auditioning for movie roles. The two had played football together for years and still stayed in touch. Dougherty would know exactly what to do but Chip didn't feel like getting into it.

He pulled a first aid kit from a noisy plastic bag. It was branded by Johnson and Johnson and contained a finger splint, a roll of trainer's tape, scissors and a bunch of stuff he didn't need. The drug store wasn't big enough to shop for first aid items a la carte, so he was stuck with extra supplies. Although he was right-handed, he was most-impressed with the job he did on his hand.

The room phone sounded like a school bell to Chip as he turned and stared at the blinking red light.

"Hello?" he said, almost as if he was on the run from someone.

"It's me. Are you ready?" she asked.

"Oh – I'm ready alright. Look, I spoke to my..." he was interrupted.

"Come over here," she said and put the phone down.

Chip popped two aspirins for the finger, grabbed his wallet from the dresser, and dashed out of the room. As he stood in the hallway outside 707 he began to get a little nervous. He stared at the peephole and took a yoga breath.

The heavy door swung open and the *knockout* staying in 707 smiled at him. She led him in and told him she was finishing an email to somebody. Chip looked around the room, it seemed nicer than his. The bed was made, everything was well organized and it smelled like the makeup counter at Bloomingdales. Cheryl sat at the desk and pounced on the tiny keys while Chip stood and watched her.

"You look great by the way," she managed to say without looking up.

"Thank you. You look great as well. You look..." he stopped himself. Cheryl arose from the chair and faced him. She clutched her phone and put her hands on her hips casually. "I look *what* exactly?"

He wanted to tell her that he wasn't into games but he used a different tactic. "Let's get something straight – let's just put all the cards on the table. Cool?"

She lightly pushed him onto the bed and sat beside him. "We don't really have time, but I'd actually like to hear this. Why don't *you* start?"

"I'm a little intimidated by you, it's true. I think you're very beautiful – I like your *look* and I – you ironed this outfit and fixed up my clothes – I don't know exactly what to think about you – forget the whole *getting to know you* thing – I can't figure out the part of you - the part before one figures some-one out – for real – ya know? Its like you're a tough career woman who seems fearless and determined but then you ironed my – and I'll be honest – when you put your hand on me in my room, I felt all torn up inside, I didn't know if we were about to have sex or what. I *still* don't know – but then I think we could somehow work together? Maybe – I don't know? I view you in that regard too - somehow – and then I have already considered the possibility that you and I could be friends – not like – I don't know – *friends*. And then sometimes I think you're just going to attack me and bring me to some kind of next level. Whatever that level is – and even if it doesn't exist, it exists in *my* mind. I *like* you – okay?"

Cheryl stood up and faced him. She was a little rattled but she *did* look great. She had on a tighter black skirt which stopped just above her tan knees. Her top was a long sleeved, rich cobalt blue and it made her sparkling blue eyes beam like polished tanzanite. She wore a simple, sterling necklace with a tiny heart pendant. Her blonde hair fell just past her shoulders and framed her high cheekbones perfectly. She had the slightest of gaps between her two front teeth and her makeup was like that of a highly-rated news anchor.

The athlete looked just as exhausted as he did after the first half of the Sugar Bowl. He took his eyes off of her as he waited for a response.

"Okay," her voice cracked a little. She cleared her throat and sat on the other side of Chip so she could hold his good hand without reaching over him. "At least one of your scenarios is probably not a good fit; I'll be hon-est with you; even though I suspect you already know all of this. Let me take each one of your points in sequence – my own though. On paper, Chip, I'm going to want kids in the next few years. I'm *looking for a husband* according to statistical data. You're still a young guy with a whole – *your* whole life ahead of you. And now you've decided to run for Congress. Plus you'll win, I know you'll win. Then what? Right? As for working together, maybe we can talk about that another day but it's unlikely - given where we've already been together and I realize that doesn't seem far. I probably have toyed with you a little, and I apologize for that. My ironing your clothes, that was the real me. My standards for sex have to do with duration of courtship. Believe me though, if I were going to break my *one-night-stand* rule, you'd be the perfect guy. I find you incredibly attractive, accomplished, sweet and even sexy. You seem a bit naïve at times with me but I promise you that it only adds to your charm. I know you've *got it* Chip, I knew when you spoke – the first time we met – at the Embassy Suites. You're special. Look at you! You've got a great name, you come from a great family, you've got an irresistible face and your body – I'm not even going to – that shouldn't matter. It seems like you were an unlikely Marine, an unlikely captain for the Gators and now an unlikely member of goddam Congress. Chip you're *special*. When I think of what those staffers are going to do to be close to you... part of me wants to take advantage of you right here right now, but I'm not going to. I think if anything is going to happen between us on this trip – if it gets – I don't know – hot, I guess - it's got to happen after we do the *House of Blues*. Otherwise we're going to get busted."

The cards were on the table. The truth was out there but no decisions had been made and that kept both of them slightly on edge. Chip half-wished they'd never met, he was simply burned out, but he still liked her. Neither of them could get their arms around the feeling in the air.

Cheryl used both hands to adjust her hair and turned slightly toward him. "How was that?" she asked.

"That was well-crafted. Thank you for clearing some of that up," he replied.

"Yea, well..." she smiled. "Don't let it go to your head."

"Wouldn't dream of it," he said with a hint of arrogance.

"We'd better go," she warned, looking at her timepiece.

Chip and Cheryl exchanged smiles during the elevator ride to the lobby. The concierge wouldn't hear of calling them a taxi and instructed the shuttle, by two-way radio, to carry them to the restaurant.

The two spoke about everyday things on the way to the *House of Blues* and kept their hands to themselves in spite of their attraction. New Orleans was teeming with people. Customized motorcycle pipes and loud music filled the night air. Chip wondered if the girls flashed their breasts even if Mardi Gras wasn't for another month.

"What's your mother like?" Cheryl asked out of the blue.

He immediately stopped thinking about spicy girls on Fat Tuesday. "Mom? Uh, she's a little out there. But she's no crazier than any other mom I don't think. She talks kinda – she's from Virginia. And sounds like it," he said. "I pretty much just tell her what I think she wants to hear most of the time. It works, right?"

"I guess so," she said, wondering if her mom was crazy. "Yea, my mom's a little crazy too."

"All moms are crazy, it comes with the territory," he joked. "You wouldn't quote me on that would you?"

"Chip the newsletter thing was made up. I'm not even remotely responsible for it," she confessed.

"So that message you left me was fake? Seriously?" he asked.

"One hundred percent, but that's also what I told your dad, so keep the white lie going if it comes up tonight," she said.

"He's in on this?"

"No baby, he's not in on anything. But he did give me your number."

"I'm confused. Where did you spend enough time with my father that he gave you my number?"

"You're not mad are you?"

"Hell no I'm not *mad*. Was it at Maxes - the reception - where?"

"We both enjoyed the game – your game – from above."

"And you told him you were doing a story or something and he just handed it over, huh?"

"Pretty much," she said with a half grin.

"And now we're showing up to dinner *together* – what – seven hours later?" he asked skeptically.

"Lighten up Charles the Third. We're almost there," she said as she reached into her purse for a ten.

He got up and went to the other side of the shuttle bus. They were facing each other now. She crossed her legs and winked at him.

"That's a pretty tight little skirt for the Director of Alumni Affairs. Ain't it?" he said, sounding *extra* North Floridian.

She rolled her eyes and shook her head but the smile had never left. The driver indicated they'd arrived at their location. Chip followed his friend to the front of the bus and watched her give him ten dollars and a warm 'thank you.' The linebacker also thanked the driver and exited the microbus. It smelled good on the streets of New Orleans, Chip was kind of surprised. The music was loud but uplifting, more Cajun than jazz. Everyone seemed happy.

"Ya'll set there *Twenty Four*? Do we need to go over anything before we go in?" she asked.

"Ready to rock, *Thirty One*. Let's do this," he replied.

"Oh my God! Look!" she gasped. "Weezer is playing tonight!"

"Sweet," he lied, wondering who in the hell 'Weezer' was.

They made it inside and were escorted upstairs to join the group. Chip looked like he was giving everyone the bird as he kept his left hand out in front of his chest. The upstairs lounge, bar and dining room had been reserved for invited guests only. The two were greeted in the lounge area by a few of the university's distinguished alums. Chip briefly noticed the furnishing and decorations then started picking out people in the room he recognized. Cheryl turned up her charm to full blast with the big wigs and introduced Chip as the captain of the football team, not as a candidate for the House. They all seemed to know about his candidacy regardless.

Most of the guests inundated Chip with ideas, questions, and advice. At first he wasn't in the mood for politics, he would rather have played grab-ass with Cheryl over what was happening between them. He saw her direct a few scrunched eyebrows at him to "get into character" so he came alive. His handshakes got firmer, his eye contact got stricter and his shoulders receded a bit. Chip started making the rounds and felt comfortable in doing so. He had briefly lost sight of his new friend but found his parents near the stage-viewing area. They were with the Davenports.

Mary slightly berated him for being so late. "Hun most of us have already had dinner! Where've you been?" she said in her Virginia plus two glasses of Chardonnay voice. "How's your hand?"

"Did you have it x-rayed?" asked Charles.

"I'm okay," Chip replied. "Hello Mr. and Mrs. Davenport. Good to see you."

The linebacker and the two men recapped the first half and the trophy presentation but no one mentioned the second half of play, when Chip stood idle on the sideline and guided Kevin Williams through his first full half of play. The two women broke free from the group and wandered off. Walt brought up the campaign and Charles scanned the room for eavesdroppers.

"Son," Walt began. "I'm impressed with your decision to run for Reynolds' seat. You're going to do just fine – and I think you can win. I've already heard from four or five guys who can help us pull this off. Chip, people are going to come out of the woodwork for favors. I'm not sure how much you know about the system. There are people I know – who know I know your dad – and have offered to help. The minute you get back to Gainesville, I want you to get the paperwork ready. You're going to need signatures and a bank – *campaign* – account as soon as possible. I've got some dough for you and so do others." Walt turned to Charles, "and we need to set up a meeting with Reynolds – a one on one with Chip here."

"I've already been contacted – sort of. I'm supposed to call him when I get back to town. He wants to meet me at his river house. I think it's in Palatka," Chip remarked.

"Sort of?" his dad asked.

"I guess he called the coach. Haynes. And the coach told me."

"Good," Walt said swiftly. "'means he's at least potentially on board. That's very good; we're going to need him."

"Thank you Mr. Davenport – for offering to help out with my campaign."

"You bet, call me Walt though. Oh, and – uh – we've got to get you out of that goddam Jap mobile before the press starts taking pictures. So, uh, start thinkin' 'bout Fords," he said with a wink. "I'm sure we can work something out."

Charles had become a GM guy in spite of his friendship with Walt and in spite of the fact that Jay was still driving the professor's Explorer after all those years of above-average reliability.

"Don't listen to him Chip, he's a damn Chevrolet turncoat!" Walt said as he jabbed Charles' ribs. "Suburban my ass!"

Charles finished his scotch with a three second chug. "The Suburban is the King of the Road!"

"It's got *nothing* on the Expedition, do some research History Man!" he retorted. They sounded like sixteen year-olds.

Chip just nodded and turned from their loose huddle. He noticed Cheryl across the room and realized they were both now in the exact same business - and that she had way more experience. She looked graceful and professional. He noticed things about her that he would have never picked up on about other girls he had known. The old guys flocked to her. She flirted with them without seeming like a flirt or a tease. Cheryl was friendly and she knew how to play the game and Chip was realizing it more and more as he observed her.

Out of nowhere a girl approached Chip from his side.

"I just wanted to say hi. I'm Meagan Herrin; I'm a sophomore at UF – too. I've seen you play or whatever. Did you hurt yourself at the game today?"

She wasn't bad looking, not by any stretch. Chip had to adjust his eyes; he'd been carefully giving Cheryl the long eye for the past ten minutes. Meagan looked like Jessica to Chip, only her hips were wider and she had a bigger bust.

"Glad to know you Meagan, Chip MacIntosh," he extended his hand slowly to her. "I thought I was the only undergraduate at this thing," he said with a slight chuckle. "Where 'ya from?"

"I'm from Jacksonville. And I – my dad's a big supporter of the program. Like, the University," she said. "So you're running for the Senate or whatever – the state senate? Do I have that right?"

"You're close," he said, trying not to sound patronizing. "US House. I have yet to formally announce though, so just think of me as a fellow coed."

The nineteen year old felt stupid. She looked down and adjusted her top a little. Her boobs got bigger and Chip tried not to look at them. 'Good idea,' Chip thought to himself, 'when your mind fails you, lift your tits a little.'

The tactic was working, Chip soon felt very comfortable. This girl was shorter than Cheryl and had short dark hair. She had dark eyes and her tan seemed more permanent than the woman's. Her voice was much higher and she had on more casual clothes. Meagan looked fun, albeit not terribly sharp compared to what Chip had been dealing with all afternoon.

The *woman* working the crowd noticed Chip and Meagan chatting away. Cheryl wasn't the type to swoop in with a cut block, but she remained mindful and it bothered her that it made her a bit angry. She wouldn't dare use the 'j' word, not even in her thoughts. Plus, she privately rationalized; Chip *couldn't* be interested in a teenager, not after his initial interaction with an actual woman.

Cheryl quickly found her group dissipating and couldn't find another tiny party to join. She was all alone in an instant. It was the perfect time to be with Chip had he not been chatting it up with the Mickey Mouse Club. She found herself running out of options and panicked slightly. 'This isn't like me' she thought to herself. Her safety net was her cell phone-computer; she yanked it from her purse and pretended to read emails.

Five minutes later Chip was still speaking with Meagan. The teenager had rebounded nicely and Chip was enjoying her ramblings about music and movies. They actually had a lot in common from a multimedia perspective. For a minute, he had forgotten all about the gal in the alumni office.

Cheryl stored her phone unit for a conversation with the guy who had invited her; Ray Smith walked up with an unlit cigar in his hand and a happy frown.

"Glad you could make it Cheryl, truly," he said as the two did the *shake, lean and peck*.

"Nice to see you Ray," she said, looking around for Mrs. Smith. "Some turnout. Who do I have to thank for hosting this – I'm embarrassed I don't even know."

Chip approached and caught Cheryl off guard.

"Ray? Have you met the captain of our defense, Charles MacIntosh III?" she asked him wondering if that made it sound like she knew him too well.

"I believe that's *former* captain," said Chip in a friendly voice. "Chip MacIntosh, nice to meet you."

"A pleasure Chip. A real pleasure. Ray Smith, with *the University*. How do you two know each other?" he asked with a slightly raised eyebrow.

They answered together: "We met at the…" but she said "Embassy Suites" and he said "the pool at the W." It was a classic screw up but Cheryl covered it like a can of tennis balls. She went over most of the story – to the point where Smith was no longer interested. He excused himself politely.

"Not bad, woman," he said as they watched the older man trail away.

"Let's cover it right now before that happens again."

"First can I get a beer?" he asked. "It's cool if I have a beer right? Cheryl?"

"Of course," she confirmed, "let's go get a beer."

"Bottle or glass, I've seen both tonight – I mean – *here*."

"I'd go with a glass. Come on."

They were stopped halfway to the bar by Meagan and her dad.

The chat was cordial but focused mostly on the run for Congress. The doctor was friendly enough but offered no assistance to the candidate. Cheryl ended up being slightly bitchy towards the end of the conversation.

At the small, private bar, Chip let Cheryl order first and she noticed his manners. "House Cabernet please," she said. "And I'll have a Sierra Nevada please." The bartender made a face like he had to urinate badly. "I'm not going to have that up here. Can you hang on for a minute?"

"Sure, if it's no trouble."

"No trouble at all," said the bartender. He picked up a headset from behind the bar. "I need Sierra Nevada upstairs please? Bring a twelver."

The bartender poured Cheryl her red wine, set it on the bar, then stepped away to meet the busboy at the stairway.

The two were alone again; the closest guest was at least twenty feet away. Cheryl took a small sip of wine and leaned closer to Chip. "I'm not going to sleep with you tonight," she said in a very sexy and unconvincing way.

The Marine pretended to look shocked. "I'm surprised you said that," he said.

"Really? Why?"

"'Cause I was just about to say the same damn thing to you."

Cheryl laughed out loud and said "yea right."

The bartender showed up with a bright green box of Sierra Nevada. "I am soooo sorry for the wait," he said dramatically. "Here you are, young man."

Chip smiled without showing his teeth and stepped away from the bar. She followed him in the least pathetic-looking way possible. The two were alone again at the opening to the main area. They could see the rest of the place eating, drinking and waiting for Weezer to take the stage.

"Shouldn't you be talking to people?" he asked her nonchalantly.

"Shouldn't you?" she asked freshly.

"I don't think I'm going to stick around."

"But your parents are here. You should probably spend some time alone with them."

"Cheryl, I see my parents all the time, we live in the same town and now that football's over..."

"Speaking of *live*. Where are you – I mean – you're not going to live in that brick house while mounting a campaign for Congress are you?"

"No. I need to find something."

The two stood silently, looking out at the rest of the venue. The crowd started to clap and cheer when Weezer walked onstage unannounced. The DJ killed the background music. Chip was ready to listen to the band that he'd never heard of.

The band opened up with a cover tune by Cake called "Let Me Go." And they were nailing it. Even the older ladies up in the private Florida gathering started moving closer to the opening for a better view. Chip nodded with the beat and played it cool. Cheryl watched him to see if he recognized the song and she was pretty sure he did.

"I know this song!" he yelled to Cheryl.

She smiled at him and moved her head with the baseline just like he was doing. Chip's parents approached, it was far too loud to introduce Cheryl so they all motioned to each other to proceed to the lounge area.

After shuffling across the loft they got to the private lounge area and went inside. There were only a handful of people who had already escaped the loud music. Cheryl and Charles had already re-introduced themselves and Chip presented Cheryl to his mother for the first time.

"Mom, I'd like you to meet Cheryl West, with Alumni Affairs. She and I met up at the pool today – at the W." Chip said as if he'd studied it.

"So nice to see you Cheryl. Have we met before Hun?" Mary asked as she tilted her head.

"I'm sure I've seen you. Perhaps in the skybox or at the Alumni Reception the other night. Very nice to formally make your acquaintance Mrs. MacIntosh. I've just gotten to know Chip and I am – well, we can't wait to tout his story in our next newsletter," she said, realizing Charles was paying attention.

Mary had a look on her face that concerned everyone else. She bounced her eyes between Cheryl's hips and Chip's open beer.

"Would you all excuse me while I use the ladies room?" Cheryl asked with a splash of a southern accent.

"Of course," Mary said pleasantly.

"Chip, are y'all?" his mom asked. "Hun what's going on there? Is she after you?"

"*After* me?"

Charles interrupted. "Maybe we should hit the road Mary; we've got to drive eight hours tomorrow morning. Wait! Chip, are you coming with us? We're leaving first thing. Hell I completely forgot."

"I actually have a ride," he said. "I'm all set."

Charles cough-laughed. "Lemme guess son, the gal in the ladies room is carrying you home?"

"She can help me. Seriously," Chip offered on deaf ears.

"Chip, what about the – what about Jessica? Is she no longer in the picture?" Mary asked.

"It's not like that – nothing has – she isn't... there's nothing between Jess and me and she knows that," Chip was slipping. "Why can't I just?..." The linebacker realized he was caught. He wanted to finish the rest of his beer but it didn't feel right in front of his mom.

"Honey we're gonna go. Are you sure you won't ride with us tomorrow?" Mary asked.

"I'll see you guys in G-ville. Okay?" he said. "I should do this. It feels right."

"Oh yea, I'm sure it does. Just use your brain Chip. You're in a whole new type of game now. And the mistakes are more costly than anything you're used to," Charles said as he looked over his shoulder.

Chip said goodbye to his parents and found a loveseat, he was tired. It was pretty quiet in the lounge. He sat back in the comfortable couch and briefly closed his eyes.

Cheryl had gotten pinned by a few guests but managed to free herself and secure reinforcements for Chip and herself. When she opened the glass door to the lounge Chip heard the music and opened his eyes. She was walking toward him with a topped off Cabernet and a fresh Sierra Nevada. He sat up and smiled at the very sight of her.

"I'm falling asleep – this happens," he said.

"Well," she began, "I assume it's the bowl game you played this afternoon."

"Yea, that and my mother. Right?"

"Where did they go?" she asked, looking around.

"They left. Their hotel is kind of far away and they are leaving at first light."

"First light? Oh... Dawn. Should we leave too?" she asked.

"Maybe I should just get a cab. I mean, don't you have to represent a little more?"

"Hell no I don't have to *represent*. I've been on vacation since the game ended – technically speaking. Do you want this or no?" she asked, holding up the beer.

"Might as well. Thanks."

Cheryl handed him the beer and took a seat in the high-back next to the loveseat. He couldn't remember the last time he had two beers in a row. Chip took his training seriously and while he might have had a beer with a steak dinner in the past six months, he certainly hadn't had two in a row. He was starting to feel the effects.

The two of them sat quietly while they enjoyed their drinks. Chip finished his beer, slapped his hands on his knees and said "I've got to go."

"Me too," she confessed. "But why don't you walk out first. Actually, meet me at the corner, we'll share a cab."

"Okay. Wait, is your car here?"

"Hello! We came together on the shuttle bus thing. Are you okay Chip?"

"I know we came – I mean in New Orleans – how did you get here?"

"I drove – it's at the hotel."

"How would you feel about driving me home-home."

"Oh, now we're road-tripping buddies?" she said with a raised eyebrow.

He just smiled and reclined a little in his seat.

"Don't sit back, I'm worried you're going to fall asleep. Leave that beer on the table. Come with me, I don't think we need to leave separately. Who gives a damn anyway? I'm ready to go."

Chip just nodded slowly.

The cab ride back to the hotel was pretty quiet. Chip and Cheryl eyed each other a few times but spoke very little. He was nervous. Cheryl was too. She finished at least three glasses of wine but was more accustomed to social drinking than her new friend. She spent the whole ride back wondering about the sleeping arrangements and how the slightest mishap could lead to eight miserable hours in the car the next morning.

It was the first time in recent memory that Cheryl was in a situation she didn't know how to handle. She liked Chip and she knew he liked her. She felt vulnerable and excited but her cautious nature and her own ambitions kept her from jumping the guy in the back of the cab.

They made it to the lobby of the W Hotel and she pulled him aside.

"Can we talk a sec?" she asked him.

"Of course. Yea," he replied.

They found a pair of comfortable chairs near a massive potted fishtail palm in the atrium.

"Chip, before we go upstairs. I thought we should just have a quick brainstorming session," she said, like they had just partnered up on a marketing plan.

"Okay," he said attentively. "*Shoot.*"

"I have a plan."

"Good. I can't wait to hear it."

"I'm going upstairs; alone. But I'm going to leave you a key to my room and that's... That's pretty much it." She had a more serious look on her face as if she wasn't waiting for a response. "I had fun with you tonight. Good night," she almost whispered and kissed him on the cheek.

Cheryl disappeared and Chip just sat there in awe. He had never heard anything like that and didn't know what to think as he studied her room key. He noticed that the bar was still open and decided to see if they had any Sierra Nevada. The linebacker had rallied. He wanted one more beer to eliminate any fears of the woman upstairs.

Chip made sure to note the exact time as he ordered the beer. He figured he had fifteen minutes, any sooner and she might not be ready yet any later and she might change her mind or fall asleep. Of course he didn't have to show up at all, but he was going to.

It was go-time. He finished his last drop of liquid courage, tipped the bartender and set off towards the elevators. He looked over his shoulder as he opened the door to his room. He undressed, peed, brushed his teeth, washed his hands and face and looked in the mirror. As Chip was leaving the bathroom he noticed a thick white robe folded neatly on the counter.

With only a pair of boxer shorts, two different room keys, and the house robe, Chip stepped across the hall. He held his breath as he slid the little card into the door marked 707.

Cheryl had drawn only the thin set of curtains, allowing the city lights to slightly illuminate the room. He could tell she was awake but decided not to talk. Chip took off his robe, laid it on a chair, and slid into her bed. He wasn't sure what to do, so he just lay still waiting for her to make the first move, even if it was conversational.

She rolled over to him and put her hand on his stomach and her lips on his shoulder. Chip turned to his side and put his injured left hand behind his back. With his right hand he explored her smooth body. The two started kissing passionately and she pressed her bare breasts up against his strong chest. Cheryl let out soft moans as she grinded her pelvis into his thigh. It was a level of foreplay Chip had never experienced before. They went after each other like wild animals for a solid ten minutes until Chip stopped moving.

"I don't have any condoms," he embarrassingly admitted.

Cheryl attempted to work on her breathing. "I didn't think you would – so I got some from the concierge – and I knew you wouldn't – that's where I got the idea – whatever – I have some."

Chip was impressed. She leaned away from him and grabbed them from the *bible* drawer next to the bed. "Here," she said, ripping one off for him.

"The concierge really had rub' – I mean – *condoms*? For real?"

"I swear... Chip – should we do this?"

"I'm up for it if you are. I don't want to if you don't – *obviously*."

"No! I want to. Are you thinking it will be weird though?"

"The sex?"

"No, the other stuff – the after-sex stuff – I'm not worried about the actual sex for christsakes."

"I – we've had team speakers come in and present on this exact situation. Professionals. Even in high school they spent a lot of time on these moments – just like this. Believe me when I tell you – I am fine with *not* doing it. I like you and I think you are outstanding, but there can be no doubts on your end."

Cheryl got out of the bed and walked to the bathroom. The Marine noticed how good her backside looked in a thong. She quickly emerged from the bathroom with her phone and a small portable speaker. She set it on the nightstand and pushed a few buttons.

Chip couldn't identify the musician but he knew what it meant.

Chapter Eleven

Cheryl awoke at eight thirty, the wine had had a bigger impact than she originally predicted. She sat up in her bed, rubbed her eyes and noticed that Chip was nowhere in sight. She got out of bed slowly and scanned her room for a note. It was on the desk and read: *Good Morning – I went for a run. Should be back at 8:30 – Chip*. Rather than write a heart symbol for the salutation, he had decided on a simple happy face. It made her happy indeed.

She glanced back at the alarm clock and dashed into the bathroom. She walked out naked to the sound of a flushing toilet. She threw on her underwear from the night before, grabbed her terry cloth robe and started brushing her hair. Cheryl threw her hair up in a quick tie then located a package of makeup wipes. She brushed her teeth then added a conservative amount of lipstick and base. Then she went back into the main room and turned on the television. There was a knock at the door.

Chip was sweating and breathing heavily. He had on a grey t-shirt and a pair of blue, mesh shorts with a *Florida Lacrosse* logo on the bottom. He had located a towel between the entrance of the hotel and the seventh floor and he had it over his shoulder.

"Hey!" she said as she waved him in.

"Did 'ya get my note?" he asked as he strolled in confidently.

"Yea – how was it? The *run*..." Cheryl asked as she checked herself in the mirror without his noticing.

"Rough! The beer, this damn finger... Can I lay down for a sec?"

"Sure. I hadn't planned on going back to bed."

"That alcohol smell comes out when you sweat – it's pretty gross. But I feel better. What time did you want to hit the road?"

It was clear he wasn't going to bring up their tryst from the night before. She felt relieved and assured herself that they'd bring it up on the car ride home. She studied him as he lay in her bed stretching his legs out and the very sight of him crushed any notions of guilt she may have had.

"We should probably take a shower, get our stuff together and head out," she instructed.

Chip froze slightly, it sounded like she meant they should shower together and he liked it. He had done the hot tub thing, but had never showered with a woman. He used the weight of his legs and feet to sling himself off the bed to a standing position. He kicked off his sneakers, pulled off his quarter socks and removed his sweaty shirt.

"I'm up for it," he said as he smiled and walked to her bathroom.

Cheryl covered her smile with her hand. She watched as he turned on the shower and removed his pants. She retraced her words to see if there was any way a reasonable individual could have deduced that she had implied that they actually take a shower together.

He turned his head back to her. "You coming?"

She wanted to laugh at his youthful interpretation of her idea but she couldn't help but be a little turned on. The trip to New Orleans had already been one for the record books so she decided to hop in with him. She debated whether to make it cleansing and playful or seductive. She had no idea what was on his mind but she figured he'd be up for anything she could throw at him.

She entered the bathroom, shut the door and turned off all but one light. Cheryl was amazed at how dark it had become. She used another make-up wet-nap on her face and de-robed. Chip was facing her through the frosted glass door but he could only see her silhouette.

He reminded himself not to say a word as she stepped into the large shower stall. She liked the hot water, the steam was getting heavy and it started clearing her head of the white wine sensation from the night before. Cheryl reached to the floor and pumped an ample amount of her sensitive-skin body wash onto her hand. She forcefully turned Chip around and began to lather up his back and message his shoulders. He became fully aroused as she pressed her breasts up against him and breathed heavily. Chip spun back around and started kissing her. He went for her neck and she started to moan a little. She grabbed the side of his head and pushed it towards her chest.

Neither of them could move by the time their shower had finished. Chip asked for permission to get out and she granted it between breaths.

It looked like it had rained in the bathroom; he tried not to slip as he reached for the light switch. "Is it okay if I turn on the lights?" he asked politely. "Sure – go ahead," she replied. Chip couldn't even see himself in the mirror; he wrapped a towel around his midsection and cracked the door to alleviate the fog. He looked over at the shower and deduced that Cheryl was washing her hair.

"Should I – uh – hang out for a minute?" he asked, unsure if the rules required him to stick around for a few minutes.

"No! Go get ready, we've got to leave."

"Okay!"

She peeked out of the shower, hiding her body. "Hey," she said. "That was fun."

"It sure was. *Sugar*," he replied sincerely. "Do you want this door open?"

"No, you can shut it; I'm going to turn the heat down a little."

Chip grabbed his clothes from the floor, pulled his room key out of his pants and dashed across the hall. He found it refreshing that his wardrobe was neatly stacked and organized. He laid out his clothes for the road trip and went to the bathroom to re-dress his broken finger for the last time – at least until he could have the team doctor give it the final remedy.

He combed his hair back and over, rolled on some deodorant, re-brushed his teeth and threw on his clothes. He crammed the rest of his stuff into his duffel bag and folded his blazer neatly over top of it. Chip's phone was the last loose item in the room. He figured he had to give Cheryl at least another ten minutes so he searched his phone for messages. It wasn't a voicemail from Jess; it was another dirty text message from Christian Ross. Chip shook his head as he read the details surrounding the quarterback's wild night with his steady hook-up partner and her model-friend from New York. Chip resisted the urge to text him back in an effort to one-up him, plus Ross wouldn't have understood.

The hotel phone in Chip's room rang like a fire alarm; it was Cheryl, of course. "Ready?" she asked. "All set," he replied. He hung up the phone and headed for her room.

Cheryl was all packed up and ready to go. "Give me your jacket. Can you take my bag and I'll take this hanging stuff?" she asked.

"Yep," he replied as he looped his duffel back over her black, rolling suit-case.

She looked relaxed in her faded red Bermuda shorts and loose white top. She had on leather sandals and her hair was in a fun ponytail. The two left the room looking like an established couple. Chip started to wonder what kind of car she drove; he certainly didn't want to ride eight hours in a compact. Then he considered the phones – what if Jessica called – or his mom.

"Are you hungry?" she asked as they boarded the elevator.

"Look at me. I'm always hungry," he said.

"There's a buffet off the lobby, we can get you something in there – maybe you could bring it with you in the car."

"Great."

They stored their bags at the front desk and checked out. Chip gave her plenty of elbow room as they walked through the lobby. She shouldered a small canvas tote bag in lieu of a purse and she walked with a purpose, something Chip had never really seen in a girl with whom he was involved.

The breakfast buffet was like nothing Chip had experienced. The guys in the white gloves were scurrying about refreshing the individual stations, which were loaded up with everything from fresh fruit to Belgian waffles. It was the first time the Marine had ever seen actual carving stations at breakfast.

"Hey, is there anything else you need to do before we leave town? Do you need anything?" Chip asked without looking at her.

"No. Why?" she asked.

"Cause this could take a while," he said as he turned to her and smiled.

A large hotel staffer approached and said "Go on cher – get ya some breakfast."

Cheryl just smiled and proceeded to the mega fruit stand.

"How did she know your name?" asked Chip.

"She didn't. They call you that here."

"They call you – *what*?" he asked as he grabbed a pair of dinner plates and handed her one.

"They say *cher* – it's French and short, I think, for Che*rry*."

"For real?"

"Yes, I heard someone say it in a movie. And last time I was here with my friends we had a tour guide who called everyone *cher*. You no-doubt noticed the French influence on the city during your visit."

"Yea, that - and the whole: *my father is a History professor* thing. Plus there was that guy – the maitre d' at Maxes, the night I totally struck out with you. He was pretty goddam French."

She just looked at him and slightly rolled her eyes. "Okay," she said.

"I'll come find you in a minute," Chip said as he headed toward the real food He found the pancakes, bacon and sausage and loaded it onto his plate like he hadn't eaten in days. He found grits and bowls and coffee and orange juice and managed to carry it all to the table Cheryl had selected. He laid all of his provisions out on the table then left again. He returned with two pints of milk, a donut, and a halved grapefruit.

She looked at the kid like he had a tapeworm. "You can't seriously eat all of that can you?" she asked.

"Sure I can *Cher*. And I'll probably grab a few of those bagels for the road," he said as he tore into his pancakes and wondered if any anti-gas tablets had found their way into his shaving kit. He knew he couldn't go eight hours without letting one go.

"So... Charles the Third, what's your plan? When will you make your formal announcement, organize your staff and volunteers, establish a campaign account, all that good stuff?"

"I need to call Congressman Reynolds – tomorrow probably - and go out and see him. Then I need to find a place to live, I've got to get someone to replace me in my house – which will be easy. Then I've got to find a little office somewhere, I'm pretty sure my current landlord will have something in town, close to campus. Momma's got a damn good banker; I'll probably call him tomorrow too. And it seems I've got to get rid of my truck, being that it's Japanese and all - which I find pathetic."

She was impressed. His delivery wasn't terribly sophisticated, but the boy knew what he had to do.

"How many classes do you have this semester?" she said looking to her left and right. She couldn't believe she was possibly dating an undergraduate.

"Well, I've signed on for three classes – nine credits – which I need to graduate."

She interrupted him. "You need *those* nine credits or you just need nine credits."

"The latter. But I was thinking," he paused to chew his breakfast without grossing her out. He took a sip of juice. "I'm going to try to see if I can get three credits for a political internship – though I'd be interning for myself in a sense. Surely running for US Congress has to be as credible as answering the phones for a member of the State Senate. Right?"

"Who came up with that idea?"

"I did Cher. I did."

She was impressed and showed it with one of those frowning nods. "Not bad Chip. Not bad at all. Have you given any thought to where you might make the actual announcement?" she asked him.

"I saw that there's a Ducks Unlimited banquet coming up in a week or two – but I wanted to talk to Congressman Reynolds about that. Maybe there'll be a dedication ceremony at a preserve or something. Do you know what Ducks Unlimited is?"

Cheryl immediately picked up on the idea that Chip knew to separate himself from the university. She wondered how he knew that – she knew he hadn't brainstormed or written any kind of a plan.

"Do you?" he asked again.

"I'm sorry. Do I what?"

"Have you ever heard of Ducks Unlimited?"

"Yes. I do – wetlands – duck hunting."

"Wetlands *conservation*, it's actually a pretty fascinating story; I'll tell you about it sometime."

"Sometime?" she said far too soon after he finished his sentence.

Chip sensed the slip. He knew that was womanly code for 'where is this all going,' but he covered it up so she wouldn't have to.

"I could tell you now if you like," he said casually.

"That girl at the game... The reporter who asked you about your platform and the issues and all of that... Have you thought? Don't get me wrong, those were great answers – but those questions are going to come up," she said.

"I'm for helping people out – those who really need help. I love nature and the environment and I feel it's worth protecting. I know a thing or two about being a veteran and I think character is best developed in good homes and in schools that produce results."

"Chip, what exactly don't you like about the *Republican* Party?" Cheryl asked him, seemingly seriously. It had turned into a complete interview but Chip decided to roll with it.

"I don't dislike the Republican Party. I just have come to associate their records as being weak on civil rights, social programs, the environment, and healthcare. I think with respect to national security and economic policies, perhaps I'd be more in step with the Republicans. My goal here, Miss West, is to represent the concerns of the people of this district – not just the Democrats, not just the voters – the *people*. I plan to use the values that have been instilled in me by my family, my peers, and my life experiences. I have honed my leadership skills on the field of battle – maybe that's a stretch – but certainly the field of play. And I realize I don't fit the bill of the stereotypical Member of Congress, but I'm not here to remind folks of the way things have been, I'm here to let them know how things *could be*. I bring with me a fresh perspective on the future of the state I call home and the country I love."

Cheryl leaned forward, looking side to side, and took his good hand. "That was pretty good Chip. Seriously – are those your words?"

"Hell yes they're my words. The thing about the parties, I'm not even sure about those records, clearly I've got a lot of research to do. There are an equal number of Democrats and Republicans in the district but look how popular Reynolds is. I've actually voted for a Republican – a couple of 'em I think."

She let go of his hand and sat back in her chair. "Well I think you're off to a great start, truly Chip, I'm in awe."

"I know I can tweak that a little. I've got someone – another guy I need to meet with – who can help me with this stuff."

"How's it going over there?" she asked, eyeing his family-of-four-breakfast. "Can we get going or what?"

"Yea," he said, taking the last sip of his coffee, "let's hit it."

Cheryl's two year old beige Jeep Grand Cherokee was out front ready to go. A doorman had their luggage neatly stacked on a chrome plated baggage cart. Chip asked the guy to hang on for a second while he fished out his shower kit.

"I'll just be a second," he told Cheryl as he handed her a five dollar bill and left to find the men's room. Chip made it to the roomy facility and rifled through his toiletries. To his delight, he possessed a healthy surplus of Gas-X and proceeded to pop them into his mouth like candy. He contemplated doing some jumping jacks to see if he could force out a few snaps before they set off for Gainesville, but he didn't want anyone to see that.

Chip bolted to the passenger side of the Jeep and found Cheryl sitting inside with her seatbelt on. "Why don't you take the first shift Big Guy," she said with a wink. "Okay," he replied and jogged around to the driver's side.

"Have you ever driven with a broken finger?" she asked him.

"I can do a lot with a broken finger," he confirmed. "You sure you want me driving this? This is a pretty nice ride."

"*Pretty* nice. This car is my baby, don't wreck it."

"Don't worry," he said as he put the vehicle in gear and hit the accelerator.

"Easy Chip!" she cautioned him.

"Damn! Is this a V8 or something?"

"It's the big one, the 5.7 liter I guess. They call it a *Hemi*, I don't know why."

"Right... You're into speed I take it?" he asked as he pulled away from the hotel in search of Interstate 10.

"The truth is I could care less what's under the hood. I wanted Light Graystone Pearl and the only two they had was a base model and this one. It does fly though, so watch your speed," she said as she fooled with the GPS navigation system. "Here, this will show us to I-10, I know it's close."

"Pretty Hi-Tec, Miss West."

"Indeed Mr. MacIntosh."

Cheryl tugged her iPhone from her tote bag as they took the ramp to Interstate 10. She hit the 'random shuffle' music application and sat back in her seat.

"I like this truck," he said as he blew past a semi. "It's very comfortable and it's fast as hell. She handles nicely too."

"Thanks," she said with a nod.

The Jeep glided down I-10 with the sun in its grill. Cheryl looked out the window and noted the hurricane damage still evident after all those years. They made it all the way to Gulfport, Mississippi before they ever really spoke to each other. Cheryl had messed with her iPad; they had pointed things out to each other – mostly hurricane damage and fellow returning Gator fans. Chip had been scouting for deer, turkeys, hogs and other wildlife.

The exit to Gulfport was about eighty miles from their hotel and Chip made it in a respectable hour and ten minutes. "I could use a bathroom break," he said as he slid into the right lane. "Good call," she said without looking at him. "Oooh, Polo Outlet..."

They found a gas station and Chip pulled in. Without asking, he used his credit card to gas up her tank – he even used premium grade fuel. She exited the vehicle and walked around the back. "You didn't have to – thanks." "You're welcome, it's the least I could do," he said as he reached back in, grabbed the keys and locked it. "You're coming in aren't you?" "Yea," she said. And they walked across the shaded concrete deck.

Chip eyed the warm fried chicken through the curved glass counter near the register. It smelled great but he could wait at least until Pensacola to eat again so he settled for a liter of bottled water and a small bag of plain pretzels. He waited for Cheryl to get out of the bathroom. She met him near the snacks and put her arms around his midsection. "Hey," he said. "Can I get you anything?" "Diet Coke I guess – thanks," she replied "I'll go grab it."

They walked back to the vehicle; it seemed colder out and Cheryl found herself hurrying. "Do you want me to drive Chip?" she asked, waiting for him to unlock the doors. "I'm doing fine, you take it easy," he said as he opened her door for her. She liked that.

"Ready Cher?" he asked as he fired up the Jeep.

"Let's do it. I'm sorry, but I have to turn on the heat for a sec," she said.

"You're cold? It's like seventy five degrees outside."

"Well I can't help it," she said, turning her attention back to the music library on her phone. "What kind of music do you like? Did we cover this last night, I can't remember."

"We covered a lot last night Cher."

"I thought we weren't going to talk about last night."

He looked over at her. "Who ever said that?" he asked. She couldn't see his eyes through his glasses.

"Huh?"

"I'm up for whatever."

They were back on the interstate. "I don't have to know what your thoughts are. I mean – I wouldn't mind. It's cool. It is what it is..." he said.

"Should we get into it?" she asked.

"I don't see what the big deal is, we're both adults. What are you worried about?"

"We both really poured it on last night – before we went out. Those were some serious feelings – ya' know? And I just think if we get into definition – I don't want it to get weird between us."

"I totally understand, believe me," said Chip, "I want what you want. But I think if we avoid the dialog for too long, it's destined to get 'weird.'"

"So what do we do? Talk about our *feelings*, our *emotions* over the past twelve hours – our *experience* together. Do we come up with a clever classification for it? Then do we each vote on the future?"

She sounded lost and had just teetered on bitchy, but Chip wasn't about to push her. "Cheryl, I didn't mean to upset you. We can drop it right now and go on down the road and never mention it again if it suits you. Let's just wait or whatever, I'm not worried about it – sincerely, I've got enough to think about this week. Right?"

"I'm sorry. I didn't mean to be rude about it; you're such a good guy Chip. And you didn't upset me – fuck I knew this was going to happen. Sorry. I didn't mean to say *fuck*."

There was a rest area just ahead and Chip eased off the highway.

"We're stopping?" Cheryl asked.

"Yea," he replied. "I can't concentrate on both right now."

Chip followed the signs to the parking area. He overshot the area by the vending machines and they ended up way in the back by the woods. He put the car in park and raised his glasses to the top of his crown.

"Is it okay if I turn the heat off now?" he asked.

"Of course, sorry," she said. Cheryl removed her glasses and seatbelt and turned in her chair. She tucked her left leg under her right thigh and looked right at him. Chip scanned the area for vagrants then turned to her.

"We like each other, we had sex, we both live in Gainesville, and we're both adults, what's the big deal? We can't just roll with that Cheryl? I'll admit it's not how I usually operate, and I assume you've been a bit out of character these last days, but seriously... We haven't done anything wrong. I could see if your job dealt with current students or something but you're in the former-student business; hence, *alumni affairs* and not *student affairs*." It sounded scandalous when he heard himself say 'affairs' so he tried to spin it. "Or is it Alumni *Relations*?" That also sounded dangerous.

"Actually, there's kind of an unwritten rule to say 'affairs' to the older, male donors and 'relations' to everyone else. And don't tell anyone I told you that – I'll just deny it. There is currently an internal memo going around proposing switching the official name to *alumni resources*. But the card that's in my wallet right now reads "Director of Alumni Affairs.""

"Got it. So what about the other stuff?"

"It's so complicated Chip. I felt so *in control* before we slept together. Now I feel like I'm... this isn't easy for me. I feel like I only have two choices."

"No chance I could hear 'em I suppose."

"No chance at all."

"Come on Cheryl, we've got another six or so hours together with no interruptions – besides your goddam iPhone. Let's have it out!"

"You sound like you want a fight."

"No, I don't want a fight – I don't want to fight with you at all, I just – you look miserable over there – this whole time you look sad or something and it bothers me. Just be straight with me. No games, just you and me – miles from home. C'mon just say it. Please..." His tone was firm but far from a shout.

She stared blankly through the windshield and twirled her hair, then she looked at Chip. He had patience in his eyes again.

"You said you want what I want. How can that possibly be accurate? What if the choices don't sit well with you?" she asked.

"I'm prepared for that Cheryl. Two weeks ago there was a chance I'd be working out with the Miami Dolphins this summer. A week ago I was ready to sign on as a goddam park ranger at Yellowstone or wherever." He raised his left hand for her to see it. "And just *yesterday*, I spent the second half of the biggest game, the last game I might add, of my athletic career on the sideline with a less-than-respectable injury. I'm wired for things not to go my way. If your choices don't sit well with me - hell, that's just another day at the office for *Charles the Third*."

She started to tear a little. He was good at this. He had great delivery and it resonated with her. She thought about making up two new options for herself then went ahead with her original thoughts.

"I didn't realize. You're a gifted actor Chip; I thought you were on top of the world when I met you. I'm actually surprised."

"Wait – I am on top of the world – for the record. But the key is – what I do – I bring the top of the world with me – wherever I go," he said with a smile.

"My God," she said. "I've never seen anyone go from humble to confident so fast in my life! And such style!"

"Cheryl." He tilted his head as if he was ready for her to come clean on her options. "Let's have it."

"Okay." She drew some air. "Here are my two best options – don't feel like you have to respond though. I mean, right away. If you want to pull out of here and get to say... oh... the Florida border, that's okay with me."

"Fine, what are they? I feel like a goddamn federal agent – *talk* Woman!" he whisper-yelled as he shifted his weight to the center console and covered his mouth with his hand.

"I'm thinking I can either push you away or try to make you into my - uh - boyfriend."

Chip remained still. He lifted his left eyebrow and squinted at her. He processed her reaction to her own words to see if she showed any signs that favored one option over the other. To ask her to repeat herself wouldn't be fair. He considered just putting the vehicle in gear and driving back on to I-10, which was certainly the most mysterious course of action he could have taken. Chip began to consider his emotions rather than his perfect reaction. He knew why she was considering a relationship with him but he didn't know exactly why she'd deliberately push him away. He was sure she was into him and that made him pretty certain she couldn't just let him go.

He could handle being pushed away and briefly fantasized about random and 'forbidden' meetings with her. He envisioned a secret relationship between the two of them where they'd meet up for weekend excursions and no one would know. His mind wandered further – he could imagine seeing her at civic events after having just spent an erotic weekend together. They'd pretend they didn't know each other very well, if at all. It provided Chip with the perfect situation; it was a lily-white scandal with all of the elements of an outlawed affair and none of the typical stigmas associated with a committed relationship.

He wasn't worried about committing to her; he was worried about committing to a relationship. Chip was a one-woman guy but he was immune to loneliness and that made him a lousy boyfriend for the classic American female.

The idea of a serious relationship was more unsettling than he had initially thought. He had actually hoped that was one of her two options but when faced with it, he began to panic slightly. Thoughts of the campaign trail started entering his head. He questioned the effectiveness of the candidate with a girlfriend, an older woman on top of that. It would come up, he was sure of it. They'd have to get their story straight. Chip quickly threw fire on the idea of a secret love affair confined to weekend trips at the ranch or Cedar Key. He was starting to feel screwed either way. Maybe he should let her push him away after all, especially if she was looking to get married and have babies. The race for Capitol Hill pressed him, he wondered if bachelorhood would be perceived as instability. The Florida delegation didn't need another skirt-chasing Congressman for the press to prey on. Chip turned square in his seat and let his head roll back against the headrest. He took a deep breath without making it sound like a sigh.

"Are you okay?" Cheryl asked.

"Yea, I just need a..." Chip stopped himself.

"Why don't I drive?"

"Cheryl?" he asked as he turned back to face her.

"Yes?"

"I feel like I've changed a little since we first met. And since we sort of got-together, I'm really enjoying things. Why don't we just... Can you be seen with me? I mean – could we actually go on a date in Gainesville? Or would it have to seem somehow professional?"

"I don't really know the answer to that question and I'm not even sure how to find out. There's no one I can ask about that - at least off the top of my head. But honestly, I can't think of who would have a problem with it. Chip, I want you to know that I'm really enjoying things too. Look, I am as blind-sided right now as you are. And I'd love to have a date with you."

"Good! We'll just leave it right there. Hey, *logic* didn't put us in this car together today? This doesn't all have to be figured out right now, let's just have fun and do whatever comes naturally. And if, for you, that means finding a nice, happy medium between pushing me away and taking me home to meet your parents, then I'm on board!"

The air had been cleared; they were both smiling again and breathing easily. Chip scoped the parking lot then put it in gear. They took off down I-10 and shared stories and theories about everything from politics to religion. The one thing they couldn't agree on, apart from a few random music selections, was the climate control. He preferred it rather cool in the Jeep and she liked it a bit warm. Chip had won the battle when Cheryl caved and pulled a sweatshirt from the backseat.

They had blown by dozens of cars, mostly SUVs, all decked-out in Gator gear. Some people had used white shoe polish to write the score of the game on their windows, some had flags holding on for dear life and others just had a few stickers or magnets.

Interstate 75 was pitch black by the time they had rolled into northern Alachua County. It was nearly seven o'clock and Gainesville was just down the road.

"It's good to be back," Chip said as they exited to University Avenue.

"I bet you're starving," Cheryl said playfully.

"How did you know?"

"Well you just had that little sandwich near Pensacola, though most humans could go at least three days on that breakfast you had. What are you going to do about dinner? I'm a big fan of McAlister's and it's right up here. Do you want to get a quick bite?"

"Yea, what – to go?"

"Either way," she said.

"My house is not an option though – they all got back yesterday. There's no way I could put you through that – even if you wanted to. Where do you live?"

Cheryl took a parking spot and put it in park. "Northeast – not far from campus – near fifth and eighth. Should we?"

"Unless you want to just eat here."

"Does everyone know who you are Chip? Can you actually go anywhere without everyone..."

"Usually. Come on, let's go in and see what it's like in there."

They decided on staying. Chip loaded up with a pair of smoked turkey sandwiches, a baked potato, a bowl of broccoli and cheddar soup and a large sweet tea. Cheryl had a chicken Caesar wrap and a bottle of water. Their chat was light-hearted, their food hit the spot and they made it out of there undetected.

Chip had decided long before the home stretch that he didn't want to spend the night with her. He was tired and ready for a good night's sleep. His house was lively but far from out of control when they pulled into the driveway.

"Thank you for the ride Cher. This has certainly been an adventure," he said.

"Oh you're welcome, I was glad you came back with me. I'm sure my dad would like it too," she replied.

"Good. Should we make a plan now or should I call you – or – call me whenever. Right? There aren't any rules. We're just seeing how it – seeing what..." He was losing ground. His nerves had caught up with him. He could close the deal but slacked a bit when it came to customer care. His traditional mindset finally kicked in without her reaching the point of frustration. "Tell you what... I'll call you for a date."

"That sounds really nice," she said. Chip leaned over and kissed her on the mouth.

"Goodnight," he said. "Hatch open?"

"Yea."

He got out of the Jeep, retrieved his gear from the cargo area and waved goodbye as he hustled to the side door.

Chapter Twelve

Tens of thousands of students had been continuously returning to campus for their spring session. It was the *long* semester for many kids now that football was over. While most of the town's youth were sleeping one off, Chip MacIntosh was loading up his truck with fishing gear at seven in the morning for a trip to Palatka. He had been back from New Orleans for two nights and spent most of his down time studying political news and records on the Internet.

Bob Reynolds was heading back to Washington that evening and Chip was supposed to meet him for a quick fishing trip on the St. Johns River. It was only about forty miles to the east but the road was pretty rural by Florida standards and Chip planned on an hour drive. The Landcruiser had a full tank of gas but Chip needed his own fuel. He found an open convenience store down the street from his house and pulled in. He grabbed a large black coffee, a banana and a pair of protein bars for later.

It was plenty light out as he headed down University Avenue toward the small river town. It sounds like it would be a scenic drive, like the drive from Savannah to Charleston, but it wasn't. The road's shoulders and medians were a mix of sugar sand and sticker-blooming weeds. Most of the foliage along the sidewalk was cut with a giant mower deck suspended from a tractor making the trees seem two dimensional. The mobile home parks had been hit with too many storms and the vine-laced chain link fences needed help.

Every ten or so miles there was a decent looking horse farm with white split-rail fencing but most of the terrain was unsightly. The actual road was in perfect shape though. Chip noted the recent widening and the addition of ample bicycle lanes. He wondered if Reynolds played any sort of role in the upgrade.

Even though Chip had tunes on his phone, he preferred the primitive sounds of his cassette player. The Alpine deck was a dealer-installed upgrade when the original owner bought the Toyota back in the late eighties and Chip stayed true to it. One of his hobbies, when time permitted, was to browse garage sales and thrift shops for country and rock tapes. He had never paid more than a dollar per album and he figured the music was the music; he was far from being a sound snob or audiophile.

Chip's phone started humming. At seven thirty in the morning, it could only be a family member. Without checking the screen he answered the phone.

"Hello, Chip MacIntosh," he said.

"Chip? It's Cheryl West... How are you?" she said cheerfully.

He lowered his voice a little, "Hey Cheryl. I'm doing pretty well – how 'bout you?"

"I was thinking about you."

"Yea, I'm uh, I'm sorry I haven't called you – just been trying to come up with a game plan," he said.

"Oh, don't you worry one bit. I'm sure you've had a lot to think about lately. I wondered Chip – I've got this thing in Saint Augustine on Friday – I thought maybe you could come along."

"A school – university event?"

"Well, not really. It's a - uh – it's actually, *technically* a bridal shower."

"Did you say a *bridal shower*?"

"Well it's actually on Saturday morning but I thought I'd – we could – go over Friday night. Together. You obviously wouldn't have to go to the thing with me. You could go to the beach or something, and then I could meet you. I got a room right on the sand – very private. It might be fun, I was just thinking. Are you in the car?"

"I'm driving to Palatka."

"Oh, the – to meet with Bob Reynolds?"

"Affirmative, he asked me to come out and fish with him for a couple of hours. Cheryl - let me think about this weekend."

"That's fine, take your time. I don't need to know right now, just think about it."

"I will, definitely. And thanks for the invite."

"Sure. I've got to run. Have fun with the Congressman – you need him ya know – Charles the third. He can make or break you."

"I know."

"Let me know how it goes though. Okay?"

"Yes. I'll call you later."

"Sounds good. Bye."

Chip hit END and tossed his phone to the empty passenger's seat. He turned up his stereo. It was Dwight Yoakum's *Guitars, Cadillac's* album. He cruised down the road and began the process of dissecting Cheryl West's phone call.

He kept repeating the words *bridal* and *shower* in his head. It sounded serious to him. He wondered why it couldn't have been a seminar or something else that had nothing to do with long-term commitments. Another concept that would keep him awake was the fact that it was an overnight trip and one that was basically way out of town. Chip liked the idea of staying a night away with her, he even liked the idea of spending time on a private beach with her, but he was torn up over the whole bridal shower concept. He wondered if the shower was at the actual hotel or if it was down the street somewhere.

Chip arrived in Palatka with plenty of time to take the scenic route. He traversed St. Johns Avenue towards the river. The Christmas wreaths still adorned the lamp posts and the sleepy town of around ten thousand seemed more charming than Chip had remembered.

Palatka was like the Ancient Greece for Florida. English settlers began farming the east side of the river in the mid 1700's. Citrus played a major role in the shaping of the town as did a behemoth cypress mill. Cannons were fired in Palatka during the Civil War. The combination of a great freeze and an even greater fire ran settlers out of town, essentially for good. Jacksonville stole the shipping industry and the citrus companies fled farther to the south.

Chip drove up the relatively well-maintained white rock road led straight to the Reynolds' property. It was lined with sabal palms and slash pines and palmetto bushes. There were a few decent canopy trees, but it looked mostly scrubby to Chip.

The Congressman's pickup was half-backed into one of his outbuildings and the light inside was on. Chip parked between the big garage and the main home. He got out of his truck and looked around. This was his kind of property.

"Congressman Reynolds?" Chip yelled politely.

"In here! MacIntosh?" he replied, sounding strained as if he was lifting something or trying to loosen a rusty bolt.

Chip walked over without retrieving anything from his vehicle. Bob Reynolds was standing in the bed of his truck reaching for something in his overhead storage rack.

"Good morning Congressman," Chip said. "Can I help you with that?"

"Good morning Chip. Here, take this," he said as he handed the kid an older looking fly rod. Chip took it willingly and offered his hand to the aging angler as he looked for a way down. "I've got it, thanks." The Congressman slipped off the tailgate to the concrete floor without incident.

"Nice to see you Chip," he said as he extended his hand to the linebacker.

"It's a pleasure Congressman, thank you for inviting me out. This is quite a spread you have here. I've always loved the St. Johns."

"Thanks. I'm going to move my truck so this door will close. Why don't you grab your shit and meet me on the back side of the house?"

"Sure."

Chip did as he was told and the Congressman fired up the diesel, moved it out of the way, closed the big door and locked it, then drove around to the side of the house. Chip had his gear and was standing near the back porch of the main house when the Congressman approached on foot. He was wearing a pair of mid-weight, olive-colored, cargo fishing pants with a tan, long sleeved and breathable shirt. He wore classic topsiders with bright white soles and dark mahogany uppers. His straw hat was right off a Dominican banana plantation.

"How do you like your coffee?" Reynolds asked the boy.

"Black, please. Uh, thank you," Chip said. He was impressed with the offer.

"Come on in Chip, *black* we can do. Mrs. Reynolds went back yesterday – to Washington."

The kid stood in the old pine kitchen and looked out over the river as Reynolds fixed two coffees to go. Chip studied the place and thought to himself how open and clean everything looked. There was no clutter and it didn't even really look as though people lived in the home. It looked like a model home, but it would be the oldest model home Chip had even stepped foot in.

"Y'ever caught a bass on a fly?" the Congressman asked.

"Yes sir, I have." Chip answered.

"Impressive," he said as he handed him a large metal coffee cup with a lid securely fastened to the top. "What happened to your hand there?"

"Oh – it's nothing. I banged it up during the Pittsburgh game, it's getting better though."

"Oh yea, nice game by the way. Sugar Bowl eh? Good show. Come on, let's catch some fish."

The two of them avoided conversation as they walked to the edge of the river. Chip noticed the Egg Harbor.

"Now there's a beautiful boat sir," Chip said.

"Thanks Chip," replied the Congressman. "I first saw one of those at Bayside down in Miami - years ago - wanted one ever since then."

The Congressman gave Chip hand signals as to how the bass boat would be launched and where the gear would go. The smaller boat made it into the water, the engine fired right up and they were ready to shove off.

Just before they left the dock, Reynolds pulled a large bait bucket from the river and filled his livewell with about a dozen wild shiners. "Just in case they aren't hitting the flies," he said with a wink. Chip smiled and nodded but hadn't personally fished for bass with live bait since he was a junior in high school. "Good idea," he reaffirmed.

The ride down the river was serene and beautiful. The homes that lined the shore had a certain stateliness about them. There was a subtlety to them and many still enjoyed a decent canopy of foliage to break up their presence. The houses abruptly disappeared and the river looked original. Chip assumed they had made it to an area he knew as *Seven Sisters*.

Reynolds pulled into a small tributary and killed the motor. "Chip, lets put you back here and I'll take the trolling motor up there. Years ago, they used to call this area *Seven Sisters*."

"Sounds good," Chip said with a half-smile.

The men took their places in the boat and Chip began throwing flies at the shoreline beneath the overhanging Cypress trees. Reynolds had planted himself in the forward pedestal seat and worked the small motor that was quieter than an electric toothbrush. He had yet to whet a line.

"So what's the deal Chip? Running for Congress."

"Well-sir, I think I can carry the torch and continue to address the issues you've been tackling," Chip said unconvincingly.

"That's bullshit Chip, and everyone's going to know it. I don't mean to discourage you son, but you've got to come up with something with bigger balls than that."

Chip set the butt of his rod on the deck and looked the member in the eye. "I'm new to this whole thing; I'm still testing the waters. I certainly didn't mean to mock you or anything."

"Keep throwing Chip. And don't sweat it; you've got plenty of time to brush up on this stuff. Politics can be an ugly business, but the truth is – it's no dirtier than anything else. What's the real reason you're taking this on then?"

Chip couldn't throw a fly and talk to a Congressman at the same time. "It won't leave this skiff?"

"No. You've got my word."

"Okay. A bunch of my dad's friends came up with it. They were all at the hunt camp and saw the article about you retiring and I don't know if they were drinking or what, but they set their sights on it and just kinda hit me with it. At first I wrote it all off as an all-too-crazy idea but then it stuck with me. I couldn't get the idea out of my head." He lifted his rod and began casting again. "So as I thought about it, I realized it wasn't such a foolish idea. I met with the lieutenant governor in New Orleans – and some others – and I signed on for it. Plus I couldn't think of anything else to do with my life."

The Congressman stopped the little motor and laughed. "You couldn't think of anything else to do with your life?"

"I didn't know what I was going to do. I didn't have a *plan*. I'm sure something would have come up, but I didn't have... I didn't have a *plan*. I know that sounds awful, doesn't it?"

"Chip, no one has a plan."

"They don't?"

"Hell no. So what's your pitch? Why you? Or what did they tell you? How'd dad's friends sell it to you? In a word?"

"Leadership," Chip said without a pause.

"That's got legs. You were a Marine and a captain on the Gators football team?"

"Once a Marine..." he stopped himself. "That's correct."

The Congressman returned to his little motor. "There's a pair of cypress under the surface up here. Put that fly right on the reflection from the cabbage palm." The boat made a wide turn toward the channel and Chip sent his lure right where the bossman said. With a loud crash a massive largemouth bass consumed the fly. The Marine looked like he was taking on enemy fire. Reynolds kept the boat steady as the kid fought. The bass had a mouth like a five gallon bucket and fought like a sailfish. The water was full of cypress knees and branches but Chip maneuvered him beautifully and never made a sound or lost control.

Reynolds calmly produced a massive landing net from a compartment below the deck. Chip had never used a net on a bass but made sure not to resist the concept.

"Holy crap!" Chip said as he reached for the giant lower jaw of the great bass.

"Jesus Christ," yelled the Congressman as he pulled a compact digital camera from his Velcro-secured chest pocket. "See if your fist will fit inside." It did, and Reynolds snapped a few photos. "Hold on, we've got to weigh him real quick." From another compartment the Congressman produced a spring scale and quickly secured it to the fish. "THIRTEEN – EIGHT! Christ!"

To Chip's surprise the Member of Congress threw his hand on the deck, leaned in next to him, extended his arm way out, and snapped a few of the two of them with the bass.

"Awesome!" yelled Reynolds.

"I know! How did you know he was in there?" asked Chip.

"I didn't know! Hell, it just looked like a good spot."

Chip carefully released the big fellow back into the dark water. "Here, let me take that troller, you take the back deck."

"Naw, I'm okay." Reynolds looked at his watch. "We should probably quit while we're ahead. My ride to Jax will be up at the house soon. And I want to talk to you some more. Thirteen-eight! Its – I just can't even believe it. Shit!"

"What's the record?" the linebacker asked, trying not to sound too cocky.

"In Florida? Seventeen something – confirmed. Just over twenty – unconfirmed. The Perry bass in Georgia was twenty-two and four. Say – did you see the picture they found? 'Got in on the Internet. 'Course then you've got that fella in Japan, I think that tied the world record."

"Yea, I saw the Perry bass online, the picture with the little kid? That bass was as big as that kid!"

"Oh yea," replied the Congressman as he fired up the big motor and pointed to the storage area for Chip to re-stash his rod. "Ready?"

"You bet."

Bob Reynolds secured a few items, including his straw hat and put the hammer down on his bass boat. The two men sped down the river at a steady sixty miles per hour and watched as the egrets got up and the alligators stayed put. Chip wondered how soon he could get the digital files from Reynolds' camera.

They were back to the house in no time. It felt like light speed to Chip who quickly jumped up to help with the lines at the dock.

The two of them walked to the little cabin in the backyard and hung their rods up on a custom rack by the door. Chip was in awe of the Congressman's cozy outbuilding. He was treated to a quick tour and expressed his humble approval. "Every man should have a place like this," he told his potential predecessor.

"All it takes is the right woman. Something to drink?"

"Sure. Whatever," Chip answered.

Reynolds pulled a pair of small, glass Coca Colas from the vintage ice box, popped the tops on an equally vintage bottle opener and handed one to the linebacker.

"Speaking of women, how's that going for you?" he asked as he sat in his chair and pointed for Chip to take the other one.

"Pardon me?" Chip asked.

"What's the girl situation?"

"Uh, I have no girlfriend."

The Congressman crossed his legs and drew from the pony bottle. "You answered that like *English* is your second language."

"While I'm no fan of the saying *it's complicated*, I'm afraid I don't have a better response."

"Don't make me ask you your opinions on Climate Change and that kind of stuff Chip, tell me about the *complicated* broad situation. Then you can ask me anything you want about Congress."

As far as Chip knew, Cheryl was the only one who knew about their situation. Chip sat back in his chair a little and took a deep breath. He briefly studied the walls and soon became very comfortable. Reynolds was fidgeting with a pipe and a decorative tobacco tin.

"There's someone with whom I think I have become involved. And the situation is not a typical one for me and I assume she too is in uncharted waters with respect to me."

"Does the smoke bother you?"

"Uh, no sir."

"Good. Continue," he said as he ignited the bowl of his pipe with a tiny blowtorch.

"Okay. Well, she's a bit more mature than I'm used to. She's a *woman*."

The Congressman nodded with his pipe between his teeth as Chip told him the whole story about Cheryl, leaving out only the racier details. He was nearly out of breath by the time he was finished. Reynolds had a grin on his face that rivaled the one he wore an hour earlier when they fished the huge bass out of the river.

"That's a great story Chip," he said. "Hell, I wonder if I have ever met her."

"I think you'd remember her. She kind of has that effect."

"Yea. Sounds like it."

"You won't – uh – say anything to anyone – right?"

"I'm in the business of secrets, kid. Don't sweat it."

"It's just I haven't told anyone and I'm not sure why I just told you – I mean I barely know you. Jesus. This all *just* happened too."

"No – that's a great story! I'm not a dirty old man or anything. Anyone, any *guy* would think that's a great story. So, what are you going to do?"

"I don't know. She's incredibly beautiful and smart and just has it all going on. And she's cool. It seems so sudden, but she seems to understand me," replied Chip. "Hey, can I ask you something?"

"Sure."

"Politically, what should I do with regard to all of this? I mean... As a candidate? Bachelor? Girlfriend/Older Woman? What would the people – the voters think?"

"Has she looked into the policy? What I mean is – is there anything in the University HR handbook that would preclude her from being able to *see* you socially? Plus, if I were you, I wouldn't refer to her as an older woman or anything like that. Get it in your head now – that she's a contemporary. The important thing is finding out what the school's policy is."

"I think she was going to look into that but didn't know where to look."

"So she's in?" asked Reynolds.

"Well I don't know if she's in – that's part of the whole issue. We haven't decided on what to do about it – the *attraction* I guess."

"Politically, I think it only helps you. Most members' wives are a pain in the ass Chip and it takes everything some guys have just to keep their asses out of sight. Conversely, some are incredibly effective at snagging votes and even representation – say – in the home district. If the university says it's alright, I don't see how it can hurt to be somewhat involved with someone like her. She sounds *incredible*. I will say that I would discourage involvement with some self-absorbed undergraduate. *Maturity* is going to be a tough sell for a twenty-four year old guy running for the House. Thirty years ago, there was no such thing as *the older woman*. These days though, it's a long way from a scandal."

Chip had made it to the edge of his chair for the Congressman's opinion. He liked what he heard and he remained amazed that the man was so insightful and interested in Chip's story.

"Mom and dad are Democrats. I assume you are too?"

"Yes sir."

"So you're okay with that big "D" trailing your name?"

"Shouldn't I be?"

"I'm not into extremes MacIntosh. The far left, I must admit, is scarier to me than even many on the far right. A lot has changed since I first took the oath."

"Really?" Chip asked, apparently very interested.

"Yea. I'm not trying to tell you what to do. This district is about half and half I think. A Democrat with a pump shotgun in his hand has a better chance than some suit-Republican from New York in my opinion. I will say that it's good to have friends though. Whoever has the most friends will win every time."

"Could I have another Coke?" Chip asked.

"Of course, help yourself to whatever you want. What's mine is yours."

"Can I get you something?" Chip asked politely.

"No thanks, I'm all set."

Chip walked past his chair on the way back from the icebox to study the photos on the wall.

"Friends? That means *money* doesn't it?" he asked the Congressman without looking at him.

"Pretty much Chip. You'll need money but you'll also need support. I can help you with that."

Chip turned around fast enough to show that he was grateful but not fast enough to seem totally surprised. "Thank you Congressman," he said while raising his Coke bottle up and slightly dipping his head.

"You're welcome Chip. Glad to help."

Chip was wondering what that help would end up costing him, but he could also hear Cheryl's voice in his head "you need him Chip."

Both men eyed the ceiling of the small building as the sound of a helicopter grew louder and louder. The Congressman got up out of his chair and asked the kid to follow him outside.

"Oh," Chip said. "That's your ride to Jacksonville, isn't it?"

"Yea."

"And that's?"

"Legal?"

"I'm sorry Congressman, I shouldn't have..."

"He's my second cousin, the pilot. Jax is under a hundred miles – there are a few things about it that make it totally legitimate. The main thing, at least for my peace of mind, is that he's going there *anyway*. And I don't think I have ever done him any special favors." Reynolds was yelling by the time he had finished his sentence. The big bird was landing on his property.

It was a beautiful piece of equipment. Chip had seen and had ridden in his share of helos, but leather interiors and plush carpeting would be a totally new experience for him. The engine and rotors came to a halt and a man jumped out of the door. He wore dark glasses and carried a small canvas duffle bag.

"Chip, this is Rich Hawkins. The builder."

"Pleased to meet you Mr. Hawkins. Chip MacIntosh."

"Nice to meet you Chip, call me Rich."

"Very well."

"If you guys will excuse me, I'm just going to grab a quick shower. Chip are you sticking around? Will I get a chance to see you in a few minutes?"

"I'm actually heading back - here in a minute," replied Chip. "To Gainesville."

"I know who you are, Chip. Good luck in November. Bob, are we going to help this young man out?"

Reynolds smiled, "we sure are."

"Good," said Rich. "Take care Chip." And the pilot raced inside the big house.

"He's got the largest private construction company in the state Chip. He lives in Ponte Vedra, works in Orlando, and spends his free time at his camp in the Everglades."

"*In* the Everglades?" Chip asked doubtfully.

"Yea, not inside the National Park per se, but it's definitely *in* the Everglades. There are half a 'dozen camps left out there. They're only accessible by airboat or helicopter. He's trying to get one of the last places in Stiltsville – Biscayne – as well. He has a hundred year lease with the state on the place in the glades."

"How's he get power – does he have power?"

"He's got a generator that'd light up Florida Field, sends airboats out with diesel. It's amazing, we'll get you out there someday. Is that your truck?"

"Yea. The Land Cruiser."

"I'd look into getting an American car."

"Yea, I've heard that from someone else. I just love that truck; I'd hate to get rid of it. Those are classics now," Chip answered, kind of bummed at the suggestion.

"Oh yea, I know Toyotas, solid trucks, but it could cause trouble for you. There's a Hank Williams Jr. song that goes..."

Chip interrupted the representative "don't give em a reason?"

"Exactly. Good call. Walk with me Chip."

They walked toward the outbuilding where they had first met that morning. Reynolds opened the small door and led Chip through the large shop to a far off corner. There was a vehicle with a large grey cover over it. Only the bottoms of the wheels were showing.

"See what you think of this," said Reynolds as he slowly yanked the cover off the vehicle.

Chip's face lit up. "Ho-ly..."

The ride back to Gainesville went by fast. Chip kept thinking about his meeting with Congressman Reynolds and wondering if he'd done well. Clearly the support was a good indication and Chip figured the story of the great bass might help Reynolds remember him better.

Chip feared the novelty of his intentions was wearing thin. He felt he needed to brainstorm – he didn't have a plan and wasn't sure how to draft one. He thought about who could help him strategize. His parents were basically smart and reliable but that sounded immature to Chip. None of his friends were terribly political; his only true friends were a long way from North Central Florida. The only trusted advisor-type he could think of was Cheryl.

Chip began to think about her. It wasn't the sex that stuck out in his mind, it was the feeling he had when she smiled at him or when she rolled her beautiful eyes at him. He could remember her scent and the way her earrings sparkled on the rooftop deck at the W Hotel. Even the image of her driving down I-10 in oversized glasses made him smile slightly.

Chapter Thirteen

Chip's first stop back in Gainesville was at a local office supply store where he loaded up with notebooks, folders, binders and pens. While passing through the stationery aisle, he remembered the fine note cards he had received as a Christmas present two years earlier. He just couldn't remember where he had stored them.

The young female clerk eyed Chip's fishing outfit like it was a Halloween costume but checked him out pleasantly enough. His phone rang as soon as he exited the store. The screen read "Boca Raton, FL" and without thinking, Chip answered it.

"Hello, Chip MacIntosh," said the linebacker confidently.

"Good afternoon Chip, my name is Les Lockhart, I got your contact information from Walt Davenport - he thought you and I should connect."

"Oh, sure, sounds good. Thank you for calling." Chip knew who he was.

"You're most-welcome Chip. I understand you're throwing your hat in the ring for the House up there."

"Yes sir, I am."

"Well, so far as I can tell, it's only been rumored. When and where are you planning on making it official?"

"I thought I'd scope out St. Augustine this weekend. That's the biggest city in the district and I assume I've got more work to do there than Gainesville."

"I can see where you came up with that, but I'd advise you to make it official in your home town. If you don't, it's a snub. Period. You announce *in Gainesville* then have a big-time St. Augustine guy, or gal - a local - introduce you at a press event on the coast. It's all about *community* now Chip, your *community* is Gainesville. We can rally the troops in Gainesville – make it all about you."

"I'm sorry, do I – I'm not sure what to expect here."

"From what – running for Congress?" Lockhart asked with a laugh.

"No sir – well, yes that – but I was talking about your, uh, services."

"Don't worry about it. Walt's sending me one of those new Mustangs, a convertible with a V8 motor in it."

Chip went silent; he couldn't tell for sure if his new advisor was pulling his chain.

"Just messing with you Chip. Ha! Got you didn't I?"

"What? Yea, you got me."

"Sorry, I couldn't resist. You've got to loosen up a little. Are you excited?"

"Yea – I'm excited. I still – I'm having trouble with the next move though. I don't know what to do."

"Couple things Chip – very important. You'll need to form a committee. 'MacIntosh for Congress.' Some candidates use the word 'friends' in their committee names, but I'd advise you against that. You have to get a CPA you trust to be your treasurer. He or she doesn't have to be a CPA, but it's a better move. And it wouldn't hurt if that treasurer had a very solid relationship with a bank. You are going to need to set up a checking account. Once you have raised or spent $5,000, you have fifteen days I think to file with the FEC. There are two forms, pretty simple really. But your very next move, Chip – is the party. You have got to get in with the party. If they aren't on board, none of that stuff I just told you about is even relevant."

"Okay. Good. How do I get in with the party?"

"Bob. Reynolds. Any chance you could meet me in St. Augustine this weekend?"

"Sure but..."

"But what?"

"Well," Chip seemed to be struggling, "I – do I pay you for this? I mean, I don't know how this works. You're a consultant aren't you?"

"I am a consultant. Don't worry about that right now."

"It's just that – I don't want to kick off my campaign with anything that the opposition could use against me. I could just hear it now: *MacIntosh taps Boca big-wig to get things rolling.*"

Lockhart laughed. "You're cautious Chip. That's a good thing. Let's call it a favor for now, I've done lots of pro bono stuff in the past. When you get your war chest going, we'll talk money. I'll be up near Jacksonville this week-end anyway. You sure you can swing over?"

"I'll be there."

"Good. Store my number in your phone. Call me with questions. And don't announce until you've spoken with Reynolds."

Chip interrupted him. "I have spoken with Reynolds."

"When?"

"Today – this morning I fished the St. Johns with him in his bass boat."

"Shit – what'd he say?"

"He said he's going to help me – my campaign."

"That's big Chip. Did he mention the party?"

Chip thought for a moment. "He did – and he..."

"He what?" asked Lockhart.

"Well, it was weird actually. I think he might be at odds with – I don't know – the *base* maybe?"

"He meant *nationally* though I bet. What'd he say about the local - the state party?"

"Well he asked me about my views – not on any actual issues but on the party. I don't remember exactly what he said but it sounded like he wanted to make sure I was on board with the Democratic Party. He's a Blue Dog though right? No one would call him a liberal would they?"

"No, they wouldn't. I think there are probably too many minorities in your district to get elected as a Republican – otherwise, he'd probably be a Republican. The liberals can't really stand Reynolds actually. Hey – speaking of that, do you have any black friends?"

"Mr. Lockhart, I've been playing football since I was eight years old and I was an enlisted Marine. Of course I have black friends," Chip said candidly.

"Okay, just checking. But, you can't quite say it like that. It sounds stereotypical. You can say it to me, because I know that's true, but practice the PC thing. You know the drill – one comment and you're off the ticket."

"I - guess. I mean, okay."

"I've got to go, plan on breakfast Saturday in St. Augustine or Jacksonville. I'll find out if you've got the full weight of Reynolds with the party. Don't worry. And if you aren't sure about something – keep your mouth shut. Plus, Chip – treat every single person you meet, from now on, as though you *need* them. It's time to turn on the charm. If you get favorable reactions – if people seem fired up about your chances or about you – ask them for a donation. It's going to suck, believe me, but it's the only way to go about it. And don't rule our undergraduates, especially at that school."

"Wait a sec - sir," Chip said, "the local party - how could they select some-one to be their candidate without a primary?"

"Well, they can't really. Good question," replied Les. "The local county chairs will sort of be required to stay neutral - but if they like you, they won't recruit others to run and they could possibly even discourage others from running against you. If you kiss up to them early, they'll start saying you're the one with the best chance of keeping their district blue - Democrat. Their goal is to block Republicans and send dems to DC. Look - if Reynolds is on board, it'll more than likely send a signal that no one could raise more money than you. The way the party sees it, the state party too, is that they want to use grassroots money in the general election. You show muscle early and you get all of the grassroots money for the general, not the primary. Does that make sense Chip?"

"It does," said the linebacker.

"Good deal, I have to go."

Lockhart hung up the phone. Chip hopped in his vehicle and headed to his house.

1308 University was pretty lively when he pulled in. There were a few cars, a Suzuki moped and a handful of unsecured bicycles that weren't nice enough to steal. Chip noticed dancing in the living room and heard music as he neared the rear entrance.

With a handful of fishing gear, Chip walked in the back door. He fielded a few questions and some slight ball-breaking then clamored up the stairs. He needed to talk to his landlord about a more suitable place to hang his hat.

The linebacker enjoyed a long, hot shower without any sort of interrup-tion. As he dried himself off, he could hear LL Cool J on the speakers down-stairs. It reminded Chip of his Marine Corps days and made him want to lift weights.

He needed to call Cheryl about the weekend but it was a shade too loud to talk in the house. Chip called her anyway.

"Hey there," she answered in an eager-sounding fashion. "Where are you?"

"I'm at the house."

"What house? Home?"

"No, *home* is where my parents live. I'm at *the house* – that's the brick house you seem to..."

"I see. What are you – having a party? I can barely hear you."

"No, we're not having a party. I'm afraid it's always - usually like this," Chip said as he looked at his watch. "Could we meet for a beer or something?"

"It's almost dinner time, why don't we grab a bite? Let me buy you dinner!"

"Sounds like a plan. Where do you want to meet?"

"I could swing by and get you if you want. I just need to run home and change real quick," she said youthfully.

"Uh, here?"

"What? No good? Chip who gives a...?"

"I thought you would."

"I don't. I have some news on that actually. I'll see you in forty five minutes. Bye."

Chip wondered about her news as he searched his wardrobe for something mature but fun. Within five minutes, he settled on a pair of classic blue jeans, a gray undershirt, and a plaid, long-sleeved oxford.

The music continued to play as Chip ambled down the staircase toward the kitchen. He never acted 'above' any of the guys in the house, but the feeling was there sometimes. It wasn't a snotty thing, it was a maturity thing and there never really seemed to be any resentment on the people that had such access to Chip MacIntosh.

From the kitchen, the linebacker studied the great room. There were only ten or so people in the house and it had become so routine for Chip that the scene seemed to be a blurred menagerie of the same ten kids over and over. Nothing ever seemed to change for him. These were popular athletes and people wanted to be around them. The television seemed to be a perennial video game that incited more yelling than any show or ball game that had ever aired. The music always had a steady beat whatever the genre: rap, reggae, hip-hop, rock. Chip preferred the latter but among the football crowd; he was in the minority – especially when it came to the hippie-jam-band scene. He had actually attended classic rock-style festivals alone because he could seldom find people willing to go along. His brother Jay had joined him on a few occasions but Chip's musical preference had perpetually kept him in, what Jessica Van Zandt often called, "his own little world."

Chip poured himself a huge cup of water and again looked out through the kitchen at the people in the house. He tried to recall having a normal conversation with even one of them and couldn't think of a single occurrence. He gulped down his favorite beverage and slipped out the back door in anticipation of Cheryl's arrival.

The cool air felt good and the music softened to the point of enjoyment. The backyard was rather serene and well cared for considering the nature of the house's residents. The landlord, Bart Johnson, was a slight landscape fanatic and every Monday, even during the colder months, an old lawn man showed up at nine o'clock to keep the grounds looking beautiful. Chip's housemates and their predecessors usually did their part to keep the outside looking presentable. The backyard was especially nice.

Taking in the beauty of the backyard reminded Chip that he needed to call Johnson about a few things. He dashed back inside and searched the backside of a cabinet door for Johnson's cell number. He glanced out the side window and saw Cheryl's Jeep pulling in.

"That's not a party?" she asked him as he shoveled into her vehicle.

"Hey," he smiled. "It's ten guys playing video games and looking over their new syllabi," he answered.

"I can see at least two girls from here."

"Oh? I hadn't noticed," he said, still clutching his cell.

"How are you? Do you need to make a call?"

Chip looked down at his phone. He didn't quite want to call Bart Johnson in front of Cheryl but suddenly sought her approval. "Yea, actually."

"Go ahead, that's fine," she said as she pulled out of the driveway.

"Cool," he said and he punched in Johnson's number.

Bart Johnson was sitting on the outside porch at his country club when his phone vibrated. His cigar-smoking buddies heard it and motioned for him to take it, in spite of the rather strict *no cell phone* policy.

Johnson dashed out of plain view and answered "Hello?"

"Mr. Johnson this is Chip MacIntosh, I'm at 1308 – in Gainesville?"

"Howdy Chip – I see you're – Chip I'm at the goddamn club – they'll fine me - lemme call you back in two minutes - at this number?"

"Yes sir – thank you."

Chip smirked slightly as he turned to Cheryl. "He's calling me back."

"Who is calling you back? Who is Johnson?" she asked without looking at him.

"He's my landlord."

"Oh. What are you in the mood for?" she asked.

"It's uh, Tuesday right?"

"Yea?"

"All you can eat ribs at Jimbo's."

Cheryl stopped at a traffic light just as he said that. She turned to him and briskly said "No. I know another place where you can get ribs. Hey – how'd it go with Reynolds?"

"I'd say it went pretty well," replied Chip proudly. "He said – or sort of implied at least – that he'd support me."

"That's awesome! What about the party?" she asked strategically.

Chip wondered how she knew the sequence of questions so relevant to the situation. Before he gave away his impression of her skills his phone rang. It was Johnson.

"Mr. J?"

"Hey Chip! Sorry I couldn't talk back there. They've got a ban on cell phones at the golf course; I'm in my vehicle now. So you're running for Congress! That's really cool. Just tell me you're a Republican and I'll break out my checkbook," he said with a chuckle.

The linebacker immediately wished he had done his homework on Johnson. He looked at his date who just nodded at him to keep talking.

"Well sir, the truth is I am a registered Democrat and I will be seeking that party's nomination for the race."

"That's it!" yelled Johnson. "I want you outta that house by Friday!"

Cheryl turned her beautiful blue eyes toward Chip - who looked like he'd just seen a ghost. The candidate took a deep but brief drag of air.

"Well that's why I'm calling. I *do* need to get some place more – uh – quieter I suppose." His voice immediately became more confident-sounding.

"Hell, you know I can't win this district as a Republican – after the last thirty years? Come on? Have you got something more suitable in town?"

"I'll have to check, I think so – probably. If not we'll just evict someone. How's the campaign coming? You're right kid; I don't think a Republican could win this district – not on the heels of Bob Reynolds. I bet the GOP'd have you though. How's the – have you announced yet?"

"I'm still forming everything so 'no,' it's a pretty simple but lengthy process, as I'm sure you know."

"Do you have an account yet?"

"Tomorrow."

"I see. Hey – listen, I'm having a party this weekend – over here at my home. You should – you're going to *need* St. Augustine Chip. Do you have plans Saturday? We'd love to have you."

"I could – uh – I am actually," he paused and looked over at Cheryl. "I will be out there this weekend." She didn't look back at him but gently placed her hand on his thigh and cracked a little smile.

"Great! Send me an email and I'll let you know the particulars."

"Are you sure it's appropriate – I mean – what were – what are you celebrating?"

"What are we selling? Did 'ya say *selling*?"

"No *celebrating* – what are you – the *reason* for the party?"

"Oh! I thought you said – uh - we're not *celebrating* anything really. I'm sure you know the National Championship game is Saturday night, but we aren't really *celebrating* it. I bet that's like acid in your mouth ain't it? Ohio State – Southern Cal for the title..."

"A little. No – those are two talented teams. I'm one of those 'may the best team win' kind of guys Mr. J."

"Sure you are – Congressman – ha!" he laughed. "Let's talk Saturday. I will help you find a place to hang your hat and whatever."

"Thank you. Uh – Mr. Johnson is there any chance I could bring a friend to your home with me?"

"Absolutely – is she a looker?" he asked playfully.

"Why, yes, I'd say that's the case... Okay..." said Chip with a slight drawl.

"Good, send me that email and we'll get you the particulars."

"Well, I don't think I have your email."

"Come on kid, you can do better than that. Find it."

"Yes sir."

"Bye."

Cheryl was excited that Chip was coming to the coast with her. She pulled into the shopping center that housed an Outback Steakhouse. It was really only popular with students on Sunday nights when longnecks were 'Five for Five.' Without seeking a spot she stopped the Jeep way out in the empty part of the parking lot.

She brought her right foot up under her backside and faced her friend. "You're actually coming with me? To the – to St. Augustine?"

Chip shrugged his shoulders and his thumbs turned up slightly. "Do you still want me to go?"

"Of course!"

"Well okay then," he said.

She leaned over and gave him a big hug.

"What's your news?" he asked.

"Pardon?" she said as she returned to her seat and adjusted her sweater.

"You said earlier you had *news*."

"Oh... It's nothing."

"C'mon, tell me," he pressed.

"Well," she cleared her throat quietly, "just in case we *did* decide to see each other socially or whatever, I learned today that it wouldn't compromise my position with the university – at least not with respect to the rules."

He wasn't sure what to say. "Really?" he said in a more positive than surprised tone.

"Uh huh."

"I'm actually kind of surprised. Did you look it up or did you ask someone?"

"I looked it up. It's because I don't teach classes and there's something about student contact. The way I read it, I'm covered on one or two separate clauses. Should we eat?"

"Yea," Chip replied contentedly. She was blushing slightly.

Cheryl drove to a closer parking space and the two walked toward the door in tandem, with a steady eighteen inch space between their shoulders. Chip got the door for her and she thanked him.

The restaurant was hardly crowded but the bar area was loaded with nacho-pounding basketball fans. A very attractive brunette in a bright red button down and tiny denim shorts showed the pair to a booth in the corner. The girl studied Chip just long enough for Cheryl to look away and pretend it had no impact on her.

They eyed their respective menus. Chip always ordered the same dinner at *Outback*, so he was really just using the menu as a tool to think about what to say next. He wondered if she was going to order a glass of wine or a diet soda.

With her eyes still focused on the menu, Cheryl spoke first.

"So what's the deal Saturday night? Your landlord is having a party?" she asked.

"You don't have to come with me if you don't want to. I mean – if you do – it's going to be tough to come off as *friends*," he said as he set his menu down on the hard, lacquered table.

"I'll go," she said, still browsing the list of entrées. "Would it be possible to meet up with some of my friends afterwards?"

"Sure you can."

"I meant both of us," she said looking up at him.

"Why not? I've also got a breakfast Saturday morning."

"In St. Augustine? With whom?"

"Yea, or Jax maybe. Some political consultant guy from Boca Raton. He's helping me out."

"Already? Wow you don't waste any time; do you?" she said with a slight wink.

"I'd say that's something we have in common, Cher," he smoothly replied with a quick nod of the head.

She smiled and turned to look around the dining room. "What's the guy in Boca's name?"

"Les Lockhart."

"And the landlord?"

"Bart Johnson."

"Oh. He's a supporter – alum right?"

"Damn you're good. What are there like three hundred thousand alumni?"

"Over three forty. Thanks."

"He's – Bart Johnson – he's been a lawyer in Northeast Florida for something like thirty-five years. I think he's a good contact to have since I know so few people over there." Chip paused and looked around for a server. "And I sure am hopeful Reynolds pulls some strings for me on the coast."

"Yea – how'd that go? He's on board?"

"It sure looks like it. He left everything so open-ended though. I felt like he wanted me to get the ball rolling and all, but he wasn't very specific. He seemed more intrigued by the bass I caught than my candidacy. I'm used to pretty specific instructions; NCOs, coaches, etc. I think that's why I have had trouble with girls."

Before Cheryl could tackle that last statement a waiter showed up with disheveled, gelled hair and thick, black-framed glasses. "Did either of you have any questions about the menu?"

Chip focused on a button clinging to the server's suspenders that read: TODAY IS THE FIRST DAY OF THE REST OF YOUR LIFE.

It caused Charles III to fully grasp the reality of his situation. His football playing days were over, he was graduating from college, running for Congress and - in all probability - he had a new girlfriend.

Chapter Fourteen

Christian Ross was in the gym stretching when his friend Chip rolled in wearing earbuds and an uncharacteristic, dejected look on his face.

"MacIntosh!" yelled Ross.

"Hey Ross," Chip said in a somber tone. "Kinda early for you isn't it?"

"I'm going tubing later with some ladies - wanna look good," he said with a grin between stretches. "You should come along Chip - these girls are smokin hot. I thought I texted you. One's from the Soviet Union or some-thing - she's like my height. Think of those legs in an inner tube!"

"I can't bro," said Chip with a half-smile. "I've got this campaign, it's a lot of work."

"You still with the Alumni lady?" asked Ross.

Chip took a seat on the floor and started stretching. "Not really," he said.

"I thought you dug her," he said. "What happened?"

"I do dig her - I think," said Chip. "It's kind of a long story."

"I just got here," said Ross. "Why don't you spot me on the bench and you can tell me about it?"

Chip sort of nodded in the affirmative and followed his teammate over to the bench press area. He had never really talked to Christian about serious stuff before and was almost a little worried about doing so. Ross had never had a girlfriend for more than a semester and wasn't known for giving sound relationship advice. It wasn't even his fault. Chip had become convinced that the girls in Christian's life used him just as much as he'd used them. He had mastered the art of sport sex. He generally thrived on action and pleasure and most who knew him thought his success was the result of luck and charm rather than determination.

But that was off the field. When the play clock was active, Christian Ross was like his idol Tom Brady: alert, focused, sharp and tough. He exhibited the wisdom of a much more seasoned football player.

"So tell me the deal MacIntosh," Ross said as he settled onto the bench and aligned his grip on the weight bar.

"Things we're going pretty great I'd say," Chip began. "I guess part of me had doubts the whole time - just because of the age factor and all that. Plus there's a lot up in the air - it's possible I'm moving to Washington, D.C. in January."

"Then what happened?" asked Christian in a strained voice.

"We were in St. Augustine for a fundraiser - at Bart Johnson's place," Chip said. "And then we met up with some of her friends."

"How'd they look?" asked Ross, resting the bar on his chest.

"Pretty good. *Fat*," answered Chip with a laugh.

Ross began to crack up "dude don't make me laugh - I'm trying to lift!"

Chip helped his friend return the bar to the rest and Ross sat up on the bench.

"So what happened?" he asked.

"We're hanging out with her dumbass friends and I just felt - like - targeted or something. They asked me a million questions about my plans if I don't win the House seat. They seemed to trivialize my campaign and gave me shit about my age. They were just rude," explained the linebacker.

"So her friends are bitches, so what?" offered Ross.

"Yea, fine, but Cheryl didn't really defend me - or anything. She was a bitch about it too," said Chip.

"Did you call her out?" asked the Quarterback. "Did you tell her she was being uncool?"

"No. I just sort of started to avoid her," Chip explained. "I miss seeing her and everything but I have to stay so focused on shit right now. Maybe the timing with Cheryl wasn't right. It's not just the campaign but the other timing. She's looking for a husband."

"Are you looking for a wife?" asked his friend.

"I mean - no. But aren't we all? Kind of?" Chip wondered out loud. "I know you're not."

"Bro, come on the river with us," Ross said with a concerned look. "You don't have to shag anyone - but you can't be a downer either. It'll be a big time."

"I'd really love to but I can't," Chip explained reluctantly. "All I need is a story about being half naked on a river with a Russian national... the Soviet Union was dissolved in 1991 by the way."

"So what would you call someone who was actually born over there prior to '91?" asked Ross.

"Probably Russian," said Chip. "But she could be Armenian or a few other nationalities I think. I should probably read up on that. I highly doubt that your new friend was born before 1991 though Chief... Hey, before I forget, watch out for poison ivy out there, my brother said it's really bad right now. He's been fishing that river a lot."

"Ten-four," said Christian, returning to another set of lifting. "So what are you going to do about Cheryl?"

Chip thought about it for a few seconds as he looked around the gym. He saw a handful of cute girls in small clothes. "I'm not going to worry about it," he said. "I miss seeing her, but not enough to chase after her and plead with her to pay attention to me. If it's meant to be, it'll work out. If not, then - I don't know. I'm practically too busy for a girlfriend right now anyway."

Chapter Fifteen

The chair of the Alachua County Democratic Party was Rosie Lawson. She was a fifty-five year old African-American homemaker and fifth generation Floridian. Her family history could be traced back to the racially motivated 1923 massacre in Levy County. She approached Chip as he walked into the uncrowded reception area of the Gainesville Episopal Church for their monthly meeting.

"You must be Chip MacIntosh…" she said nicely.

"Yes ma'am, are you Ms. Lawson?" he asked humbly.

"Call me Rosie," she said - still shaking his hand. "You're a charming looking young man Chip."

"Thank you," he said. "I'm excited to be here - to meet you."

"Carolyn Miller is our featured speaker - the state representative? You know her?" asked the lady.

"Uh, no - I don't," he admitted.

"Well you've heard of her right?" she asked.

"Of course," he lied.

A few more people showed up and Chip found himself standing with nothing to say as the chair briefly greeted her fellow democratic activists. She introduced Chip to a few people. The football player couldn't remember one name. He wondered if he was dressed properly as he looked down at his starched plaid oxford and pressed chinos. His loafers were getting tired and worn. And his socks, though barely visible, showed signs of age. He was starting to second-guess his decision not to wear a blazer.

"Ah - here's Carolyn!" Rosie said, refocusing her attention back to Chip. "Rep. Miller, please say hello to Chip MacIntosh."

"Yes, Chip MacIntosh - the pride of the Gators," she said with a big smile, "nice to meet you honey." She was accompanied by a pimply twenty-something with a shitty tie.

"Representative Miller - it's a pleasure to meet you" he said.

Carolyn had on a bright blue jacket over an indeterminable black outfit. She had on a fair amount of gold and smelled somewhat floral to Chip.

"Have you made it official?" she asked the aspiring Congressman, leaning into his personal space.

Chip looked around a little "I've not officially announced. But it's official," he said, perhaps too playfully.

"Are you signed up to speak tonight?" Carolyn asked.

"No - I am just here to get a sense of the local - chapter," he said. "I'm here to learn tonight."

Carolyn head-tilted and walked between him and the chair. "Come here a sec," she whispered.

There was less light and fewer people in the hallway; they were basically alone.

"You're running for Congress right?" she asked.

"Right," he said.

"Chip - you fucking speak. You speak every chance you get," she instructed. "There's no time to kick tires. These people need to know your intentions - they need to know your values - they need to know YOU. If you don't get up there tonight they're all going to go home and say that there was a guy at the meeting running for Congress but that he clearly didn't want their vote. You can't do that - you address the crowd."

Chip just nodded quietly.

"Who are you here with?" she asked.

"I'm - no one," he said like a deer in the headlights.

"Okay - not only do you always speak - but you always bring someone to these. It doesn't matter who - just not your parents - no offense. You bring a buddy, a girlfriend, a student - probably a guy - and it looks like you have a 'staff' - even if you don't."

"Copy," said Chip.

"Copy what?" she asked.

"I copy. I understand the - directive," he said.

"This isn't the Army, Sugar, just say 'you follow' - or 'got it,'" offered the state representative. "Shoot Chip - you make me want to take your little butt on in the primary," she said. "Tell the guy with the clip board you'd appreciate an opportunity to address the group tonight."

"Okay - will do," said Chip. "And, thank you."

Ms. Miller walked away feeling smart and Chip headed to the clipboard man. "It's just you and Rep. Miller then Mr. MacIntosh. Obviously since she's an elected official and our keynote speaker so she will go first. She will give remarks, take questions, then the chair will introduce you. I'd tell Rosie how you'd like to be introduced," said the man.

The room filled in a bit and people began taking their seats in the front.

Carolyn swept over to Chip and told him to meet her in the lobby area after he speaks. The football player nodded. He was worried about the speech as he wasn't even remotely prepared. It was almost as if he was invisible. The people walking in had no idea who he was. Most had pleasant faces but he thought the crowd looked a tad sloppy.

He saw an open door to the sanctuary and decided to look for something to write with. He found a stack of flyers for Easter lily tributes and plucked a golf pencil from the backside of a pew.

Using a hymnal as a backing, he wrote down:

About Me

My Values

Why I'm Running

Why You Should Support Me

It was the best he could come up with, there wasn't time to pen a full speech. He was sure he could talk about a few basic features of this situation he'd put himself in.

He scratched a few more details and folded the paper into his shirt pocket. With a polite bow toward the great cross at the end of the room Chip returned to the gathering.

One of the helpers approached him with a name tag stuck to her ring finger "here ya go" she said without intros, "we like to know who everyone is."

His name looked so informal below "Hi, My Name Is:." He wasn't a huge fan of lowercase letters. For a minute he considered going by *Charles*.

Chip told himself it was 'go time' and decided to start pressing the flesh.

He introduced himself to a few random people as the group ushered into the main meeting room.

A shorter woman with loose jeans, a black tee shirt and a majority purple overshirt gave Chip a somewhat dirty look as he slow-walked toward the front.

Carolyn Miller waved Chip over to her seat. "You'll speak after me then we'll walk out after you speak - they conduct sort of a business meeting once the speakers go - we can leave," she said.

"Great," said Chip, taking a seat between her and the 17 year old kid who was acting like Secret Service.

The Chairwoman opened the meeting by griping about Republicans and thanking everyone for attending. Chip scanned the room to get a sense of his constituents and potential volunteers. They seemed like a nice group of people - they looked like his neighbors, teachers - one lady was obviously a nurse.

They did a treasurer's report. The cash on hand amount was a respectable $28,000.

Rosie covered a few more topics then introduced Representative Carolyn Miller.

Chip watched her movements from the moment she stood up. She was good, he thought. She moved quickly and with purpose. Rather than looking hurried, she came across more like she was mindful of everyone else's time. She gave individual shout outs - mentioned at least four people by name - and thanked everyone there for their commitment to their collective cause. This woman knew the value of the activists.

Carolyn had a great disposition, she reminded Chip of some of the better female politicians he'd seen on television over the years. He began to think she was younger than she looked - like it was an act. He wondered if it was the kind of tactic he needed.

She spoke about the legislative work going on in Tallahassee and how she remained laser-focused on Education and Healthcare.

The state rep took a few ambiguous questions from the crowd, spun them into confusing but acceptable answers, and returned to her seat.

Rosie Lawson returned to the podium, "Our next speaker is going to be a very familiar name to our football fans. He's considering a run for US Congress, please join me in welcoming Chip MacIntosh."

The linebacker was nervous but he got up and tried to mimic the moves of the previous speaker. He made it to the podium and looked out at the crowd. He estimated the attendance at about 35. Chip silently reminded himself that he'd spoken 'football' in front of 30,000 people - he could handle a small group of mostly elderly Democrats. He adjusted the mic to account for his large stature.

"Thank you all for coming tonight - I'm Chip MacIntosh and I am planning to soon announce my candidacy for the United States House of Representatives!"

Golf claps all around. "Fuck" he thought, "tough crowd." Carolyn had them eating out of her hands and Chip looked like he had just delivered relatively bad news.

The congressional hopeful told the crowd a bit about growing up in Gainesville, serving overseas in uniform, returning home, going to college, and leading the Gators to some very memorable and significant victories. He liked where he'd left the crowd at that point; they actually seemed pretty warm.

"I admit I am new to this process - I don't want to take up too much time - so - does anyone have any - uh - questions?" he asked. He didn't look like a serious candidate and he knew it. There were some nice smiles in the crowd but they were pitty smiles. This group had been in the game for an average of twenty-five years - a year longer than Chip had been alive.

"Very well then - thank you everybody. Thank you Ms. Rosie," he said; and he walked off.

Carolyn and her intern stood up and walked out to the lobby area with Chip. The three of them were slightly accosted by a lone, male gay rights activist. He asked a bunch of questions of Chip - barraged him about some sort of pledge.

The state rep intervened, "Sir, thank you for your passion on this - Mr. MacIntosh is committed to hearing from the voters - and from your coalition. He's still mapping out his platform - he hasn't even announced yet. Let's table these important issues until the next time we're all together. Sound fair?" she asked.

"Okay," said the man. He handed them each a home-printed business card and went back into the meeting.

"Thanks Rep Miller," said Chip. "I owe you one."

"Careful with that phrase" she said with a smirk. "Have you met Tyler?"

"Hey Tyler," said Chip, extending his large hand.

"Nice to meet you Mr. MacIntosh," said the scrawny teen.

Carolyn told Tyler that she'd get back to her hotel and told him to head back in and take notes on the rest of the meeting. She asked him to help Rosie to her car with empty brownie tins or file boxes.

"You're good," said Chip, impressed. "You're staying in Gainesville tonight?"

"Yes, it's kind of a hike to my place," she said.

"Makes sense," he said. "Can I give you a lift?"

"I thought you'd never ask," she said. "Why don't you let me buy you dinner?"

Chip thought about where to suggest, he knew she wasn't a rib or wing girl - probably hated beer... "We could go to La Vieille Maison - maybe..." he offered. It was remarkably fancy for Chip's taste, but at least no one would see them.

"Sure," she said.

They walked across the dimly lit church parking lot toward the Land Cruiser. "This is me," he said.

"Perfect," said the woman as she hopped in the front seat.

Fortunately for Chip, Carolyn used this time to return some work calls. He was impressed with how she spoke to people - she was a businesswoman - direct and to the point with every sentence. And she did it without sounding too demanding.

The truck bounced into the quiet parking lot of one of Gainesville's most elegant spots. Chip ignored the VALET PARKING sign and stashed his ride in the back by the dumpster. He waited while his new friend finished her phone call.

"Sorry about all of that," she said. "I appreciate your letting me tie up those loose ends. You ready?"

The linebacker nodded and reached for his door handle.

They made their way to the entrance of the restaurant without speaking. It was a giant, old home-looking building with candle illuminated coach lamps every ten feet. The smell of burning wood added to the charm of the French-themed establishment.

An athletic-looking girl at the hostess station recognized Chip but managed not to say anything. "Two - for dinner?" she asked pleasantly.

"Somewhere private please," suggested Carolyn.

"Of course," replied the hostess as she led them to the back corner.

The place wasn't full but it felt popular to Chip. He scanned for familiar faces and noted the beauty of the restaurant. He'd only been there one other time and it was sophomore year of high school. One of the kids in their group was related to the head chef.

Non-annoying French music played in the background as they studied the upscale menu. Chip decided on the pistachio-crusted pheasant within sixty seconds but kept eying the lists in spite of the low lighting that made it tough for him to see. He looked across the table at Carolyn. Her tortoise shell reading glasses framed her hazel eyes nicely. And he thought her skin looked nice in the softer light.

The waitress showed up with two large glasses of water and asked if anyone wanted a cocktail or a glass of wine.

"House cab for me please," said Carolyn without looking up.

"Same. Please," said Chip. "Ms. Miller are you ready to order," asked Chip, wondering how long it would take to make the pheasant.

"I think I'll have the salmon," she said.

"And I'd like the pheasant," Chip said.

"Two excellent choices," said the waitress with a smile. "I'll be right back with your wine." She stopped herself "would you rather a bottle of the house cabernet?"

"Yes please," said Carolyn. "That's a better idea - thank you. Chip, I'm gonna run to the ladies room - please save my seat." She gently touched his shoulder as she walked away.

'Don't read into that' he told himself silently. He tried to think of some questions that would make him sound somewhat clued in. Nothing came to mind. A basket of French bread appeared with a small vessel of soft farmhouse cheese. The Marine zoned out of his mission at hand and went straight for the bread. The wine also showed up - it was good. He was draining his first glass like it was room-temp water when Carolyn returned to the table.

"How long have I been gone?" she asked with a smile.

She had removed her blazer and was wearing a sleeveless black top. She looked much daintier without the clunky jacket and her arms were tan and well defined. He also noticed that her waist was much smaller than he thought.

The state representative placed her jacket and handbag in the chair next to her and reached for her glass. "What should we drink to Chip?" she asked.

"To... *new friends*?" he asked, already showing signs of a wine buzz.

"Okay," she said "and to new experiences."

"Definitely," said Chip, taking another heavy pull of the house red.

They talked biographically while waiting for the food to arrive. Carolyn tried to seem younger than she was; her dinner date - just the opposite. It was getting playful, Chip had put away two glasses of Cabernet Sauvignon and was starting not to give a shit about his congressional race.

When their dinners arrived Carolyn asked Chip if they should get another bottle of wine. "Of course we should get another bottle of wine," he said with an uncharacteristic smirk.

He ate much faster than a normal person, especially at a swishy French restaurant. Chip used the opportunity to ask a series of *yes or no* questions so Carolyn could finish her dinner at a regular pace. He asked about recruiting volunteers, raising money, attending and speaking at events and other mechanical questions related to running for office.

A busboy with a fauxhawk haircut appeared with water. "I'm finished sweetie," she said, sliding her plate toward the edge of the table. The kid nodded, filled their waters and retrieved her plate.

La Vieille Maison had gotten quiet, only a few other people still lingered. Carolyn was having fun. "So Chip, do you have a *girlfriend*?"

"Isn't that kinda personal?" he asked, scrunching his eyebrows at her.

"Well, no - politically I think it's pretty important," she said.

"And - uh - why is that?" he asked.

"Because running for Congress is a big deal and it usually requires someone's partner to understand what comes with it," she replied. "It's a time-suck."

"A what?" he asked.

"It takes pretty much all of your spare time Chip," she said, taking a sip of red. "Honey do you have any idea what your schedule is about to look like over the next few months? You're going to have to tell your little chica - or *chicas* - that you don't have time for them."

He was still sober enough to gather intel. "Carolyn - what about these county events - the meetings and the potluck dinners... What's their *game*?

Like the guy that we spoke to in the lobby tonight. I guess - what's - like - out there - waiting for me?"

The state rep had hoped they could have had a more youthful discussion but she played ball. "Well, you can expect more of what you saw tonight. You've got something like ten counties in your district - some are just tiny slivers of certain counties - but you still show up to their meetings and visit with *the folks.*"

"I'm happy to do that - but 'why?'" he asked. "Why is that necessary?"

"It's called *kissing the ring.*" she said. "These people have to get to know you. They're important and they want you to know it. Plus - Chip - you've got to remember something. These are the activists. Not only are these the people who help out at shit - they're known around town as the people *in the know* - with Democrat politics. Ms. Rosie goes to Publix tomorrow and spends an extra thirty minutes talking to people about the state of the local party. She is going to tell someone - tomorrow - guaranteed - that she met you - that you came to the meeting last night. And she's going to tell those people what she thought of you - her first impression. And the ten people she talks to - they're going to tell an average of three or four people - and that's how the grassroots works."

Chip was pretty engaged. But he looked like a puppy.

"And that guy tonight," Carolyn continued, "he was a gay rights activist - its like a subcomittee - theres a bunch of them: environmentalists, civil rights, abortion, immigration, etc. The party is the best place for all of these folks to air their message. It's like a tavern in the eighteenth century - you come to a T in the road. Picture two public houses - on the right they're in there talking about having more guns and less taxes - a stronger military perhaps... And *Jesus.* In the tavern on the left - you've got people in there saying we need cleaner energy, safer schools, more diversity, stronger regulations to protect workers, gender equality..."

He was smiling and she didn't know why. "What?" she asked - trying not to smile.

"Carolyn!" he yelled quietly. "That was fucking awesome."

"You're not making fun of me are you?" she asked.

"Hell no!" he said, "My dad is a History Professor - even he's never explained anything so - historical context - I dunno - I was *really* into that."

"You're sweet," she said, taking a drink.

"Question tho," he said. "Why doesn't the whole tavern just say 'of course - we agree - we're all on the same sheet of music - there's no need to have a sidebar discussion?'"

"They do that - in a sense. It's like - they call it a 'platform' and that's the part that everyone theoretically agrees on. They vote on this stuff - it's a democratic process. Imagine if everyone in the huddle - on Florida Field - got to vote on which play to run..."

"Yea," he said, "only one guy calls the play - otherwise it'd be chaos."

"There you go - it *works* in football," she said. "In politics we'd call that a monarchy."

Chip was pretty drunk, he'd already decided that driving home was not an option. "I like you," he said to his new friend in a friendly voice. "You're good at this."

It got a little too silent for the seasoned politician "we should probably figure out this check and how we're getting home - I don't think either of us should drive."

"Oh - yea - last thing I need is a..." Carolyn knew what he meant. "What hotel are you in?" he asked.

"Park Place," she said. "But you never answered my question. Do you have a girlfriend Chip?"

"No, I don't think so. There is - *was* - someone," he said in a slightly sad fashion. "I haven't talked to her in a while, we sort of had a fight. I can't even remember what it was about. We had a pretty big initial attraction and seemed to be..."

"A student, right?" interrupted Carolyn. "Baby you're in the big leagues now, it'd be hard for an undergrad to play in that field."

"Yea," Chip lied, "she's a junior. It's okay, I'm over it I guess. So, the *Park Place*? Nice."

For a minute Chip wondered if he'd see the inside of her room but pretty much dismissed the idea when he recalled the centralized lobby situation. There was no way those two could walk through that lobby together - not even at eleven o'clock during the week. He actually breathed a sigh of relief. Plus she was twice his age - what the hell was he thinking.

"I'm actually in one the the guest cottages in the back of the property - it's all they had," she said. "It's huge in there, I even have my own hot tub."

Jesus, thought Chip. *Private entrance and hot tub...* He felt a little speechless.

Their server showed up with the tab. "Chip, let's just split it even - will that work?" asked Carolyn.

"Sure thing," he said as he fished his credit card out.

"I'll run these and be right back - take your time, I see you've got a bit more wine, there's no rush at all," assured the server.

It was awkwardly quiet again. The kid tried to think about other lingering political questions but came up short. He was pretty sure Carolyn was giving him the eye but just couldn't know - in many ways she was out of his league. He decided to keep his mouth shut, she'd have to make the first move - if there was one.

"We still have a half'a bottle of wine left," said Carolyn, signing her part of the dinner bill. "Should we stay here and finish it - or..."

"I'm - or... *what*?" asked Chip.

"I think you know, Slugger," she said like a teacher. "I've got a suite baby, it's far too big for one person. But if you're not up for it, I totally understand."

Chip pulled up his phone, ignored a bunch of missed calls and texts. He messaged his brother Jay: *Land Cruiser at La Vieille Maison - need it moved to the brick house ASAP - key above visor. THX.*

Seventeen minutes later Chip was on the couch in her suite wondering what exactly was on the mind of the woman in the bathroom. He was pretty drunk so his goal was simply not to fall asleep or otherwise embarrass himself. He thought he could hear her on the phone but couldn't be sure. Plus, who could she possibly be talking to at such an hour. The linebacker avoided his own phone - it made him nervous just thinking about what was on there. He had hoped Jay moved his car but had enough faith not to check.

Carolyn appeared from the other half of the suite. She had on a very small silk robe and her hair was up. She reached for the light switch and killed the spotlights. It was almost completely dark. She grabbed the stereo remote and quickly found an adult contemporary station.

"How's that?" she asked before sitting next to her new friend on the gray couch.

"I like it," he said, hoping it was the right answer.

It was.

Chapter Sixteen

The home of Stephen Swenson was well known to everyone in Gainesville over the age of thirty. It was an original Frank Lloyd Wright home situated in the woods just outside of the main town. The property overlooked a relatively ancient sinkhole. Almost completely surrounded by massive trees and ferns, the only open area was at the bottom of the sinkhole, which housed a natural spring lake with uncharacteristically clear water. While most fifty acre parcels in the region contained either cattle pastures or row-planted pines, this native forest estate was a rarity.

Swenson came to Florida in the eighties to get away from the brutally cold winters of his native Wisconsin. He was a wealthy man who inherited his money from his grandfather's business. They had been in everything from manufacturing to oil to cellular phone towers. Steve made more money on interest per month than most people made in a year. His big charity was youth football programs in the inner cities across the south and the midwest.

He'd reached out to Chip through Rosie Lawson and offered to host a gathering at his home. Rosie explained to Chip that this was his chance to shine in front of a guy who could inject a ton of cash into his campaign - by bundling. Yes, he was a bit of a loaner, but he was the kind of guy who rolled around with the richest people in America. "If he likes you Chip - that's a really, really good thing," the chairman of the party had told Chip.

It had been almost a month since Chip announced. With the help of a few friends, relatives and seasoned political operators, Chip had decided to kick off his campaign at the local community center. It was where he played his first football game at the age of seven.

The kickoff event was pretty flawless. The press was there, hundreds of supporters and potential supporters had showed up. The weather held up. As Chip's unofficial digital media strategist, Jay MacIntosh knew he could get everyone in the dorms to attend the event by offering free ice cream. The ice cream truck was a mere $1500 for the day and the kids completely cleaned the guy out.

So successful was the kickoff, Chip seemed to have warded off any primary challengers. He also snagged a ton of online support. His number of followers on social media was fast approaching a record number for a congressional candidate. Jay was also doing constant research on the three Republicans vying for the house seat his brother was seeking.

Chip's remarks to the crowd were tight but everyone agreed he needed to get better at asking for money. The Swenson party was his opportunity to fine-tune his message to the donor class.

He wanted to get there early and help set up but Steve told him not to dream of it. He told Chip to arrive fifteen minutes after start time and to show up with a crew - some sort of staff-types to make him look more important.

As instructed, Chip pulled up fifteen minutes after start time. Jay drove their dad's big Suburban and they had two fellow football players who were sharp looking - and they idolized Chip.

From the front, the place looked boxy and small. Jay pulled the Chevrolet around to the left of the house and found the parking area. "You've gotta get me permission to hike down there - I've seen the satellite image, that hole is insane," said Jay as he put the truck in park. Chip had butterflies and ignored his brother.

"Go time MacIntosh," shouted one of the football players in the back seat.

The young men walked in together as instructed. They had never seen a house like Steve's. It was the epitome of Mid Century Modern, pretty rare for north central Florida. It was Scandavian by design, everything was squared off beautifully and yet it flowed together perfectly. There were book shelves from floor to ceiling housing everything from Sports Illustrated to big vinyl records.

The furniture was also period-specific. There were built-in cabinets and desks. The only rounded objects involved lighting and a football helmet, which caught the eyes of Chip and his teammates. It was from the University of Wisconsin. Steve saw the young men eying it from across the room. He approached them with a big grin.

"I played for the Badgers my freshman year - strong safety," he said, extending his hand to Chip. "Hey Sport - I'm Steve Swenson - nice to finally meet you in person."

Steve was about six-one with a medium build. He had a white beard and a ponytail. His skin was tan and he had less than perfect teeth.

"Were you injured? Sorry - Mr. Swenson - thank you for having me, I am honored to have this level of support," said Chip. He introduced his fellow players and his brother to the man.

"Call me Steve," he told the boys. "And yes, I sprained my neck during spring practice after my freshman season. I got a little playing time that fall but I didn't like the neck thing... It actually scared me. I almost got hit by a VW Beetle like a month later - couldn't turn my head. Nightmare. I thanked the coaches and told them I was done with the game."

The guys all made a grossed-out/sympathetic face and nodded.

A young woman appeared in front of the linebacker. "Hi Chip, I'm Shannon Grady with the national party," she said. "It's great to finally meet you!"

"Thank you Shannon," said Chip, trying not to look at her cleavage. "I'm pleased you could come down for this. How are things at the top?"

"I wouldn't miss it," she said, "things at HQ are great, we'd certainly like to keep this district in our column in November."

"Well, we'll do our part," he said.

"I'll let you mingle a little - really, really great to meet you Chip," she said with a borderline flirtatious look on her face.

Shannon disappeared and Steve Swenson quickly guided Chip toward another small congregation of people.

"Chip I'd like to introduce you to some folks - then you can sort of do a stump speech. Two to five minutes - max. Then you can have side bar conversations. Have these guys nearby so they can pull you if someone talks too long. It's kind of a block and tackle game - they can interrupt, nicely, and make sure you're hitting as many people as possible. Everyone is here because they want to know you," said Swenson. "Sound good men? Do you guys have a notepad so you can follow up with folks?"

"Damn," said Jay. "It's in the car - I can go."

"No worries, I have extras. Hey - in that second drawer there's a few blank notebooks. Just grab one out of there. Pens are in that skinny drawer," said Steve.

Jay did as instructed and returned with an olive colored notepad. It was a nice one - there were no spiral wires and it looked to be made of leather. The pen was a Parker, from Steven's native Wisconsin.

"I can be the record keeper," said Jay, sounding somewhat official.

Steve and Chip made the rounds. The kid tried like hell to remember peoples' names, he made a mental note to have name tags at all subsequent campaign events. Everyone was remarkably friendly. Each new room in the house was more impressive than the last. From the corner of his eye, Chip saw a familiar woman in a striking orange dress.

Cheryl looked beautiful. The sleeveless dress seemed uncharacteristic of her; it was practically skin tight and barely touched the top of her knees. The front opening came together beneath the middle of her chest - offering a relatively open view of her breasts. Her hair was gelled and pinned back tightly and her makeup looked like a professional applied it. She wore studded pearl earrings and left her necklaces at home. She stuck out - surrounded as usual with old guys.

Chip looked at her and wondered why they weren't together. It occurred to him that she had likely shelled out two hundred and fifty bucks just to run into him. It was a turn on. He adjusted his positions so he could see her better in the distance.

There were things that they both wanted to say to each other yet somehow they both knew it could wait. In the midst of this political fundraiser, he knew he wanted to spend the night with her.

Steve and Chip made the rounds. Jay was an earshot away the whole time, occasionally scribbling down notes, phone numbers, and emails. He forced dozens of photos and took every opportunity to mention the social media info to Chip's supporters. "I wanna see that on Facebook later tonight," he kept telling people with a softly pointed index finger.

It was time to liaise with Cheryl's group. Steve knew a few of the guys surrounding her, but he didn't know Cheryl. Chip wasn't sure if he should shake her hand and pretend they barely knew each other. She gave him a hug that was just north of *business professional* and a small kiss on the cheek - and it wasn't just an audible air kiss - she planted her lips on his cheek - then looked into his eyes as she pressed her thumb against his face "sorry about that Chip."

"I see you two know each other," said Steve.

The other guys in the group looked to be in awe of the moment.

"Yes, we are acquainted," said Chip in a cool way. "Ms. West - you look very nice this evening, who are your friends?"

She made the intros but he was having trouble keeping his eyes off her. She looked like a girl in a *James Bond* picture.

Chip did his thing - talked politics and football. It made Cheryl want him. She went around and gave Jay a less aggressive hug than his older brother. They made small chat while he listened to hear if Chip had any follow-up. Cheryl remarked at how good the online operation looked. She knew enough about Jay to know he'd probably hacked a few sites in order to have such an impressive following. She even suspected he had some kind of unfettered access to the student web portal at the college. The less she knew, the better. She asked Jay if he still saw Sarah, the girl he was with in New Orleans. Jay answered in the affirmative but assured Cheryl that Sarah was more like a friend.

As Chip was finishing up with Chreyl's guys, Steve suggested it was time for remarks. Chip turned to his brother and Cheryl. "They're ready for a few remarks," said the linebacker. "What's that Cher?"

"It's a Crown and Coke, would you like a sip?" she asked.

"Well, it's yours - I can..."

"No, it's yours," she said "it's for *you*." She had gotten it for him - to give him just a tiny bit of help with his speech.

"Thank you," he said. "That's so nice of you."

Her eyes told him he'd earned it.

Steve clanked a glass with a shrimp fork for a few seconds. "Folks if we can head out to the deck - our guest of honor is going to say a few words!" he yelled.

The deck overlooked the awesome forest and sinkhole. Steve had draped a wooden pallet with a stylish contemporary rug for Chip to have a perch. Everyone gathered around, including Chip's parents - who he'd seen but hadn't spoken with. Chip drained his cocktail and took his place on the makeshift stage.

He was in white oxford with a spread collar and a light gray suit. He wore an American flag lapel pin and opted not to wear a tie. His hair was longer than usual but it looked neat and brushed with a dash of hairspray. Chip had aged.

He looked out at the crowd. People looked sharp - they looked like him, to an extent. He immediately felt comfortable.

"First and foremost, I'd like to thank our excellent host - Mr. Stephen Swenson. I've been in hundreds of homes and I can honestly say this place is easily one of my favorites... I also want to thank my parents for being here - and for instilling in me a sense of service and civic duty... I'd also like to recognize and thank the great work of Ms. Rosie Lawson - for her help with the party over the past twenty-something years. I've gotten to know Ms. Rosie and I can tell you that I don't think we could have a better chair of our local party. And I want to thank everyone here - for your support and for taking the time out of your busy schedules to come out here this evening. I've got some people helping me with my campaign - I want to give them a shout out - including my brother Jay - he's the one that will call and hassle you to post photos from tonight on your social media feeds.

As you know by now - hopefully - I'm Chip MacIntosh - and I'm running for US Congress!

The God's honest truth is that I never thought about being in Congress - this is something I first explored just this past Christmas. The way it worked - Bob Reynolds announced his retirement. I was spending the weekend with some of my most revered role models - some of you are here tonight... They told me that serving in Congress was about *leadership* - it's about learning from the people you represent - getting up to date on the issues - listening - and getting the job done for the American people...

I studied it - hard. That's all I did... I talked to people in every corner of North Central Florida. I read every blog post and Twitter feed - it consumed me... And it didn't take long - after my extensive research and at the urging of so many of you - that I knew this was my destiny.

My time out in the district these past few months has shown me - here's what I have learned...

I've learned that I have the *energy* to do what's necessary to win this seat in November and that I have the ability to commit the requisite amount of time necessary to effectively represent you...

I am 100% committed to this - I'm *all in* - not just with respect to the time and energy requirements - but my *heart* is on board too...

Any time I've gone *all in* - I've accomplished my goals - my mission. I've never quit once in my life - and I won't start now...

I was an All-State athlete - down the road at Gainesville High School - I was a member of the *National Honor Honor Society*... I turned down athletic scholarships at division one schools and I turned down a few academic scholarships - one to Georgia Tech...

Why?

Because I wanted to serve my country - that sense of service to my country was the most important thing. I convinced myself that college would be there for me when I got done...

I served as a US Marine for three years - with multiple combat deployments in the Middle East and a few other places I can't tell you about...

After attaining the highest rank possible and earning multiple citations for valor, I returned to my beloved Gainesville to get my degree...

I tried out for the football team - Coach Haines gave me a shot - I earned the right to wear the blue and orange. I had teammates who were stronger - I had teammates who were faster. But no one on that field worked harder than me. Even when I messed up - the coaches would pull me aside and say things like - if everyone worked as hard as you - we'd be national champions every year...

I earned a starting position with the team my junior year and was swiftly promoted to captain - the first junior captain in three decades...

As captain I helped lead the Gators to two SEC Championships - earning multiple accolades and distinctions along the way. I was named student athlete of the week a record four times.

My grade point average was one of the highest in the conference - I never took my eye off the prize. I wasn't the smartest guy on that campus but I think you'd be hard-pressed to find someone who could outwork me...

It is with this same determination and focus that I will represent *you* in Washington...

Just like the team - just like a platoon of fresh Marines - I cannot do any of this alone. I am going to need your help. I'm certainly grateful for the support of all of you this evening - I'm going to need to build a sizable warchest to win in November. My least favorite part about running - is asking for money... It's one of those necessary evils...

I've become pretty tight with Congressman Reynolds - and fortunately for me - his favorite place to do business is on our beautiful St. Johns River... it's interesting about Reynolds...

He doesn't care if he catches a damn thing - he is happier when he puts others on a good fish. He is a kind and decent man... I'm grateful for his wisdom and his friendship - and I am very proud to have his full-fledged endorsement!

I don't want to take up too much more of everyone's time - thank you again to everyone who made this evening possible - I'm proud to be from Gainesville - I love my country - and I will work as hard as I can in order to earn your continued support - THANK YOU ALL!"

Everyone clapped loudly. Chip stepped down and hugged his parents. Jay had been snapping pictures and videos the entire time. It was a picturesque setting - perhaps the ultimate house party for a candidate.

Cheryl couldn't stay back. She appeared behind his folks with a fresh cocktail for the guy who just rallied 150 people. She had realized they were in the same business - they were both in marketing - and this guy was good at it. She wondered if she should run for office, just for the experience. Over the course of a few months he'd actually gone from a star linebacker to a very convincing politician.

"Hey Cheryl," he said with a smile. "What'd you think?"

"I thought it was really great, Chip," she said, "Very personal and sweet - leadership... You were confident without being arrogant. And I must say - very handsome - you looked so sharp up there. I'm very proud of you - if you'll let me be proud of you."

"Thank you," he said. There were people all around or he might have hugged her.

She leaned in, "Can I see you later? I just want to be with you."

He winked at her and turned to another smiler with their hand out.

Jay had gone to the Suburban and returned with a better camera. He wanted to get some candid shots and videos for his digital operation.

Chip was stuck on the deck answering questions. "Chip," said one older gentleman, "nothing about the party - I think next time you should say what it means to you to be a Democrat. Many of us are here tonight because we're looking for an issues-based candidate to fight the Republicans in D.C.."

The guy went on and on about his own DNC pedigree and why he was a Democrat. Chip originally thought he had a point but he was rambling and the Marine started not to care what he was saying. His goal was to avoid any direct questions about his political ideology.

"I think you're exactly right," said Chip. "I DO need to incorporate some of our platform issues into my stump speech. I thank you for that constructive advice. Would you excuse me while I look for the men's room?"

The guy seemed happy with Chip's answer, "Of course - there's one off the kitchen," he told the young candidate. Chip excused himself. He was pleased to see that people had left after his remarks. He was also pleased to see people grabbing bumper stickers from the kitchen counter. They read: *MacIntosh for Congress* in blue and orange with an image of his peninsular home state off to the right.

An hour later Chip was in the throws of a conversation with the remaining twenty-five guests. His voice was nearly shot and he never made it past the state of a slight buzz. His parents and his friends from the team had split. Jay was playing a game on his phone in the living room. Cheryl was instinctively helping the caterers and Ms. Rosie clean up. She was ready to go; she was fading.

"Hey Buddy," Cheryl said when she found Jay.

He sat up in the Eames lounge chair. "Hi Cheryl," he said looking around.

"You did a great job tonight Jay," she said. "I'm looking forward to seeing some of those photos online."

"Thanks," he said "he is ready or what?"

"Tell you what - I'll give you $20 if you can get him to leave," she offered.

"Deal," he said. "Just approach confidently and tell the group he's got a big day tomorrow, right?"

"Exactly," she said with a pretty smile. "I'll even give him a lift home."

"Sweet," said Jay. "Does he - uh - know that?"

"Yep," she said. "I'll pull my car around and he can just jump in. Do you need a ride too?"

"Nope - I've got the professor's 'burb," he said.

She slow-nodded, handed the undergraduate a crisp twenty and headed for the solid wood front door.

Jay approached the last group of party-goers with confidence. He had a camera bag slung over his shoulder - a pad and phone in his hand.

"Time to hit it Jay?" Chip half-yelled from the crew.

"Big day tomorrow Captain..." said Jay. "I know you'd rather stay and visit but we've still got some work to do yet tonight - with the web page and all."

Chip shook everyone's hand and gave Stephen Swenson a bear hug. "Call me," he said.

When he turned around he was face to face with Shannon Grady. "Are you guys going out for a few drinks?" she asked.

"Not tonight Shannon," said Chip in a friendly tone. "We've got more work today - got to keep that majority up in your town!"

Shannon tried to hide her disappointment. "Okay - you've got my number, please let me know if you need us for anything. Great to meet you Chip - I hope to see on the Hill in January - or sooner."

He nodded, turned and thanked everyone one last time.

The brothers finally broke free from the party. "Do you know if Miss West already left?" asked Chip.

"She's waiting to take you - uh - *home*," said Jay with a hint of sarcasm.

They opened the front door and Chip was happy to see her familiar Cherokee idling on the riverstone driveway. "You're the man - call me tomorrow," said Chip without looking at his brother.

She hit the gas pedal and the V8-powered Jeep kicked up a few stones as she headed for the long road to the highway.

"So you're giving me a lift home?" asked Chip, looking over at her.

"I thought it went great. You were really great," she said. "Did anyone give you shit about not mentioning the party?"

"You noticed that?" he asked "For real - or someone said something."

"No one said anything," she explained. "Hell - you're at a Democratic Party fundraiser - you're supposed to mention stuff like - you know - *the Democratic Party*." Her tone was more friendly than bitchy.

"I know that - now," he said.

"The rest of it was awesome though - my gosh - really awesome *Charles the Third* - I was thinking..." she started.

"Thank you," he said, "Wait! I'm not talking to you right now. How'd I end up sitting shotgun in your car? I'm supposed to be pissed off at you."

She stopped at a stoplight, "I hate to say this - but can we just deal with all that later? You know this isn't how I operate, but I just need you to shut your mouth and take me to bed. I paid good money to attend that event. Do you like my dress?"

"It's pretty incredible," he said, looking it up and down. "Okay, you own me tonight. Two-fifty ought to get you.. something."

There was a short pause then he continued, "So, apart from all of that, how do you think it went tonight?"

"Oh it went great," she said, "actually, tonight was the first time I was pretty sure you were going to be a Member of Congress. I mean - I saw it. I can see it now. You looked a little - I don't know - more 'ready.' It was solid Chip - you're coming into the role."

"It felt good. And thank you," he said. "The light changed - its green."

"Kiss me," she said. "There's no one coming."

He placed his hand on her neck and ear and did as he was told. They'd missed each other.

"My place?" she asked.

"Sounds good," he said.

Chip studied his phone messages and social media feed for the rest of the drive. Cheryl turned up her stereo - it was Tom Petty and the Heartbreakers' "Here Comes My Girl." Chip approved without telling her.

They barely made it into Cheryl's place with their clothes on. She was the aggressor - partially because she was worried now more than ever that she would lose him to D.C.. Chip went along with it - by some standards it bordered on assault.

He woke up at six and she was sound asleep next to him. Chip tiptoed into the bathroom and looked himself over. There was some slight bruising on his chest and he had a bite mark just beneath his collar bone. Neither was drunk the night before so his memory of their encounter was pretty steady - plus she wouldn't be able to blame any of the aggression on alcohol.

Chip wondered what had come over her - this was not characteristic of their previous lovemaking. He drained his bladder then headed to the kitchen to make a pot of coffee. As it brewed he returned to the bedroom and slipped into his undershirt. He checked the nightstand for a sign of unusual behavior - a magazine or a spicy novel. There was nothing that would quickly explain her attack on him. He pulled his phone from a charger and sat on one of her kitchen bar stools.

The toilet in the other room flushed. Cheryl appeared two minutes later with her hair pinned up. She was wearing a terry cloth robe with her initials on it. He smiled as she approached.

"Good morning - Sunshine," he said.

"Hi," she said, kissing his ear briefly. "Thank you for making coffee. And for staying here last night."

"Of course," he said, placing his iPhone on the counter. He was tempted to ask her what compelled her to have relatively hostile sex with him but decided to let her bring it up.

"Do you want me to make you some crepes?" she asked. "I have bacon too."

"I would love some crepes, I'm starving," he replied. "You don't have to make bacon though - that's kind of a pain in the ass."

"I got the pre-cooked kind - just goes in the microwave for thirty seconds," she said.

"Can I help?" he asked her.

"Noooo - I've got it," she said, pouring a cup of black coffee for him. "Here you are..."

"Thanks Cher," he said. "Hey - about last night... how'd you think that went?"

"The parade or the fireworks show?" she asked as she measured the flour and milk.

He smiled and shook his head a little, "Either one."

"Something came over me last night Chip, I'm sorry if I seemed a little over-the-top. I think I was a little jealous or something," she said apologetically. "Are you worried right now?"

"Nope, I just want to make sure you're okay," he explained. "I thought you might be upset with me. And why would jealousy come into the picture? Who've you got to be jealous of? You were the hottest girl there last night - by a mile. Are you mixing that in a *blender?*"

"Yes I'm using a blender - trust me on this," she said, hitting the highest setting in the appliance. "I wasn't jealous but - what about that chick from the party? The one with the big tits and the slightly red hair? She was into you - *Shannon* - I don't like her."

He was smart not to pretend to not have noticed her. "She's annoying - I talked to her for like five seconds. Ms. Rosie said to warm up to her a little - try to get financial help from the party. She wasn't into me though - I totally didn't get that vibe. Plus she's not my type."

Cheryl just kept cooking but she wasn't exactly moody about it.

The candidate studied his phone again and thought back to the girl from the national party. He remembered her rather well. She was average height, auburn red hair - thick and sort of flowing. She had a good bust and wasn't afraid to show it off in her sleeveless cocktail wrap dress. Chip never noticed her shoes though he rarely did. He wondered why Cheryl mentioned her - it immediately caused him to envision her. The jealous streak even made the girl seem sexier than Chip remembered. She was the green-eyed Irish type - fair skin with a slightly rounded face. Either way, this was probably her first and last visit to the district.

"Here you go Tiger," said Cheryl as she slid across a fabulous stack of warm crepes to the linebacker. She placed four strips of bacon on a separate plate and slid that over too. She ate standing across from him - and only wanted one of the French pancakes and one slice of bacon. Neither of them really liked syrup - both liked butter - she peppered hers with cinnamon. It drove Chip crazy, he hated cinnamon.

"These are amazing!" he said like a caveman. He devoured the entire plate in the time it took her to eat one.

"I'm glad," she said. "What's your plan today?"

"Not sure - I don't think it's terribly full - my calendar is at home - I'd have to see. One thing I know I have to do is make some calls - follow ups from last night. Jay took notes for me. I also want to look at the - I've checked a few spots but Jay knows where to look to see how last night's event played online. I'll say one thing for that kid - he knows this digital bullshit better than anyone."

"Agreed," she said between sips of coffee. "He could end up getting you over the line. Young people, as you know, are the least likely voting block...

You can get them with the Internet and free stuff. If anyone can figure that out - it's your brother."

"Totally," said Chip. "Hey - you think you could spin me home?"

"Can I shower first?" she asked.

"Absolutely," he said. "I'll do the dishes."

"I'll do them later, come hop in the shower with me," she said.

Chapter Seventeen

Jay MacIntosh had become a pretty killer campaign operator. He'd been working with Les Lockhardt and the DNC - even the local party - to maximize the use of technology and the youth vote. He had quite the operation planned for Chip's graduation. Some politicos had coached Chip not to make a big splash on graduation day. They said it would highlight his youth. Jay disagreed and figured he could register enough people to vote absentee.

As the tens of thousands of people filed into the ceremony, there'd be trained interns collecting data, waving signs, and passing out stickers.

Jay even designed a special flyer that could easily attach to a ceremonial graduation cap. It was a five inch squared card that read: *MacIntosh Congress* in blue and orange.

Chip's brother figured out how to recruit students to get community service hours. As one of the campaign officials, Jay had the power to double-up on hours - it became a magnet for undergrads looking for easy volunteer work.

Chip had moved out of the brick house at 1308 University Avenue. His new place was an above-garage apartment. The main house was vacant, Chip's place was large. He had a bedroom and two bathrooms, a living room converted to an office and a big family room with a large sleeper sofa and comfortable chairs for reading. It was way nicer than Chip's previous pad.

The new place served as the temporary campaign headquarters. The office had three banquet tables with cheap laptops and phone chargers. Jay and his buddies had helped Chip make phone calls through their cell phones. There were frequent contests to see who could log the most phone calls in a night.

Chip had switched cars with his dad, the Suburban looked way more official and Charles didn't mind clanking around town in his son's vintage Land Cruiser wagon. His only gripe was the absurd number of college students who waived, yelled, and even ran up and slapped the truck - thinking the younger Charles Macintosh was behind the wheel.

Trips to St. Augustine were far nicer in the Suburban. Chip was starting to like his potential section of the coast.

Bob Reynolds had introduced Chip to a few of his farmer and rancher friends. He had learned the lingo and the issues important to their community. The Marine even saddled up at a nearby county's annual rodeo fair. He looked like a natural - riding and roping. The local press coverage was decent but the photos from the event didn't travel too far nationally.

The candidate was in frequent contact with Shannon Grady, the DNC girl who he'd first met at Steve Swenson's house party. She was based in D.C. but called Chip, even Jay, with numbers and stats and ideas. Almost daily she would email them talking points from the national party platform.

Chip's most uncomfortable campaign stop involved one of the platform's key objectives.

While at a chili cook off in one of his rural counties, he found himself encircled by locals in blue jeans and flannel shirts. He was asked about abortion. His stock answer was to deflect and say that it was a deeply personal decision between a woman and her physician. He had gotten good at leaving it in the *weeds* every time - and it usually worked.

One of the cowboy-looking people was actually a member of the press - online at least. He pushed Chip on the answer he gave and flatly asked him if he supports the Supreme Court's decision to legalize abortion.

"Look," said Chip "I'm not someone who particularly likes the practice - I can't actually imagine how someone could kill a baby - but it's currently the law of the land and maybe if the states want to ban it - I say go for it. This isn't my favorite issue. Here - I wouldn't do it - but I don't think - somehow that if you outlaw it - that that's a good idea either."

The blogger got traction with an article online that went slightly viral *Is MacIntosh Pro-Life?* This prompted hundreds of micro debates on social media. It also meant multiple calls from local and national dems - including Shannon Grady.

She laid into Chip hard - threatening to pull funding from the national party. She ripped him for isolating the youth vote, which is largely pro-choice.

Jay got inspired by the gaff. He began working on a video series of *Women for Chip MacIntosh.* He'd get women from 18 to 98 to say nice things about his brother on social media, then he'd pay for a blast and still hack a few sites for extra exposure.

The ace in the hole was a gray-haired hippie lady - former county chair who went on camera and said: *This is a tough issue for millions of Americans - millions of Democrats. It's not so black and white and I've met literally hundreds of people in my thirty years of activism - who have an evolving view of this sensitive topic.*

It was enough to right the ship. Team MacIntosh was back in good grace with the voters and, to a lesser extent, the national party.

With graduation approaching, Chip had been going back and forth with his mother on whether to have a party at the house. He'd rather have had donations than graduation presents. They settled on a family-only party with catered barbeque. The only question was whether to invite Cheryl. They'd only seen each other twice in the past month. He decided to invite her in person - at the graduation.

Most of the candidate's days were spent mapping out the calendars for speaking opportunities and making fundraising calls. He didn't have time to chase after Cheryl. Still, when she called him, he answered. And he'd be at her house at the drop of a dime if she needed to see him. She'd been really cool about giving him the room he needed.

The Director of Alumni Affairs was also busy with work. Graduation was one of their busiest times of the year hosting receptions and giving out awards. Plus no one was more giving than an alum at his or her kid's graduation from their same college.

It was two days until graduation day. Chip called Jay and told him he'd like to review the plan. Jay said he'd assemble some of his commandos and come over to the garage apartment.

The old Explorer showed up within the hour. Jay and his pals pulled a few boxes and bags from the cargo area and clambered up the wooden stairs to the MacIntosh Campaign Office. Jay told Chip to grab his cap for Friday. He pulled one of his clever fliers from a cardboard box and slipped in around the button on the top of the cap. He told his brother he had a thousand of them. Chip nodded approvingly and hoped it was legal.

Next Jay produced a list of volunteers with names and numbers. He showed Chip the *run of show* - an impressive event memo showing exactly where everyone would be and what they would do.

It was all there - swag, messaging, voting forms, decals, and a very clever way for a sea of graduates to show support for their candidate.

Jay's online operation was all set too. If anyone at the graduation *Googled* Chip, they'd instantly see an awesome photo of him in a suit and tie in front of the Capitol Dome with a "Donate $25 Now" link.

Chip was scheduled to attend two breakfasts and a brunch on graduation day. He was a member of the prestigious Florida Blue Key and the Society of Collegiate Scholars. Members of both groups were treated to breakfast and a large bronze medallion that pulled on ribbons of blue and gold.

Chip only spent a few minutes with the Scholars - he used that one for food. He ate two plates with a group of random parents and basically left the event without anyone even talking to him.

Full of scrambled eggs and bacon, the linebacker checked himself over in a men's room then headed for the Blue Key breakfast. This was where the money was. MacIntosh wasn't the most active member of the club, but they all knew who he was and many were eager to help his candidacy.

The moment Chip was free, a thirty-something with thick glasses approached and told him there was someone who wanted to talk to him. Chip acquiesced and was led to a side room - it was like a sitting area at church where a mom would feed a crying baby.

A man who looked like Woodrow Wilson was seated in a reception-style chair. He had a cane tilted against his knee. He invited Chip to sit next to him and the younger man with the glasses disappeared. They were alone.

"I ran for Congress in Tampa twenty years ago," he said. "I'm a Republican MacIntosh - and I think you might be too."

Chip just looked at the guy and waited for him to say something else. He didn't.

"Forgive me," said Chip politely, "I don't think I caught your name."

"It's Sidney Green," said the man.

"Well, it's nice to meet a fellow - Blue Key Member," said Chip, wondering if he could trust his fellow society member.

The guy stayed quiet so Chip continued "I'm not sure what you meant by your comment Mr. Green, I am in fact running as a Democrat."

"You're getting beat up in the press for not being enough of a Democrat," he said.

Chip was wondering what the guy's point was and he started asking himself how talking to this guy was in any way helpful to his future. "Look, I don't think it's any secret that I am what you would call a 'soft' dem. I have a few concerns - differences with the national party platform. They're cutting me a break though - they know this isn't Berkley down here."

"Why didn't you just run as a Republican?" asked Mr. Green.

"Because I'm a Democrat. Also - this district - you know it leans Democrat right?" asked Chip.

"Yea, I suppose," said the man.

Chip was annoyed. "So is that all, sir? Did you just want to ask me why I am a Democrat?"

"I'd like to help," he said. "Financially. I can bundle a stack of maximum individual contributions. Sorry for giving you a hard time earlier. I have a group of friends who would like to meet with you in the next few weeks. They're all Republicans though, that's why I tried to get your answer earlier - forgive me - I was clumsy about it."

"Thank you Mr. Green, I would be happy to meet with them. Whatever you want to do," said Chip.

This was a jackpot situation for Chip, he stayed and visited with Sid Green for another ten minutes. He told him he had to run to the next event - the football brunch - but they exchanged cards. Chip felt the need to hammer home his point about the party. He told the man that he had met both kinds of Democrats and that he obviously sides with the moderates more than the radicals. It was good enough for Green. Chip excused himself and calculated that his visit to the Florida Blue Key reception would likely yield around $30K. Not bad.

The graduating football player's brunch was a shade too *knucklehead* for Chip. He wasn't in the mood to talk about big games and tackles. The boys were bumping fists and chests and reciting war chants. It all seemed like a million years ago to their former star linebacker.

He had a very adult conversation with Coach Haynes about helping out with the team in the summer and fall. The coach offered to pay him a salary for a part time gig as a linebacker's coach. Chip was honest about his time commitments for the election. He told the coach he'd think about it and offered to help for free at local games. The coach understood and thanked him.

They didn't entertain the idea of a somber goodbye hug. Haynes said to call him.

It was nearly go-time. Chip left the brunch for the O'Connell Center, he was about to graduate from college.

It was just over eighty degrees outside and Chip was feeling warm in his all-black outfit. He felt anonymous as he walked along the breezeways and pathways across campus. There were people all over the place. Everyone looked great to Chip - *camera-ready* he'd grown fond of saying.

He spotted a few of Jay's comrades - cute ones in sundresses - passing out MacIntosh lit and voter forms. He could see at least one cap with his logo on it. "Pretty cool," he mumbled to himself as he continued his final stroll as an undergrad.

Most graduates sit with their respective department or school. Chip was in the front ten rows with the rest of the medallion-wearers from the Collegiate Scholars. Jay was way up in the press box with a two-way radio and a pair of open laptops. He had free-reign of the University with his network of teckie student helpers. Jay watched from his perch as hundreds of graduates affixed the sign he created to their caps. By the time an Air Force Sergeant belted out the National Anthem, the number of MacIntosh cap signs looked to be in the thousands.

Jay watched the $25 dollar donations flood his website during the provost's monotonous remarks. His plan was working. Twitter and Instagram started showing the cap signs.

Chip sat in his folding chair waiting for his name to be called. He was excited and he thought he'd reflect on his time at UF, but he didn't. All he could think about was Congress and Cheryl. He wanted both.

Cheryl had been in his life for nearly six months - about the same amount of time he'd spent trying to become a Congressman. They were like separate factions competing for Chip's attention. He liked her more than running for Congress - but the campaign got his full attention.

He was grateful for the space she had given him and though they had never settled on exclusivity, Chip felt guilty about having spent the night with Representative Carolyn Miller. She had only called and texted him a few times after their tryst and none of their communications even remotely mentioned their affair. He was impressed with her discretion.

Jay was up in the crow's nest of the arena, sweating about the next trick up his sleeve. He'd gotten a friend to hack the P.A. system at the graduation. When Chip was being called, they were going to play a voice clip of an older-sounding gentleman introducing Chip as their next Member of Congress.

It was finally Chip's group and Jay was freaking out, "oh Sweet Jesus," he said softly as he closed his eyes... "ELLA KYLIE, SUNG KYM, PETER ANGELO MACKENSIE...YOUR NEXT CONGRESSMAN: CHIP MACINTOSH!"

The clip was perfect - everyone clapped and cheered and yelled for Chip. The announcer had a puzzled look on his face, the crowd thought it was him. He tried the next name to make sure his mic was working "PETER CHAPMAN MACVANE." It all flowed too quickly for anyone to second-guess what happened. If no one talked, the college would never find out how it happened. Even Chip, grinning as he walked off the stage, had no idea what had just happened. Jay decided to never mention it to him.

The linebacker thumbed his news feed back in his seat as he waited for the rest of the seniors to walk. His name was trending on Twitter - it was a combination of the cap signs atop so many graduates and the audio intro of Chip.

The recent graduate scanned the area around the stage for Cheryl. She was nowhere to be found so he texted her: *Can you meet me after the ceremony?*

She wrote back: *Hey! Sure - greenroom right behind the stage - up one level.*

Finally, the last graduate with an unpronounceable Slovakian "Z" name walked across the stage at the Friday commencement. Most of the scholars poured out toward the street entrance while Chip went to look for the Director of Alumni Affairs.

She was the first thing he noticed when he entered the green room reception area. She was wearing a light tan suit with a royal blue top underneath. Around her neck was a vibrant, vintage scarf with pronounced blues and orange. She had on more gold than usual - Chip enjoyed seeing her. He watched her work the donors like keys on a piano.

She spotted him on the edge of the room and didn't wait to approach him.

"You look so beautiful," he said as she approached him.

"Congratulations Charles MacIntosh, you're officially an alum," she said under the guise of a business-like hug.

"Does that mean you get to *direct* me?" he said with a wink.

"Of course it does," she replied.

"How's the rest of your afternoon look?" he asked.

"Pretty open," she said, "Why what's up? Oh - by the way - how did you get introduced as our next Congressman or whatever? No one can figure that out - like a spliced tape or something?"

"I wish I knew!" Chip whisper-yelled. "I thought I was hearing things. Are people pissed?"

"No, I don't think so," she said. "They'll probably just say it was some kind of technical malfunction. What's in store for later? Aren't you having dinner with your mom and dad?"

"Mary is having a few people to the house for a barbecue. Can you come?" he asked. "There are a million parties later tonight - will have to see how I feel."

"Yea, same here - but I'm not really required to attend any of them; I could swing by," she said. "How do you feel right now?"

"Amazing," he confessed. "It feels like I just crossed a big life-hurdle. It also feels like I am just entering this new world too - like it's time to take my life more seriously, if that makes sense."

"It does - and in a sense, you graduated in New Orleans the day you won the Sugar Bowl" she said. There was a brief pause, "So what - like - an hour? Your mother's house?"

"Yes," he said. "Small group. Glad you'll be there."

"Certainly," she said. "I also have a little something for you - a graduation present."

Chapter Eighteen

By the end of the summer, campaigning had gotten easy for Chip MacIntosh. He was on a strict regime of appearances, special events, fundraisers at homes and hotels, and calls to donors. The money was coming in and the grassroots were growing strong. He still got badgered from time to time about being a Republican. He stayed firmly in the middle and tilted left when he was with the tie-dye crowd and he tilted right when he was with the race fans. It worked for him because it was who he really was.

He was doing great with his staff: Jay, some volunteers, their family friend banker/treasurer and Chip - the *talent*. They were saving a fortune but the party essentially forced them to hire a communications person.

Shannon Grady had called Chip and told him that she was sending a woman to be his press secretary. She also instructed Chip to find her a place to sleep for four months.

The girl was from Michigan. She was loud and somewhat crass. After one conversation with Shana Horowitz, Chip quickly called Shannon Grady and begged her not to send her. He told her that Shana would not fit in in north central Florida and that this was a waste.

Ms. Grady repeated the girl's resume to Chip and reassured him that the party was going to pay for her out of their general fund. Shana had just been working as a junior communications person for a Senate candidate in Illinois. Chip's race was her big break.

Jay wasn't going to be happy but the team had no choice. She was on her way down - in her trusty white Honda Civic.

Chip called Rosie Lawson to see when the Victory Office would be ready. It was slated to be in a shopping center just off campus. Every two years the party would pull together enough money to rent a storefront, load it with computers and phones and decorate the hell out of the windows with candidate signs and graphics.

She told Chip it'd be ready in a few days. He offered to help paint or whatever but she assured him it was covered. Finally he asked her if she could think of anyone who could host his new coms person. He asked if she knew anyone from Michigan. Nothing came to her mind, she promised him she'd ask around.

Hopefully Shana could work from the Victory Office while Chip and Jay and the others operated from Chip's place. Rosie reminded Chip that the general election involved a lot of door knocking and to make sure they were recruiting folks to hit doors and drop literature. He vowed that record numbers would turn out for his *front porch brigade.*

Jay had already started a massive database he created himself. It incorporated all of the lists that campaigns traditionally pay big money for. He used fancy computer math and probably a few cut corners to acquire and prioritize Chip's target voters. Best of all, he had already figured out a way to integrate his lists into the outreach app being used by the national party.

Chip was confident in his ground game, he was doing well online, and his messaging was usually spot on. He felt like Gaineville was a complete lock and his farming and rural constituency was looking good as well.

Jay wanted to do more on the coast. The district had a sliver of the beach and downtown St. Augustine - an area he didn't know terribly well. Jacksonville had a major newspaper that covered his whole district.

All of the Republicans in Chip's race were from the coast. They'd been duking it out in their primary for six months. Only one person had dropped out and he was never a serious candidate. The remaining candidates were constantly touting themselves as 'the one who can beat MacIntosh.' At first it bothered Chip, he mistakenly took it as a personal attack.

Jay and Les knew that in reality, it forced voters to know who he was without making his own headlines. "Take the free press," Les would tell the MacIntosh brothers from the beginning.

Chip was browsing a list Jay compiled of every special event on the coast. There were bike rides, a motorcycle ride, a boat show, a garden show, some book groups, clam bakes, charity golf matches, concerts, a beach volleyball tournament and an air show.

He had two weeks until the primary. He was uncontested in his, but the Republicans were busy trying to outwork and outspend each other. He wondered if he should use his two weeks to dominate the coast. He called Jay and rattled off the Republican-seeming events: motorcycles, boat show, and the air show. He asked Jay to build out an itinerary for the next two weeks. He

told him he wanted attractive girls in MacIntosh attire at the boat show passing out decals and fliers - he'd be there too.

Jay got to work. He called the print shop they'd been using and told them
he needed one of those 10x10 tailgating tents with the MacIntosh for Congress logo on it. He checked the rules for a non-profit exhibition at the boat
show and the fees associated with it. He called his dad to see if anyone in the
circle of trust had a Harley Davidson. Charles said he'd make a few calls.

Jay wondered about the airshow - that would involve the beach. What
could be more effective than girls in bikinis waiving MacIntosh signs? How
would Chip do that? Another booth? Chip was jump-certified in the Corps,
perhaps he could parachute in... Jay delegated some web stuff to one of his
sidekicks and started working the phones.

An hour later he showed up at Chip's place with a calendar and a tenta-
tive agenda. "I've got some ideas," he began. "I can get us a booth at the boat
show. We'll put me and two 'subjects' there with literature and swag. It's a
boat show - I think you should walk the floor with Cheryl and maybe two of
my guys. There could be no better person for a boat show than Cheryl. You
don't even have to be an item, just walk around with her and shake hands...
Also - dad knows a guy with a Harley and a trailer for it - I'm working on a
way to get it out there for the motorcycle thing. You'd just wear your Gators
jersey and we'll blow it up online. No one even has to know it's you during
the actual ride. You and Cheryl can stay in a cheap hotel and the rest of us
can return to G-Ville - unless I can get an RV. The airshow is the next weekend - would you be open to parachuting in - if we can set that up?"

Chip felt like he was in a movie. He was impressed with his brother's cre-
ativity and new-found work ethic. "Sure," he said. "Goddamn right I'll jump."

Chip's cell beeped. It was Shana - an hour outside of Gainesville. "I'll text
you the address," he said as he hung up. "Can you help me? I'm stuck with
this coms chick. She has nowhere to sleep and I guess she's coming here until
we can find her a spot. I've got sheets for the pullout couch. What a nightmare."

"Could be fun," suggested Jay.

"No chance," said Chip, unfolding the queen-sized fitted sheet. "I've spoken with her - she's a total nightmare. Let's clean some of this shit up. Thank
God I have another bathroom."

The office section had a lot going on - stacks of voter forms, boxes and bags of merch - but the rest of the place looked sharp enough for a bachelor/recent grad. Chip took the trash out to help with the scent. The Civic pulled up as he was shutting the lid on his trash can.

Shana got out and looked around. Her host was semi hidden behind some lattice work that blocked the utility area where the garbage and recycling lived.

She was petite. Her hair was practically black and fell just south of her shoulders. The glasses were huge and dark. She wore a long and loose gray exercise top, black shorts and black cross trainers. Her skin was in need of sunshine. She looked pissed.

Chip clunked the recycling bin enough to announce his presence and walked into the light. He introduced himself and was acting far more pleasant than he really felt. He explained the current living situation. She was way cooler about it than he thought she'd be. They had a nice, brief visit in the driveway then Chip offered to grab her bags.

It wasn't much stuff, nearly everything she had was in one rolling bag, a hiking pack, and a folding suit carrier.

They made it upstairs and found Jay buried in a MacBook Air. He was dismissive, then he looked and saw her and his manners improved. She was good looking. Jay wondered how his brother was so bloody lucky to have this girl crashing on his couch for up to four months.

Shana lifted her glasses and shook hands with Jay. She had dark blue eyes and a stunning smile. She looked pretty natural and crisp for someone who'd just completed such a serious road trip. Chip showed her the pullout couch and explained that he hardly ever went in the family room. He even offered to see about getting some kind of screen to put next to the bed to give her some privacy.

It was better than she had predicted. The oversized bathroom helped. She studied the large tub and shower, the toilet was clean and there was plenty of room to change.

"My parents live close by, I can see if they have one of those clothing racks with the bars," said Chip when she stepped back into the main area. "You could even put it on this side of the bed - like a wall."

"It'll be fine," she assured him. "This is the office too?"

"For right now - sort of," he said. "The local party is finishing up with their local Victory Office, we'll have two rooms in there to operate. And they'll have a big phone banking area. I've also put out some feelers for more suitable sleeping quarters."

"I'm easier going than you'd think. Do I call you - Chip?" she asked.

"Absolutely," he confirmed. "We're pretty casual around here. I can't speak for the victory office - but you're fine in - whatever you want to wear."

"Okay," she said.

"My mom comes by with food - there's a stack in the garage fridge and I usually just reheat it up stairs. There's a decent rotation of people in and out but everyone is - well they're good people - students mostly. Jay has been running the grassroots and digital operation thus far. Shannon said you had experience with booking radio and tv hits - maybe we start there. Tell you what... Jay and I will take off for a bit. Why don't you get settled and we'll grab some takeout for dinner? We can talk shop then I'll show you around Gainesville if you're not too tired from the trip."

Chip grabbed Jay and they headed down to the Explorer.

"She's kinda hot," Jay remarked as he threw his truck in reverse.

"I know," replied Chip. "She sounded quite the opposite on the phone. Fuck."

"What, Cheryl?" asked Jay.

"Yea... she's gonna freak," he said.

"Are you guys like - exclusive? What exactly is the deal there? I've never really asked you - it's always mom. She even asks me about Cheryl when you're not around."

"Shocking," he said sarcastically. "I don't exactly know the deal. We are pretty strong when we're together. We're also pretty good at being apart.

"Do you love her?" asked Jay.

"Honestly, I would be hard not to man. She's unlike any girl or woman I've ever known. There are just so many other factors - the timing isn't right somehow. I know it's cliche, but it's pretty complicated. I do know this though: if I awoke from a coma - she's the first person I'd want to see. That's gotta mean something."

"Then why aren't you WITHHH her?" he asked his brother.

"Because," Chip started, "because she's seven years older than me and she is ready to get married and have a family. And I'm not. As much as I love her I cannot just get engaged and settle down with someone - I'm not there yet. I want to win this goddam contest - then I can reassess. She knows that."

"I think you're going to win," Jay announced. "I also think that will make you one of the world's most eligible bachelors in the south. Could you survive with Cheryl in that sort of climate?"

"It's not likely," he guessed. "I'm strong-willed, but it only takes a decent body, a good smile and fifth of whiskey and I am like every other man on the planet."

The Explorer pulled into their childhood home. "Are ya'll exclusive? How've you left it?" he asked Chip.

"I don't know if she's been out with anyone," he said. "This will sound crazy to you, but I don't want to know. I've been pretty good in spite of our arrangement - I assume she has too."

They waited as the garage door opened slowly. "So do we like her for the boat show?" asked Jay.

"We do," replied Chip, dipping onto the garage, avoiding their dad's MG.

They found the coat rack, spent the requisite ten minutes visiting with their parents and headed back out.

"Hey - let's take her out to dinner - she's been driving for two days, I don't want to stick her with Chinese to go," said Chip. "You drop me off - go home and get cleaned up - see if your two main guys are around - we'll meet up for - I dunno - pizza or something."

"Okay," said Jay.

Chip announced his presence before actually opening the door. He wiggled the coat rack in and waited for her to yell something to him. "Shana?" he called.

"Hi Chip," yelled the girl in the other room. She walked in wearing just a towel, "Nice rack," she joked. "That's a big help. Thank you."

"Terrific," he said. "Listen I think we'll go out for dinner if you're cool with that."

"Perfect! What should I wear? College casual?" she asked.

"I'll be in jeans and an oxford - I guess - wear whatever you like," he said. "Fifteen minutes?"

"Sure!" she said with a nice smile.

The MacIntosh Campaign was seated at a high-top table at the best pizza joint in Gainesville. They were lucky to be up in the loft where they could speak relatively freely and Chip was able to go basically unnoticed.

Unlike 90% of the town's eating establishments, Joe's Pizza wasn't all decked out in UF gear - Joe was a New Yorker and his Yankees reigned supreme. There were murals of Yankee Stadium, the Statue of Liberty, the Brooklyn Bridge and Washington Square. The walls were dotted with signed 8x10s of every Italian in Hollywood - and not one of the salutations was "To Joe." It was a complete *eBay hit job*. Joe didn't care - he wanted his 'boyz up there.'

The group consisted of Jay and his two loyal helpers: Mick and Preston, Shana, and Chip. The only one missing from the team was their sixty year old treasurer. The old guy handled the money and kept everyone out of trouble with the Federal Election Commission. He wasn't much for pizza and domestic beer specials. Chip had only seen him once since announcing his candidacy.

Jay brought Shana up to date on the ground game. She had told Jay that their social media was the best she'd ever seen. He took the compliment but wondered how many campaigns she'd actually worked on. Shana told the group she was fine with Jay running the digital side of things and that she would direct her focus on the actual press: radio, TV and print media. She sort of asked Chip if that was cool with him and he nodded approvingly.

Mick and Preston were pretty quiet at first. They were both sophomores and lived down the hall from Jay.

Shana was a talker. And a doer. She pulled an iPad mini from her purse, took a sip of Miller Lite and said that she wanted to hash out the next two weeks. Whether planned or proposed, she asked the guys to rattle off a list of events. Fortunately that's what Jay and Chip had just discussed; it was fresh in their minds.

They went through the list while Shana used her iPhone to identify media outlets that might cover the young congressional candidate. The boys were good at this. She was encouraged.

"This is legit, fellas. What about the next two?" she asked.

Chip spoke with a mouthful of pizza "I forgot I'm going to Washington too. But that's not really campaign stuff."

"When?" she asked her new boss.

"Next Tuesday and Thursday." replied Chip after a big swig of the ice cold beer.

"Aren't they in recess?" she asked.

"Uh - it's right before I think," he said. "It's a meet and greet. Reynolds set it up - there might be a fundraiser involved. But definitely no press."

"It's D.C. Chip - there's always press. I should go with you."

Jay tried not to seem bothered. Chip just nodded; he'd check with Congressman Reynolds.

"Okay," said Shana. "We've got St. Augustine this weekend then DC. And the Victory Office is coming on line - what - in two days?

"Yep, that's the drill," he said like his dad.

Chip was feeling good about the team. Jay had really stepped up to the plate. No one had seen him so passionate about anything outside of schooling and computers. Mick and Preston were utility gophers. They would do anything asked of them and wanted the experience. Chip knew very little about either of them but he made sure they never paid for anything when he was around. Preston was a chick magnet - they flocked to him because of his looks but he wasn't very cool. He had zero lady skills and Chip assumed the looks were relatively recent. He was one of those guys who didn't know he was attractive. Mick was in the marching band and of all things - played the flute. He was a nice kid though and he idolized Jay, the dorm-dwelling upperclassman.

Shana was nothing like she was on the phone when Chip originally met her. Not only was she pretty cute, she was sharp as a tack and fun to be around. Her voice went from "Press Secretary" to "Buzzed Midwesterner at a Bowling Alley" over the course of the evening. The Floridians got a kick out of her. Chip had told himself twenty times not to sleep with her - no matter what.

Shana spoke up, "so we've got the boat show this weekend - then it's off to DC - ask Reynolds if you pay for that out of campaign funds or personal funds and I'll call Shannon to see what she thinks - then we've got the motorcycles. That sounds dangerous but whatever. Talk to me about the boat show - I have no idea what that looks like."

Jay ran through the *run of show*, explained every detail with precision and confirmed that he could borrow an RV - an in-kind contribution from an associate.

"I don't get it," she asked. "What's the story-story?"

"The story is that... *where there's boats - there's votes*," said Jay.

Chip spit his beer out and laughed out loud. Jay smiled at him then looked back toward Shana. She cracked up then repeated Jay's silly one-liner in her bowler accent.

"So you just see a booth with three staffers or whatever and Chip walks the floor looking at boats?" she asked.

"I was thinking he takes his friend Cheryl - and maybe Preston and Mick. Actually - we could do a little outreach and set up meetings with the principals. That way these folks know to expect him or whatever."

"Blow it up on *social* that he's at a boat show?" she asked. She turned to Chip and smiled without opening her mouth "And who is Cheryl?"

"I need to hit the head," said Chip, excusing himself.

"He has a girlfriend?" asked Shana, professionally. "There's nothing in the press - how'd you guys..."

"She's not his girlfriend," confirmed Jay. "They're just friends."

"Oh," said Shana, sensing there was more to the story. "I'll call the Times Union and see about an interview on site. He can tool around with his friend and talk to a reporter about it I guess. Boating does have some underlying topics important to voters I guess. Business meets the environment - jobs, etc... I can come up with something. Jay - you wanna research who is going to be there - look for Democrat donors and former Seminoles - kidding... *Gators*. Set them up from 10am to 12pm. He can hope to get invited to join someone important for lunch then I can do the interview for 1:30 or 2 and he can talk about all of the great jobs supported by the industry."

"Good call," said Jay. He was impressed. "I don't need an RV. Do I?"

"Nupe," she said "we'll be back in Gainesville in time for dinner."

It got louder downstairs - rowdy but fun. Shana looked out beneath the loft railing and saw Chip MacIntosh bro-hugging and high-fiving a bunch of people. She was pretty green but tried to even conceptualize a candidate for

Congress getting that kind of attention. Shannon had told her he was one of a kind - she was starting to see it firsthand.

Chip returned to the loft and the conversation switched from business to pleasure. They had morphed back into a group of twenty-somethings - enjoying good food and exceptionally fair beer prices. The music was upbeat and bluesy.

Chapter Nineteen

Charles MacIntosh III sat alone in the Gainesville Regional Airport. He was reading the local newspaper in a brand new navy suit by Ralph Lauren. He would have prefered to carry the suit in a garment bag and wear casual clothes for the flight but those days were over for Chip - he had to be "on" going forward. He was waiting for his flight to Charlotte - then Washington's Reagan National Airport.

Representative Bob Reynolds had insisted he travel solo for his first trip up. He had arranged for his protege to meet with staff from House Leadership, a few lobbyist friends, and, most importantly, his D.C. staff.

Chip pulled his phone from his jacket and reviewed emails and texts. Shana had given him some talking points to memorize. He lost interest and went to his photo album. It was somewhat depressing - images of signs, statistics, graphs and documents and news story screenshots. His life of pretty girls and trips to the ranch were replaced with his postgraduate lifestyle - his political reality.

In the era of running for Congress, Chip had to check the web if he wanted to see pictures of him doing neat stuff.

At the top of the online laundry basket of photos and stories was a brand new shot of Chip at the North Florida Boat Show in sunny St. Augustine. He could see part of Cheryl in a few of the shots. She was good at staying out of the frame. Chip found her to be a welcome presence at the show - he wished she was accompanying him to the nation's capital.

The boat show had been successful. The campaign was able to connect with hundreds of likely voters and Chip was the only candidate there. Shana was right about the messaging and it played well online and in print. Jay had flipped images and taglines to every boating magazine and environmental organization. The girls in the campaign tent were just as popular as Chip - Jay had them in MacIntosh tees and the smallest shorts that decency would permit. The team left St. Augustine completely out of bumper stickers.

The manufacturer's reps appreciated Chip's knowledge of boats and plenty of attendees were grateful that he bothered to show up and shake hands with people.

Those were his people though, D.C. was going to be different. Chip was younger than most of the people *working* on the hill. He had butterflies about going up. He reminded himself that being prepared was the key to his nerves so he pulled out Shana's talkers and worked to memorize them.

After an uneventful day of flying and reading, the congressional hopeful jumped in an Uber and headed to Bob Reynolds' favorite restaurant.

Traffic on the George Washington Memorial Parkway was lighter on the way into the city. The driver was from Africa and Chip talked to him the whole time and still managed to look out the window at the sites. It felt surreal to the kid from Florida.

Pennsylvania Avenue, past the Capitol Dome, was packed. There were groups of young kids, college kids, staffers, tourists and cops - cops everywhere. The Uber driver pulled in front of Tune Inn and thanked Chip for the nice conversation. It looked like a college campus but everyone was dressed up. It was warm and everyone seemed to want the sunshine on their shoulders.

Chip was confused when he entered the restaurant. It looked like a dive bar, there was no way he was in the right place. As he traversed the bar area he found the dining room - which consisted of vintage black vinyl booths and only enough of them to seat about fifty people. The candidate looked the place up and down - he actually liked the decor. There were stuffed heads and an ancient mounted sailfish. It was kind of a dump, but Chip liked the place. There was one empty booth. It was larger than the others and had a RESERVED tent sign in the middle of the table.

A fast walking Spanish lady asked Chip if he needed a table. She was out of range by the time he could answer. She disappeared into the packed bar area while he stood there like an idiot with his luggage, waiting for her to return.

"Hey Chip!" yelled Congressman Robert Reynolds from the back of the restaurant. He waved the kid toward the kitchen. "There's another table back here that no one knows about. You don't mind do ya?" he asked.

"No sir - this is your town," he said.

"It's turkey night - best in town Chip..." said Reynolds.

The two men made it back to the secret booth. It was totally private, there was even a backdoor to a smoking porch. Chip was introduced to Barry Smith and Michael Schindler.

"I've known these guys my entire time in Washington - they both worked on campaigns and in house offices and committees. They're some of the best lobbyists in this city. Principled, dedicated - and just - good," confirmed Reynolds.

Chip shook their hands, made eye contact, smiled, and took a seat. He planned to give complete sentence answers to their inquiries and to keep his mouth shut as much as possible.

The older men at the table did nearly all of the talking.

Ninety minutes later Chip was exhausted - he wondered what he'd gotten himself into. As he politely ate dry turkey and sipped barely-cold IPA, the men had told him how "Washington *really* worked."

They made it sound like the lobbyists ran the town - and they kept calling it a town - even a *small town* numerous times.

They basically told him that they bundle donations through a SuperPAC then they hire a strategy firm to make television and web commercials that compromise opponents. Attack ads; which run during local news. They tell the candidate what committees they can be on, they tell them who to avoid, where to live, etc.

Bob Reynolds could sense Chip's uneasiness with the conversation and at times would drop lines like "plus you get to bring home the goods - projects or whatever - to the people of North-Central Florida - *your* people!"

Chip left the two hour dinner and headed to his hotel; he knew it was nothing special but it was close to the Capitol and it was relatively inexpensive. He listened to phone messages and read texts as he walked down Pennsylvania Avenue toward South Capitol Street. There was one bar on the way that caught his eye - the Capitol Lounge. He felt like he heard of it before but couldn't recall. The place was loaded with good looking Hill-types. It didn't look like they could handle one more patron, much less a patron with a medium rolling bag and a shoulder bag.

"Chiiiiiiiiip" yelled a voice behind him as he was almost to his turn.

The football player turned, paused and looked around the semi crowded brick sidewalk. It was Shannon Grady. "It's Shannon," she said. She was right, he didn't recognize her. The last time he'd seen her was in Gainesville at Steve Swenson's house party.

"Hey there," said Chip. "You look different - *nice*."

She had on a simple black dress with a revealing cut. Her auburn hair looked darker, it was in a bun and Chip noticed some extra silver jewelry clamped to different parts of her ears. Her green eyes sparkled beneath her potentially artificial eyelashes.

"I didn't think I'd see you tonight?" she said enthusiastically. "You just get here?"

"Show'nuff" he said, trying to sound hip. "I had dinner at the Tune Inn - and I was going to head over to my *actual* inn." The dad-joke fell flat.

"Where are you staying?" she asked.

"Right around the corner - Capitol Hotel," he said.

"Okay - go drop your stuff and come back!" she commanded. "You've got to come party with us!"

Chip scanned the sidewalk for wardrobe suggestions. Half the guys on the block were in suits, the other half were pretty casual. It seemed to Chip that the trend was getting more casual as the night went on.

"Are you sure it's okay? I don't want to impose..." said Chip politely.

"Oh my god, no, of course you're not imposing," she said. "I'm gonna be mad if you don't come."

"Roger that," said the Marine. "Let me check in and I'll come find you. Right there, yes? The Capitol Lounge?"

"Yep," she said, giving him a hug. "I'm so glad I saw you. See you in a few!" She turned and walked back toward the entrance. He couldn't help checking out her backside as she swished away.

The hotel was even closer than he thought. Chip rushed through the check-in process and made it to his nice, but small quarters. He went straight to the bathroom and turned on the shower to the hottest setting. He then unpacked and hung his shirts and pants on the shower curtain. The idea of a shower sounded pretty good to Chip so he transferred his clothing to another rack and hopped in.

Within twenty minutes of checking in, he had showered and dressed for mini night on the town with Shannon Grady and her friends. Chip decided on wearing plain-front khakis and a crisp white shirt with casual brown ox-fords and matching leather belt.

He looked sharp as he squeezed into the bar while flashing his ID at the bouncer. The place was comfortably loud and the linebacker could hear Phish covering *Good Times, Bad Times* by Zeppelin in the background. The place had a good vibe. It wasn't as grungy as the Tune Inn but it had the same weathered/authentic feel. The clientele was clearly 90% Hill staff, everyone looked good to Chip as he calmly traversed the bar, trying to fit it. He could feel a few *very* friendly eyes on him but he just half-smiled and kept going.

There was an opening between rooms that was crowded, as he made his way into the other wing he felt a hand on his hip. It was Shannon. She hugged him again out of nowhere and kissed him on the corner of his mouth. She had a pretty healthy buzz and it was clear she was somewhat interested in Chip.

She took his hand and walked him toward the back door then pivoted and walked down the stairway that Chip hadn't even noticed. "We're down-stairs," she yelled. "It's quieter down there."

The big guy from Florida was introduced to five other staffers in Shannon's group. He couldn't remember one of their names and had trouble taking his eyes off the girl with the green eyes. Chip could barely feel the effects of the beers he'd had at dinner and was slightly worried about getting back in the game. Just then a delightful fifty something waitress appeared and asked if anyone needed a drink. Shannon told him of a local IPA that he had to try it. Chip complied and gave the lady his credit card to start a tab. Shannon ordered another vodka club and thanked the guy who bought it.

The group encircled Chip as he waited for his beer. They asked him dozens of policy questions that he mostly brushed aside. "Don't be so wonky!" Shannon scolded her pals with a big smile. "They're not usually like this, Chip!"

In the corner of her eye she saw someone leave a small couch alone; she grabbed Chips hand and led him to the spot. She sat down next to him, crossed her legs and leaned in toward him. "I'm so glad you're here - I can't wait till it's official-official. How's the race going?"

"We're doing great! The fundraising is exceeding expectations, our digi-tal operation is - well, you've seen our stuff - and the Republicans are bludgeoning each other on the other side. We're organized and tight. Reynolds is pushing some big buttons for us. I've been focusing on St. Augustine - the coast," said Chip proudly.

"How's your new coms girl?" asked Shannon. "You didn't sleep with her did you?"

The waitress appeared with their drinks before Chip could show her how surprised he was at the forwardness of the question. He hoped she'd forget she asked as he took a double-sip of the fresh beer.

"I like this place!" said Chip approvingly. "Is this pretty much the spot?"

"Definitely!" she said. "It's kept it's way while other places come and go with the trends. I've talked to people who have been coming here for twenty years and they say it's exactly the same. It's kinda like Vegas Chip."

He looked around the room, "why - how's it like Vegas?"

"What happens at the Lounge, *stays at the Lounge*," she said with a wink.

The candidate for Congress felt nervous, he was attracted to Shannon. The bar was packed to the gills with staff from the US House and he was starting to feel targeted. He was in the middle of a successful congressional bid and started to think about bad press and scandalous hit pieces permeating the corners of the Internet. Chip was experienced enough to know that he was one beer away from going to bed with her.

Shannon got up and excused herself as she headed to the ladies room. Chip used the opportunity to check his phone. Reynolds had thanked him for a good showing at the dinner earlier. He had a voicemail from Shana. He couldn't hear it in the bar so he saved it for later.

As he scrolled the news headlines he got a text from Shannon: Meet me at your hotel. Right now.

The alarm went off at six. Chip awoke and scanned his room for the girl from the night before. He was pleased to be alone in his hotel. He stretched and yawned. The pleasure outweighed any negative repercussions he could conjure up. He had been sober enough to recall well the events that had occured in his first twelve hours in Washington.

Chip drained his bladder then found a purple-shaded lip imprint on his cheek. He allowed himself to grin as he wiped it clean with a tissue. After a quick check of his phone, he suited up for a morning run.

At seventy degrees, it felt cool for August - cooler than he was used to. Six-thirty was still too early for D.C. commuters. There were other joggers and some cyclists, but the traffic seemed as easy as the temperature. Chip ran straight for the great domed building that housed the legislative branch. It felt surreal to see the Capitol even though he'd passed it the day before in a car.

He made the left turn before the senate office buildings and ran west toward the National Mall and the Washington Monument. The skyline was incredible and the air was comfortably thin. Chip tried to contain his excitement for his potential future city. He kept thinking about Shannon and what a terrific host she'd already been. He wondered if he could ever be a one-woman guy as he passed multiple cute girls running in the opposite direction.

He made it to the Lincoln Memorial and stopped running. Even though he'd already seen the great structure, it felt like it was his first time. Chip walked and stretched and observed the landscape. Some tourists had gathered and a few people were protesting something. He looked back toward the Washington Monument and took in the beauty of its reflection in the long pool that separated it from the Lincoln. For a brief moment he thought about Cheryl and felt a wave of guilt for having spent the night with Shannon.

The run back to the Hill was just about two and a half miles and it felt easy for Chip. He liked the tiny crushed-rock surface, the tall pin oaks and the museums that flanked the mall. He thought he ran past a petite, woman Senator from the midwest in an ARMY shirt but couldn't be sure.

Chip found a breakfast place near the Capitol Lounge and grabbed a seat at the counter. He had a good sweat going but was decent enough for a public eatery.

The morning rush through D.C. had subsided by 9:30 am. Chip MacIntosh was leaving his hotel in his new navy suit. He had a leather portfolio in one hand and a free cup of coffee in his other. He had given himself thirty minutes to get to the US Capitol.

He entered through a little-known door on the southern edge of the great building. Just as he cleared the security machines he was approached by a 22-year old round kid in a suit. "Are you Charles MacIntosh?" asked the young man with the sweaty forehead.

"Call me Chip!" said the candidate, extending his hand.

"I'm Thomas, I'll be escorting you to the Majority Leader's Office," he said. "Please follow me."

The kid seemed like a robot, Chip automatically decided not to make small talk. He looked the hallways up and down and admired the architecture. Chip smiled at the people he thought were members as he walked next to Thomas.

The Leader's office was large and beautiful as Chip had predicted. The walls were painted red and the furniture looked expensive and tasteful. There were lamps and paintings and nice looking young people wandering around carrying files and briefs.

Thomas led Chip to a side office, told him to have a seat and offered him coffee. Chip declined both and just stood in the room admiring the artwork and floor to ceiling bookshelves. He was eyeing some vintage political history books when someone called his name from behind him.

Two women and three men paraded hurriedly into the room. Everyone exchanged business cards and shook hands and took seats. Chip felt slightly rushed as he explained his background and made his pitch as if they were all casting fall ballots in North Central Florida.

When the candidate finished, the group took turns asking him a series of cryptic questions, mostly having to do with his political ideology. They were the stock issues that separate political party platforms.

Chip could read them. He sensed he was losing them on some of their core issues. He doubled-down on healthcare and the environment - offering them a jolt of progressivism.

A previously unnoticed door near the corner of the room opened and in walked the House Majority Leader.

"Sir, this is Chip MacIntosh, from *Florida*," said one of the staffers.

"Chip, welcome to Washington," said the Leader. "Anthony White, it's great to meet you."

"What an honor, Mr. Majority Leader," replied Chip.

The meeting turned from a panel-style inquisition to a *one on one* between Chip and Leader White. They chatted about families and hometowns and other biographical topics while the Leader's staff listened and nodded.

"I'm glad you're doing this Chip," said the seasoned Member of Congress. "I know it's hard sometimes, but I can promise you, it is worth it. And I think you're going to pull this off. Our youngest member of the caucus!"

The main door to the room opened. The girl in the doorway signaled to the boss that it was time for his next meeting. The big linebacker couldn't take his eyes off her. She was darker skinned and had black hair that fell just beneath her shoulders. She had dark eyes and her off-white outfit seemed perfectly tailored to her voluptuous figure.

"Mari this is Chip MacIntosh from the great state of Florida," said the Leader.

Chip stood up and walked over to the door, he extended his hand and self-introduced himself to her with a smile. She was flattered but turned to her boss and gave him the look.

Leader White shook hands with Chip again and offered to help him in any way. The Floridian thanked him and said goodbye.

The original conversation with the staff members resumed. Chip was more relaxed by having already met with the majority leader. He was thinking that he liked Anthony White and he was hoping that wasn't the last he'd seen of Mari.

He spent the rest of the time attempting to charm the group. Reynolds' lobbyist friends had told Chip to warm up to them. These weren't Gator fans though, they were dialed in on the issues, policies, and processes. They seemed very "D.C." to Chip. He wondered if the member offices were as serious as the leadership offices appeared to be.

The group wrapped up with standards and suggestions. Their final suggestions were about serving in Congress as opposed to running for Congress. One of them asked Chip if he needed to be escorted out and he politely declined, opting to look around the Capitol.

He wandered for as long as he could, taking in the beauty of sculptures, busts, paintings and architecture. The visitor pass he had clipped to his lapel was only valid with a staff escort. A capitol police officer asked Chip where his escort was. Chip had to explain that he was unaccompanied and in the nicest way conceivable, the guard escorted him to the main exit.

He had a two o'clock meeting at Congressman Reynolds' office, giving him time to grab a quick bite and head over to the Rayburn House Office Building with enough time to clear security and make it to room 2554.

The large mahogany double door was open. The office was flanked with the Stars and Stripes and the Florida flag, which was customary for house offices. Some offices added Prisoner of War-Missing in Action banners and some had the LGBT rainbow flag. Reynolds prefered state and country and had the standard bronze name plate displaying his state and district.

Chip was greeted by a friendly staff assistant at the front desk. She was a nice-looking woman with short gray hair and tan, freckled shoulders. She knuckle-tapped the door to the Chief of Staff. David W. Jasper flung open his door and welcomed Chip into his office.

They had spoken only briefly when the Congressman entered through a side door. Reynolds kept his voice low as he recapped some of their dinner conversation the night before. Bob wanted David to know some of the details before they grew the meeting to include the rest of the staff.

Jasper rattled off a few other names of folks with close ties to the office, some of their interests, and he coached Chip to call him any time if he had questions about constituents who claimed to know his boss.

They answered a few of Chip's questions about his campaign style and echoed their support for his candidacy. The three men shook hands and made their way into the member's private office. It was large and had a partial view of the Capitol. Chip figured they could see the entire complex once the leaves dropped in the fall. He also knew this was the office of a veteran Congressman. If he was lucky enough to carry the torch of the district, he'd more than likely be stashed in the fifth floor of the Cannon House Office Building.

Reynolds had deep blue carpeting and nice leather furniture. The walls were eggshell white and were adorned with historical objects including a vintage poster from a cannery in Palatka. There was evidence of citrus, Seminole Indians, the Gators, and other vintage Florida artifacts. Chip started thinking about the sort of office he'd have if elected. Reynolds' taste was exemplary.

David darted out and returned with the rest of the staff. Chip focused heavily on knowing everyone's name. Everyone was older than he was, it felt surreal. A summer intern had been placed at the front desk to welcome unexpected visitors.

It was friendly. No one had tough questions for Chip and they seemed eager to get to know him personally. There was very little discussion about policy. Reynolds used the time primarily to introduce his staff. He had a little story about each of them and it sounded almost like a roasting.

From what Chip could tell, it was like a family. It also seemed like a small company to him; everyone had a specific contribution to making the wheels go around. From a personality standpoint, he felt like he could work with everyone in the room.

What Chip didn't realize was that the Reynolds crew all worked for a senior member of the House of Representatives. He obviously knew he was a long-serving member, but didn't realize the implications. In Washington, D.C., going from a senior member to a twenty-five year old freshman carried with it a significant drop in prestige for a Capitol Hill operator. The team didn't show any sign of this though, they'd all have Reynolds and Chip believe that they would stick around if the football player from Gainesville assumed command of their worlds. Reynolds was optimistic, but he knew how D.C. worked.

The Congressman walked Chip to the reception area, introduced him to their summer intern and stepped into the corridor. "Well, what do you think?" he asked his protege.

"It's all so - exciting Sir," said Chip. "It makes me want to get back to the district and work harder.

"You want to be here, then?" said Reynolds.

"I don't know if I'm the perfect guy for this job, but I definitely want to try and find out," Chip paused for a second. "I get the feeling the shoes I am trying to fill are bigger than I thought. How'd you think it went with the staff?"

They were totally alone in the hall. "I think it went great, I can tell the team likes you. Son, they can help you - just like our friends from last night. This town - everyone needs help. I don't care who they are - everyone needs some kind of assistance. The second you think you can go it alone, the second you fail."

"I didn't think I connected with-" Chip started.

"I know what you're going to say - don't worry about it. It is what it is," said the Congressman. "How'd it go with the Leaders' office?"

"Very well, I'd say," replied Chip. "You haven't heard from anyone over there?"

"Nah. Nothing," said Reynolds. "Hey, I've gotta return some calls, you're heading back tonight, right?"

"Yessir - the hotel let me keep my luggage there after I checked out. I'll just go grab my gear and head to the airport," said Chip.

"Good deal - get back there and knock some doors," he instructed. "Just keep doing what you're doing kid - it'll all work out. I feel good about this."

Chapter Twenty

A September poll showed Chip with a five point lead over his Republican opponent. Bill Lowe was a New Jersey transplant to St. Augustine. He was the "it's his turn" candidate. After years of fundraising and volunteer wrangling, Bill was always the frontrunner in the GOP primary. He'd served on the city council and wound up serving the remaining term of a state rep who died in office. He later ran for state senate and got crushed by a former prosecutor.

The Republicans had recruited him to run against Reynolds twice - twelve years earlier - but was bested twice by the popular Democrat. The Republican faithful were certain he could beat the kid from Gainesville if he could coast through his contentious primary.

Chip was in full-time-plus-overtime mode. He walked the neighborhoods all day and worked the phones all night. He showed up at everything with a camera rolling. The opinion letters to the local papers were a constant force. Shana had developed three template letters and they were working with the older folks.

Jay stayed true to his talents, building the biggest network of voters a congressional race had ever seen. The digital campaign was as robust as the old school grassroots tactics. Jay had even pulled up dirt on Chip's opponent that no political firm could have found, but his older brother wouldn't use it.

Chip's visit to DC had yielded an influx of fresh capital - enough to help out with Rosie Lawson's victory office operation. Chip was gaining points with the party for sharing the fruits of his charisma and drive.

Cheryl was mostly absent for the final push. She was giving him the space he didn't ask for, but knew he needed. Chip was too busy for romance.

Shana still lived with Chip. Both of them had secretly considered a fling but the situation, as convenient as it would have seemed, never presented itself. They fell asleep working almost every night. It was an exercise in restraint, rare for Chip in spite of his eagle scout facade.

On Sundays, Chip tried to attend a different church service every week. If he was in Gainesville, he tried to have Sunday dinner with his folks. Shana would join the MacIntoshes from time to time.

The last thing Chip wanted to do was have a televised debate with a guy twice his age; not to mention someone with thirty years of experience in politics. Alas, the campaigns agreed to it and selected a date at the advice of the parties.

Bill Lowe's people wanted to have the debate in St. Augustine - at the community center. Team MacIntosh obviously wanted it held in Gainesville. Jay had called his older brother "Are you okay with a coin toss?" Chip said "sure, *tails*."

Jay and Rosie drove half-way to St. Augustine and met their enemy counterparts at a Publix Supermarket. They agreed to flip a Kennedy Half-Dollar on the covered, green painted sidewalk. Jay yelled "TAILS" and Lowe's guy flipped the large coin into the air. "TAAAAAAILS" yelled Rosie excitedly. The four people shook hands and agreed to hold the debate in Gainesville.

Jay offered to buy everyone a sandwich at Publix but they politely declined and hopped in a Volvo SUV and took off to the east. Rosie said she could grab a few items in the store if Jay wanted to have a quick sandwich. The soon-to-be college senior agreed and dipped in to the deli to grab a number.

He was finishing up a Boar's Head Italian when Rosie approached with two paper bags of groceries. She smiled at the young man and asked him if he was ready. The kid grabbed his large iced tea, chucked his sandwich wrapper and escorted the woman to his squeaky old Explorer.

They spent their thirty-five minute ride back to Gainesville discussing debate strategy. Jay thought half of what she was saying sounded antiquated. He still listened intently, though he was pretty sure Shana would have an updated perspective.

Jay had spent hours watching debates on YouTube, from city council races to presidential elections. And he didn't just watch the actual debates, he watched the expert commentary afterward.

Chip was in the Victory Office when Jay and Rosie returned from the coin toss. He was in his shared (with Shana) office making phone calls. Jay entered while Rosie peeled off toward the kitchenette with her provisions. He closed the door when his older brother was off the phone.

"The debate..." Jay began, "will be held - in *Gainesville*."

"Yes!" Chip whispered loudly.

Jay smiled proudly, "yea, pretty cool. I can get at least 250 MacIntosh-yelling undergraduates in there."

"Good," said Shana, "but we've got to set up a mock debate like right away. I think Shannon is coming down for the prep; she's taken quite an interest in this race for some reason. Where would the site be? The location."

"The college, right?" asked Chip. "Shannon is coming?"

"Of course the college," replied Jay. "We'll have at the Reitz Union - I can get us in there any time to do the prep. We'll know the temperature, the lighting, etc. You can do press in the lobby - they have those director chairs like on CNN."

Chip tilted his head down slightly and stared at his abused desk calendar. He hadn't been that nervous since his first stump speech. He thought about Cheryl and how on so many occasions she had given him a little push, a little extra confidence.

"Do we know the date yet?" asked the candidate.

"October 28th," Jay said.

"Shit that's like two weeks," said Chip. "We've got to get started right away. Jay, can you find out if there's anything going on in St. Augustine that night? And figure out how to promote it?"

"You want to divert the eastern half of the district?" asked Shana.

"No good?" asked Chip.

Shana shook her head, "No good. I'll check with the party but I think the better tactic is to promote the debate and kick the guy's ass on stage. In your hometown. You're a fucking *Marine* and a football star - what in the hell are you scared of?"

"I'm not afraid," said Chip calmly. "One of the things that has made me successful in certain areas is my ability to know my strengths and my weaknesses. I can promise you that debating a guy like Bill Lowe is not one of my strengths, but you're right about the strategy. I guess it's less about the debate and more about what people are saying about the debate."

"Exactly," said Shana. "We'll get some friendly reporters in that lobby and try to spin any blunders or missteps. I've got you covered. And you're right about one thing, we've got to get to work on this right away. Jay, we're going to need more people in here making calls. Shannon is coming down here and we're going to get the big guy back on the practice field."

A week later, they were in the Reitz Student Union with podiums and lights and some volunteer audience members. Les Lockhart was playing the part of Bill Lowe and Chip, the political novice, was playing the role of a seasoned debater. Shannon and Shana were at a folding table asking questions. Jay and his boys were just off stage behind a tall burgundy curtain.

The girls grilled both men but Chip got the tougher questions about his age, his lack of experience, and they even blasted him on why he even wanted to be a Member of Congress. They pressed him on the issues, one by one.

Les took a few cheap shots at Chip, forcing him to admit how green he was on economic and healthcare matters. "I don't see how we can put the care of our elderly population in the hands of someone who finished school less than six months ago," he declared. "Maybe we should send him back to run for the UF Senate."

"The problem," Chip replied, "is that YOU fit the mold of the average member of the House of Representatives and look where that's gotten us! America - this Congressional District - needs a fresh perspective and I'm - that's what I am offering? Wait.."

It wasn't a terrible answer. Shannon rolled her eyes slightly and moved on. They questioned the participants for another hour and finally called it a night. The participants filed out of the auditorium while Chip and his team stayed to discuss.

"I could use a beer," said Chip.

"Same," said Les.

"There's a bar off the lobby, it's like right there," offered Jay.

Les, Chip, Shannon, Jay and Shana found a table just off the lobby and ordered two cold pitchers of Sierra. A fried sampler of onion rings, mozzarella sticks and waffle fries showed up courtesy of the bartender, who knew Jay from the dorm freshman year.

The group talked strategy until the beer kicked in, then they started talking about all sorts of general topics. Les Lockhart was the first to leave. As a fifty-something politico he felt more than a little out of place slinging draft beer on a college campus. "Great work everyone," he said. "Chip, Jay - I'll call ya."

Shannon was staying through the debate. She set up shop at the Victory Office and worked with Chip daily on the final push. Jay and his buddies were spending their days getting people to vote early while Shana continued to book news hits and answer reporters' questions via email.

Lowe had a letter a day of support hit the papers; all of them mercilessly attacking his opponent's lack of real-world experience.

Chip's mother was no longer able to look at the negative letters. Mary spent much of her time during the final weeks of the campaign writing letters to friends. She was checking in with people she knew and she was making a last minute plea for their support of her son. Both Mary and Charles had become regulars at the Victory Office - making calls and brewing fresh coffee for the volunteers. They had also donated food and folding chairs on a continual basis. Charles was lousy on the phone, he didn't have a normal person's inflection after so many years in front of History scholars. He preferred delivering signs, he could drive out into the country and puff on a cigar between stops. And he liked the way old country music sounded in Chip's vintage Toyota.

The stress of the debate was starting to weigh on Chip again. With the big showdown just a day away, he felt the need to release some tension. He tried a two hour workout, more than his usual routine of a long run and a hundred pushups. It didn't do the trick. He wanted to spend the night with Cheryl - nothing could be more relaxing. He worried she'd say no, they'd barely spoken. He decided to call her.

She couldn't resist and Chip awoke the next day in Cheryl's arms.

They avoided all of the negative and emotional connotations of what they'd just done. She had realized that he'd met some of her physical needs and knew it wasn't the time for feelings. Still, Chip felt a little guilty for what he viewed as having slightly used her to relieve sexual tension.

"Hey," she said as she opened her eyes and stretched.

"Hey there," he said softly with a smile.

"You doing better?" she asked.

He nodded. "I'm tired Cher."

"I know," she said. "It's almost over though. You look different."

"What do you mean - different?" he asked.

"Compared to the first time I woke up with you - that guy seems like a kid now - in retrospect," she said. "And now you're this... maybe I shouldn't say it... Man?"

It was a compliment but somehow it creeped him out. "Thanks? I guess."

"What?" she asked slowly, "I think you've matured a lot since we first met. Look, a lot has happened since New Orleans. You're not upset are you? I didn't mean that to sound rude."

"No, I'm just uh - it sounds weird when you say 'man' like that," he said. "I'm not upset."

"Good!" she said. Cheryl slipped out of bed, stashed her hair in a pony-tail holder and slid her nude body into a silk, Hawaiian-themed robe. "I'll make breakfast."

He knew he had to stay for breakfast.

Chip sat in a greenroom backstage with Shannon, everyone else was working the crowd.

"How are you feeling?" she asked. "You look like JFK - I mean, really sharp."

"Thanks I feel pretty great. I'm prepared, whatever happens - happens," he said. "I'm ready. I worked out earlier, I'm well rested."

Shannon snickered a little as she sipped a can of Diet Coke.

"What?" he asked in a friendly, inquisitive tone.

"I heard you didn't come home last night," she said without looking at him.

"Oh, yeah," he replied, "I crashed at my parents house," he lied.

"Chip you don't have to lie to me Honey," she said. "I'm on your side."

"How'd you know?" he asked.

"Because - you look like you got some action last night. I'm not stupid," she said. "I'm actually glad, I think it's healthy - I wish I got laid last night. You look like a movie star right now. You needed it."

He just smirked a little.

"Was it the hot blonde in the orange dress - from that house party?" she asked.

Chip blushed a little and nodded, "yep."

"Is she your girlfriend?" asked Shannon.

"Not really," he said. "I don't know what we are. We were together but it didn't really work out. Sometimes we connect though."

"Chip we never really talked about our tryst in D.C., you probably think that's a regular thing for me - and I'm sure everyone says this but that's not typical behavior for me."

"It's not typical behavior for me either," he said. "It was fun though. Right?"

"Totally!" she said. "And, no regrets."

"Cool," said Chip, returning to his laminated list of talking points.

Shannon wasn't done. "Are you in love with her?" she asked.

Chip tapped his gold pen on his legal pad and looked up at her eyes "Probably," he said. "The timing just - it isn't ideal. Can we talk about this some other time though?"

"Of course," she said. "I didn't mean to push you. I'm sorry."

"No apologies," he said. "I just want to get through this damn debate." He wondered if Cheryl was in attendance. They had not covered what she was doing with her evening.

Jay and Shana walked into the room. "Ready Chip?"

"Yea," said Chip unenthusiastically.

"We're gonna walk out into that other greenroom area, meet your opponent, shake hands or whatever and then you'll both be announced," instructed Jay.

"Okay let's do this!" exclaimed Shana. "You got this Chip."

The Republican opponent had a similar but older gang with him. He wore a navy blazer with gold buttons and a pair of gray dress slacks. He wore his white oxford with an open collar to make room for his oversized neck. He had no discernable chin and his hair was mostly white with a splash of brown dye. Bill Lowe was finishing up with a reporter when Chip approached with his hand out.

Chip was a half foot taller and in way better shape. The cameras were rolling.

"Mr. Lowe, it's nice to meet you sir, I'm Chip MacIntosh," said the Democrat in the dark suit.

"Yea, sure Chip, it's nice to see you," he replied. "I'd like you to meet my bride, Janice."

"It's a pleasure Mrs. Lowe. *Janice*... Been some contest Mr. Lowe, I want to thank you in advance for a spirited debate," said Chip over the sound of clicking cameras.

"You betcha - shall we do this?" replied Lowe, extending his hand for another gentlemanly embrace.

Chip shook his hand and noticed his opponents eyes rolling back in his head. "Bill are you okay?" asked Chip. "Bill?"

The older man spun around and hit the floor with a loud thud.

"Someone call EMS!" yelled Chip as he threw his portfolio to the side, knelt over the man and checked his vitals. "He's having a heart attack - go find aspirin!"

Chip went to work providing chest compressions and mouth to mouth resuscitation. Bill's wife ran over and screamed loudly. The audience in the auditorium got eerily quiet. Others rushed to the backstage area and started asking questions. Everyone stood in shock. The debate was cancelled just after Bill Lowe was brought through the main lobby on a gurney.

People gathered around the Marine to thank him and show support. Chip looked like he'd just seen a ghost. His tie was loose and his whole head looked disheveled. He was breathing heavily and looking around nervously. Shannon's brother suffered from PTSD and she knew the signs - she quickly whisked Chip away to their original greenroom - yelling for everyone to get out of the way.

Jay worked on crowd control while Shana began drafting a statement on her iPad Mini. Les was off to the side, trying to think of a situation that even remotely resembled a politician saving the life of their opponent - with the cameras rolling.

Shannon got her candidate alone. He seemed out of sorts. "Chip I want you to drink this," she said, handing him a bottle of Voss water she'd pulled from her tote bag.

He complied and took a sip, staring blankly at a wall. Shannon took off her jacket and undid one of the buttons on her blouse without Chip seeing. She walked to the door, opened it and told someone not to let anyone in.

She sat across the table from Chip and tried to look sexier than serious. She tried to look cool and calm, avoiding direct eye contact. A text came through from Shana: "Prior to tonight's scheduled debate, Mr. Lowe and

Mr. MacIntosh were exchanging friendly greetings when Mr. Lowe showed signs of a medical struggle. Mr. Lowe fell to the floor and seemingly stopped breathing. Mr. MacIntosh, without hesitation, administered life-saving practices he learned during his time in the military. Paramedics from Gainesville and University EMS arrived and transported Mr. Lowe to an unknown location for additional care."

She didn't want to ask Chip if it worked for him. She texted her friend back: "Perfect, attribute to the MacIntosh Campaign."

"Will do - they want to talk to him. Is he ok?" Shana texted back.

"Not sure but he def needs a few min" wrote Shannon.

Shana: "Call the hospital so you can say he was worried"

Shannon: "Ok good call - send Jay in here."

Chip's phone buzzed. It was Cheryl. Shannon listened intently without trying to be obvious. The Marine answered a few questions then asked her to come to where he was. He said Jay would find her at the entrance to the secure area and escort her back to him.

"Shannon could you give me a few minutes," asked Chip, checking Twitter for Bill's condition. "Of course," she said. As she was walking out, Jay and Cheryl walked in. Shannon studied the blonde woman then slipped into the main hallway.

Cheryl looked like an undercover cop. Her hair was looped through the back of a low-profile, orange Gators cap. She had on a weathered denim top and a pair of white jeans that displayed a trendy, needlepoint cloth belt. Her sandals were the color of her top and trimmed in white to match her pants.

"You okay Chip?" asked Cheryl more like a friend than a lover. "I think you saved the guy's life."

Chip walked up and hugged her, "he made it?"

"Well he was breathing when he left - someone said," replied Cheryl. "MacIntosh you're a hero - but in a vastly different way."

"What?" he asked humbly.

"They were filming it - civilians saw and *will see* you bringing your political opponent back from death," she said. "This isn't some battlefield in the desert where only one guy saw it and never told anyone."

Jay walked to the door to give them some privacy, "Nice work Chip," he said. "It'd shock me if his wife didn't vote for you next week. I'll be in the hallway."

Cheryl took a seat next to Chip and tossed her baseball cap on the large conference table. "You okay?"

"Yes," he said, looking at her pretty eyes. "I actually got a little freaked out for a minute - admittedly. I'm okay. You good?"

She smiled without teeth and nodded. She took his hand in hers. "You obviously won this debate Babe. And I think it's fair to say you probably won the election. The headlines tomorrow are going to read: Chip MacIntosh Saves Life of Opponent Prior to Gainesville Debate. That communications girl with the black hair is probably talking to the *Tonight Show* producer right this second. This thing is *o-verr*."

Chapter Twenty One

It was a complete blowout. Charles Robert MacIntosh III won his district by margins that exceeded his predecessor, the Honorable Robert Reynolds. Chip was surrounded by friends and family and supporters and was on top of the world. He stood in disbelief as he promised the audience at his victory speech that he'd never stop working for the people of North Central Florida. The crowd cheered and clapped as he stepped off the stage amid the spray of champagne, balloons, and confetti.

The party was held at the Florida Theater in downtown Gainesville. Jay had rigged a camera so that supporters in St. Augustine could watch the speech live. The Gainesville Team could also watch their east coast counterparts on monitors as well. It was exciting and surreal.

Chip's parents had booked an after party. *The Swamp* had never been completely closed for a private event before. By nine o'clock, the place was filled with nearly two hundred of the MacIntoshes closest friends and supporters.

The elder Charles MacIntosh tried not to think about the associated costs as he watched people leave the bar with two or three drinks at a time. He was pleased to see that Chip was situated around a hightop table with his oldest friends, the guys who first talked to Chip about running back at the family ranch. Pete, Jimmy, and Walt were telling stories and slapping each other on the shoulders. Charles was proud of his son and how'd he won over his best confidants.

Mary was encircled by a few of her local favorites, along with some new friends she'd made through her son's campaign. She was in a tan dress with an American Flag-themed scarf with yellow accents and a fair amount of gold jewelry on.

Jay was over in a corner with his crew of underclassmen campaign aides. He looked like he was a visiting professor - schooling his pals on the ways of the world. There were even a few girls seemingly paying close attention to his oration.

Charles turned to the front door and saw a familiar sight, it was the striking Cheryl West. She had on a dark blouse with a khaki skirt. Her hair was down but looked different somehow, it fell on her exposed collarbones. The top looked open but not terribly revealing. Cheryl looked pretty and confident as usual. Charles watched for Chip's reaction to her.

As predicted, the woman stopped him in his tracks. The Congressman-elect looked upon her like she was a 1957 Corvette on a street full of grubby middle schoolers in band uniforms. She had a glow. Charles' buddies caught on and collectively inquired about the blonde in the black top.

Cheryl saw Charles unattended and went straight to him. She gave the professor a hug and they chatted for a bit about their favorite football player - equally careful not to broach the topic of whether she and the junior MacIntosh would be *together*.

Chip wasn't the only one eyeing Cheryl from afar. Shannon Grady watched with intrigue, perhaps disdain as she sipped on a gin-based cocktail.

"I guess this is good for business, tonight's win?" Charles speculated.

"Most definitely," replied the Director of Alumni Affairs. "We'll put this out in the morning newsletter - amplify it on social media. A total win-win. He's not the first one to go to Congress, of course. However, he's the only one who looked like... like *him*."

Chip appreciated that his greatest love interest was talking to his father and he figured it was the perfect opportunity to say hello to her. Charles watched as he made his way over to their side of the room. Chip had removed his tie and jacket and his sleeves were rolled up. He had a cold IPA in his left hand and used his right hand for fist-bumps, high-fives and handshakes. His face looked happy and his hair was disheveled with a splash of sweat around the edges of his face.

He went straight for the woman. She threw her arms around him and planted her lips on the side of his face. They hugged long enough for Charles to smile and turn away slightly.

"I'm so happy for you MacIntosh!" she said enthusiastically.

"I can't believe it's - real - this is crazy!" he half-yelled.

"Hey dad," Chip said without really looking at him. Charles just smiled and took a small sip of scotch.

Chip desperately wanted to stay eye-locked with Cheryl for a few minutes but the party attendees were too fired up to give Chip a free pass. He was being repeatedly bombarded with well-wishers and bear hugs.

Cheryl politely stepped to the side to give the Congressman-elect some room to visit with his people. She contemplated joining Mary's little posse then decided against it. Cheryl had wondered if Mary even liked her. On more than one occasion she caught Chip's mother giving her the evil eye. Her theory was that her son couldn't possibly take her seriously due to their age gap. Not to mention the fact that her kid was running for Congress and surely she wouldn't want anyone to derail his chances.

Cheryl felt awkward standing alone so she gravitated toward two of the women who helped the Marine get elected: Shannon and Shana. They had all met before but had never spent enough time together to build any sort of relationship. The conversation centered around Cheryl's work at the university. Shannon was slightly bitchy.

Chip looked over at the trio and got just a tad uncomfortable. He decided to give an impromptu speech. He stood up on a chair and attempted to whistle with his hand and mouth - it didn't work but the crowd realized his intentions and they got quiet enough for remarks.

"What a night! Thank you all for being here, for the tireless support and hard work! I especially want to thank my brother Jay and Shana and the staff - and Rosie Lawson... I also want to thank my opponent, Mr. Lowe, for a great contest and for running a clean operation - I wish him the best and hope to be able to work with him in my new role. I never thought I'd be standing on a chair in The Swamp - addressing a big crowd of people who just helped get me elected to the House seat held by my friend *and mentor* - The Honorable Robert Reynolds! And to be across the street from the greatest institution of higher learning *on the planet* - GOOOO GATORS!!!" The crowd clapped and cheered. Chip continued, "I want everyone to know - that - that - I plan to deliver for all of you. I know I've got big shoes to fill up there, but I WON'T LET YOU DOWN! Now... before I let y'all get back to your conversation - first - a heartfelt thank you to my mother and father - Mary and Charles MacIntosh!" Chip waited for the clapping to slow down. "Thank you for your love and support over the years - and for this incredible party!" The Congressman-elect jumped down and walked to his folks for hugs.

The short speech worked, Cheryl had broken free from the other women. "Director!" he yelled as he freed himself from his parents and walked toward her.

"Hello Mr. MacIntosh," she said.

"What are you drinking?" he asked her.

"Whitfield Cab," replied Cheryl. "It's *remarkable*. I paid for it."

"Why?" he asked, "it's not a cash bar - mom and dad are covering this."

"Are you in love with me Chip?" she asked him out of nowhere.

He looked around and realized he was basically alone with her, "of course I am. Aren't you?"

"Yes," she said, struggling with how to continue the conversation. She wanted to ask him what their next move was but she didn't want to diminish the elation he was experiencing. Cheryl was too good natured and mature to inquire about their future during his victory party.

"You look really sharp tonight," he said.

"Thank you," she said. "You look pretty sharp too. Hey - how about lunch tomorrow? Do you have plans?"

"I have a call at ten that I have to be on. I should be okay for lunch," he said. "But..."

"But what?" she asked.

"Well, what are you doing for - breakfast?" he asked with a slight grin.

She smiled a little "Chip you're going to be here awhile Honey. I'm going to bed pretty soon."

"Not true!" he assured her. "We only have this place for another twenty-five minutes."

"That's just the open bar, people are going to stay - and they're going to be salty if you're not sticking around with them to celebrate. You're still in campaign mode buddy."

He bit his bottom lip and nodded, she was right. "Yea," he said slowly.

"I'm gonna split. Have fun - enjoy this. You earned it. I still can't believe the debate - everyone I've talked to - has asked me about that," she said.

"Same here," he said. "Where should we get lunch?"

"McAllisters?" suggested Cheryl.

"Kinda far," he said, initially forgetting that was the first place they dined together in Gainesville. "What if we got subs and met at Lake Alice?"

"The bench at the end of frat row?" she asked.

"Perfect," he said. "I'll see you there at 12. Text me your order and I'll grab it at Joes." He hugged her and put a kiss on her cheek.

Chip spent the next thirty minutes talking to everyone who he thought would leave when the free alcohol tab was over - the older and certainly the younger people in the restaurant. It was the same conversation with everyone, the Congressman-elect was getting tired of his own voice. Plus he was exhausted. Even in his ideal physical condition, the race had weighed on him.

He was wrong about whether the guests would linger. At the top of the hour, everyone started clearing out. Most people said they had to be at work in the morning as they shook hands with their next Congressman. Even Charles' friends from Miami headed for their hotels.

Shana approached Chip with the "media opportunity" look on her face. "My phone is lighting up Chip - what do we want to do tomorrow? I booked the local NBC and ABC at noon - tentatively. They need to know. Yes, right?"

"Uh huh," said Chip slowly. He was going to have to cancel his lunch plans.

"We also need to talk about the next week and month and stuff. With Shannon," said Shana.

"Sure thing," said Chip. "Sounds good."

He stepped aside and called Cheryl, "I can't do lunch tomorrow."

"Then we better do breakfast," she said. "I'll wait up, come celebrate."

Chapter Twenty Two

It was one of those rare November days that pulled people from their offices to outdoor cafes and park benches for lunch. The sun was bright and the temperature was pleasant at 64 degrees with little more than a gentle breeze.

Chip had flown up to D.C. the day before with Les Lockhardt to conduct the business of an incoming Congressman.

They were seated at a table overlooking the Washington Channel with David Jasper, who had joined them at their meeting with Rep. John Angel from Oregon. The restaurant was called *Porto* and had a Spanish/Portugal seafood vibe.

Chip was spreading butter on a roll when Congressman Reynolds walked alone into the dining area.

"Don't get up gentlemen," he said as he made his way to the open chair.

Les got up anyway, "Sir I'm Les Lockhart, we met once or twice over the years - I worked with Graham in the old days."

Reynolds shook his hand, "delighted."

"Les was a big help to me this past year Sir," offered Chip before returning to his bread.

The Congressman handed his coat to a fast-moving busboy and took his seat.

"None of this was here when I got to town all those years ago. In fact, none of this was here five years ago," said Reynolds, admiring the view of the channel. "David - you remember when we used to buy fish down there - and crabs?"

"I sure do," said his Chief of Staff. "We had to run to the crab shack and back to avoid getting shot."

"They did a great job with this development," said the Congressman. "Boats and dogs and families everywhere - young people sipping wine and ordering boards full of cheese. Les, where's home now?"

"I'm down in Boca Raton," said Les, returning his hot tea to its saucer.

"Yea," said Reynolds, "so you know. You keep a boat down there?"

"I'm in that fortunate category - my best friend has a twenty-five Regulator and a very small freezer," replied Lockhart with a raised eyebrow.

"Thata boy - great boat, first-rate - especially where you are," replied the legislator. "And Chip! Man how's it feel to be up here knowing you're actually going to be a freshman Congressman from the state we all call home? You guys meet with Angel?"

"I'm sure everyone says this, but it feels surreal," replied Chip. "I don't even think it's kicked in yet."

Jasper spoke up, "he couldn't believe people knew who he was Bob. One young lady asked him for a selfie. And, yes, we did the Blue Dog meeting."

"Chip that selfie stuff is going to be out of control; I hope you know that," said the Congressman. "You've been on national television - late night too. And you're all over the damn internet."

A waiter with slicked black hair appeared with another bottle of pre-chilled tap water. "Are you gentlemen ready to order?"

"Paella for four please," chirped the old man. "That okay with everyone?"

"Of course," they all said, as if they'd planned on it.

"Also," said Reynolds slowly, "bring us a round of those little draft beers with the red-logoed glasses.

"Absolutely," replied the waiter as he spun around and walked away.

Bob Reynolds had told Chip months prior about the Blue Dog Coalition, a group of 25 Congressional Democrats who lean right on fiscal policies.

"He's in, right David?" asked the boss.

"He is," said Jasper.

"Sir, I just want to thank you for your help with that," said Chip. "I appreciate it and I think, based on what everyone has said, that I'll be a good fit for the group. I'll help out however I can."

The Member nodded and sipped ice water.

"Angel loved him," said David, "they've got a lot in common with guns and the football. We took care of some administrative items as well - he got his credentials and - oh, he got his office - *Cannon*."

"You two headed to K Street on this visit?" the Congressman asked in the respective directions of Chip and Les.

Lockhart cleared his throat and explained that he had lined up a few meetings with some trade association reps and a few friends from the Hill in the old days.

"Chip you just remember to listen and not do much talking," said Reynolds. "It's like your first visit up here with my guys. You listen, you nod. And if you have questions, don't hesitate to call me or the other guys here at this table for clarification."

He paused when the food arrived and allowed the restaurant staff to present the food in its proper form.

He continued when the waitstaff left: "I've told you my thoughts on this town and how things get done and I know Les wouldn't steer you wrong, but people are going to be after you - and they're not 300-pound lineman this time. You won't see them coming. Could be a beautiful girl from California."

Chip nodded and wondered what the California reference meant. "This looks incredible! PIE-EH-UHHHH!" He sounded like a boxing ring announcer.

The older guys just smirked at the fact that Chip was excited for the dish in front of him, he sounded like a trained bird. The men made small talk between bites of seafood and sips of beer. There were miniature character assassinations and a decent amount of laughter until Reynolds casually asked how Cheryl was doing.

Chip didn't expect to explain Cheryl, he could barely even remember telling him about her.

He washed down some burned rice and faced his mentor.

"We haven't seen each other very much," he said, hoping it wasn't somehow the wrong answer. "Have I mentioned her since you and I met back in January? I didn't realize - you remembered her name?"

"You haven't seen her much because of the campaign schedule or some other reason?" pressed Reynolds.

Chip could sense he was serious and tried not to screw up, "she's an incredible woman, I just - well sir - the timing isn't ideal - right now."

"What's she say about it?" asked the Congressman.

Chip dabbed his mouth with his linen napkin, "I haven't quite asked her."

Reynolds didn't look up from his lunch.

Chip searched the other men for answers. Les made the "I don't know Buddy" face and David Jasper just quickly shook his head as if to say "don't push it."

David changed the subject, "Chip and I spoke about my sticking around in January. I told him it would be an honor to continue to serve the people of Florida by his side."

"Well there's some good news," said Reynolds with a respectable nod.

The men remained relatively quiet for the rest of the event. Les offered to get the check but Reynolds waived him off. "David, why don't you and Mr. Lockhart head out, I want to spend a few minutes with MacIntosh."

"Great idea," said Les, rising from the table. "Congressman, thank you for the exceptional lunch, I enjoyed it very much and look forward to seeing you again. Chip, call me later, take your time."

Reynolds pulled a small piece of paper from his shirt pocket and studied it through his reading glasses. "Chip," he said, "let's take a walk."

The men got up from the table, retrieved their outerwear and found their way to the waterfront promenade along the channel. The Congressman pointed out a number of impressive watercraft lining the yacht basin as they walked. Many of the larger boats had already been winterized for the season, this meant they were shrink-wrapped in white plastic sheathing.

Chip looked up as a large flock of Canada geese flew over. The Congressman stopped walking.

"Everything okay sir?" Chip asked as he put his hand on his mentor's shoulder.

"I must say I was a little stunned to hear about Cheryl," he said while continuing the walk.

Chip wondered why Reynolds was so worried about his love life, "I'm not sure what you mean. Are you upset that we're not together-together?"

"No," said Bob, "I know it's none of my business Chip, but I was pulling for you two. Did she ever tell you we met?"

"When?" asked Chip, feeling somewhat betrayed that he didn't know they'd met before.

"She told me not to tell you - thought it would mess with your head," said the Congressman. "We met at a school function this summer, I don't know where you were." He paused while a large helicopter flew past them in the channel. "I liked her from the minute you told me the story kid. When I met her in person - I thought she was one of the most elegant young women I'd ever met."

"How come neither of you told me you met?" asked Chip.

"Her idea," he answered. "I actually don't know."

The Marine noticed the Congressman fidgeting with a pipe and a Zippo lighter, he looked around to see if anyone was watching.

"I'm retiring," said Reynolds, "no one cares if I puff a pipe on my lunch break."

They continued their stroll.

Chip returned to the conversation, "It's not about her Congressman - she's not the problem - at all. If she was a 27 year-old staff assistant for a Member from - Indiana or something... I'd be with her. But she's down there and I'm about to be up here and she's ready to get married. I'm just - not - ready for all of that. I'll be twenty-five in two weeks and I've got my whole life ahead of me. It's a timing issue, I'm not ready to get married and have a family right now."

"That's bullshit Chip," said Reynolds. "Were you ready to be a Marine? A football captain? Hell, you think you're ready to be a goddam Congressman?"

"With all due respect, those are all short term commitments!" Chip retorted. "Hell I was in the Corps for three years - captain for two and Congress is a two-year deal. If I screw up in Congress it's most assuredly a two-year commitment."

Reynolds turned to face Chip, he took a quick puff of his pipe and looked him in the eyes, "If I crossed the line I'm sorry."

"It's okay," said the linebacker.

"Do you love her?" he asked.

"Yes," Chip replied confidently. "Of course I do."

"Then you'll figure it out," he said. "Marriage and families are serious business Chip. No one - and I mean no one - is ever ready. And you're right, it's a serious commitment. I remember when you first told me about her - at the river house. She sounded incredible - and ya'll had just met I think. The way you talked about her - every man should have half of that passion when they're talking about someone special. Then I met her and I thought the world of her Chip - I truly did."

"She's one in a million - I know," said Chip. "But how can I know if she's actually the one?"

"Well I don't know exactly," said Reynolds, "but I can tell you how it was for me."

"Please," urged Chip.

"This is going way back to a different time of course," said the Member of Congress, "but when I asked myself: Would it bother me if she married another fellow?"

Chip moved his mouth a little like he was trying to remember a test question and looked back toward the water. "Interesting," he said, barely aloud.

Chapter Twenty Three

"Happy Birthday Champ," whispered Cheryl as she turned to her side and slid her hand over Chip's torso. He felt her soft pajamas by his bare legs.

"Thank you Darlin," he replied as he yawned and stretched in the small bed.

"I like this camper," she said. "It's more comfortable than I thought it would be. And less damp."

"The heater didn't keep you up?" he asked.

"Nope," she said. "I think it helped - I slept like a baby."

"How do you think last night went?" he asked her. "You think your parents had a good time? It wasn't exactly the Breakers."

"They loved it Chip, I got a text from my mom last night - they really enjoyed it," she said. "I don't think they'd ever had fried turkey before. I would bet my dad is searching the Cabelas catalog for a turkey fryer right now."

"Mary can be a little much," he admitted.

Cheryl put her hand in his, "every woman can be a little much Chip, that's our speciality. Mary was fine last night."

"I think it was a perfect Thanksgiving - one of my favorites," he said.

"Well hopefully this is one of your favorite birthdays too," Cheryl said. "What do you want to do today?"

"I have a surprise for you," he said. "I've got something - you ready for this - PLANNED!"

"You planned something other than a fishing trip with Jay?" she asked. "That's amazing. Can you tell me what it is?"

"No. Sorry," he said. "It's a surprise."

"Okay, got it. What is the attire? Or is this a clothing-free surprise?" she asked.

"I like the way you operate Cher. I think jeans, a light sweater, and a pair of sturdy shoes or boots would be optimal if you have them. We probably have boots here somewhere," he said. "You want to grab some breakfast?"

"I do," she said, looking him in the eye. "Chip, these past two weeks have really been special. I love you very much."

"I love you too," he said, kissing her forehead and rolling out of the bed.

Chip and Cheryl found Mary in the kitchen in the ranch house. She was sipping coffee and putting together a few breakfast items. The three spoke about what a nice Thanksgiving they had all had. Mary stirred a pot of grits while Chip fixed a pair of coffees.

Mary told Cheryl how much she enjoyed getting to know her parents and said she hoped they had a nice time. Chip strolled out to the front porch while the ladies chatted. He heard the squeak of old trailer brakes out on the main road and watched as a cowboy drove an old pickup truck into the driveway.

"Cheryl!" he yelled. "We've gotta get dressed."

She excused herself and walked to the porch. "Who is that?" she asked. "What are you up to Chip? Is that a horse trailer?"

"Yep, let's get ready - we're riding!" he cried. "Let's get dressed."

They told Mary they'd see her later and scrambled to get dressed in the motorhome.

Jay was visiting with the horse guy and petting one of the animals when his brother and Cheryl walked up.

"You only got two?" asked Jay.

"Sorry man," replied Chip. "We'll be back in a few hours."

"Or we could come back in an hour and give Jay a turn," said Cheryl unconvincingly.

"Next time," said Chip, helping her onto the large animal.

"I'll be by at around four to pick them up," yelled the cowboy as Chip saddled up. "You want to know their names?"

"Nope!" yelled Chip, leading the way to the trail. "Come on Cheryl. Jay - see if our friend wants some coffee for the road."

Jay and the cowboy watched as the two rode off into the pines.

Mary watched from the porch and smiled, she knew what was about to happen.

Cheryl looked beautiful on the trail horse. She had on tight-fitting jeans and a light-gray V-neck sweater. She wore rubber chore boots she had found in the ranch house and she donned a blaze orange trucker cap with a Red-Head logo on the front - also a ranch loaner.

"I haven't ridden in years," she said. "How'd you think of this?"

"Just something I wanted to share with you," he said. "It's deer season - so there's a chance we'll hear a gunshot. Your horse might get spooked if that happens. Make sure you don't tighten up and panic."

"Got it," she said. "Do you have friends out here or is it just neighbors?"

"Neighbors - sometimes poachers," he said.

They rode slowly for about an hour. Chip pointed out critters and favorite spots. She tried like hell not to talk about the future, but it was weighing on her. It was a remarkably symbolic day for Chip - turning twenty-five was his last requirement to serve in Congress.

"Follow me Cher," he said as he turned off the trail onto another one. The woods got more dense as the pine forest transitioned into oaks and sabals and saw palmettos.

"Where we going Chip?" she asked, ducking a spider web.

"We built a little day camp back here in high school," he said. "I think you'll like it."

It was pretty charming for the middle of the woods. They had dragged an old aluminum camper via tractor to the site. It was a boxy park model built in the early sixties. Shade was provided by a cluster of several live oaks laced with Spanish moss.

There was a skinning shed with a hoist and a large cutting table.

"This is crazy, Chip," she said as he helped her down and secured the horses.

"I know," he said. "Let me turn on the generator. I can get water for these two."

"You have power and water all the way the hell out here?" she asked.

Chip answered in the affirmative and fired up the generator. He let it run for a few minutes then returned with water pails. He then opened up the trailer to let it air out while the air conditioning ran. He found Cheryl sitting on the tree swing with a content little smirk on her face.

"I like to run the air in there and force out the moisture," he said. "No girl has ever been out here. This is where Jay and I used to sleep on the big weekends. Pretty cool fort right?"

"I like the festive party lights and the decorations," she said. "It's peaceful out here - these trees are amazing." She stood up and put her arms around him. "Happy Birthday Charles the Third. Is the inside worth seeing?"

"It's a little crude - there are pictures of naked ladies and beer signs and stuff," he said.

"Well now I definitely want to see it," she said, softly breaking away from him and walking toward the door of the camper.

"Cheryl - wait!" he yelled.

"Chip - its boobs and beer - I can handle it," she said without turning around.

"Okay but there's something... can you come back over here?" he asked.

She turned and walked back toward him. He slowly took a knee and extended his hand toward her.

Her eyes immediately teared up as he pulled a small velvet pouch from his shirt pocket.

"Oh my god Chip!" she cried. "Oh my god..."

"Cheryl," he said confidently but without breathing, "I am in love with you and I want to marry you... will you marry me?"

"YES," she said, holding her hands over her face. "Yes I will marry you Chip."

He shook slightly as he slid the attractive diamond ring onto Cheryl's ring finger.

"It's beautiful Chip - just beautiful," she said through tears. "I love you so much... Is this really what you want - you want to marry me? Are you sure?"

"Of course I'm sure!" he said, "of course I'm sure."

She hugged and kissed him, "I'm so happy Chip."

"Come in the camper, I have something in there," he said.

"Oaky," she said.

Chip opened the door and flipped open a cooler with a chilled bottle of Dom. "Can you grab those glasses on the kitchen counter?"

"Of course," she said, looking around the most boyish establishment she'd ever seen.

"Bruce pre-staged this for me," Chip said as he stripped the foil from the heavy bottle.

"He knew?" asked Cheryl. "Who else knows? My parents?"

"Your dad knows," replied Chip, "so I assume your mom knows too - but maybe not. Can we hang out here for a little bit? I don't think I can go back to the ranch house yet."

"Do your parents know?" she asked him.

"Of course," he said, handing her a glass of champagne. "Mary is crazy about you, but she's protective of me and I knew I'd have to convince her that I was ready for this."

"This is a game changer Chip," she said. "I mean - we've got to get you sworn in, find you a place to crash up there, maybe get a place in Gainesville, plan a freaking wedding. This is crazy! You can do all of that?"

He took an ample drink of the Dom, "I can get sworn in."

Made in the USA
Columbia, SC
25 May 2021